UNSPEAKABLE
JOURNEY

UNSPEAKABLE
JOURNEY
RINDA HAHN

TATE PUBLISHING & *Enterprises*

Published by Tate Publishing & Enterprises, LLC
127 E. Trade Center Terrace | Mustang, Oklahoma 73064 USA
1.888.361.9473 | www.tatepublishing.com

Tate Publishing is committed to excellence in the publishing industry. The company reflects the philosophy established by the founders, based on Psalm 68:11,
"The Lord gave the word and great was the company of those who published it."

Book design copyright © 2009 by Tate Publishing, LLC. All rights reserved.
Cover design by Tyler Evans
Interior design by Joey Garrett

Published in the United States of America

ISBN: 978-1-61566-693-5
1. Fiction / Christian / General
2. Fiction / Christian / Romance
10.04.14

ACKNOWLEDGMENTS

First, I must thank my heavenly Father. Without his grace, love, and guidance throughout my life, I never would have had the courage to write this story. He is the first and only perfect author, and I praise him for his faithfulness.

I owe a special thanks to Ron, Sarah, and Elizabeth. Unconditional love is a rare and priceless gift, and when I receive it from my family, I am overcome. You inspire me to be a better wife, mom, and Christian. Your support and love keep me going.

Two amazing women and great friends, Sharon Wright and Jill Gick, were invaluable to this process. From the first few chapters, your excitement about this story drove me forward. When I was discouraged, you prayed me off the edge, and I could not have finished without your help. Thank you for staying with me to the end.

Many thanks to Brian and Becky Hendley, Karen

Stewart, and Traci Jones. You were the first to read this manuscript and provide insight. Your love of the book and confidence in its potential gave me courage to continue on in the process.

Lastly, I offer a special thanks to all the staff at Tate Publishing. I am honored by your excitement about my book. Thanks to acquisitions, editing, and design for all the time and effort you put into making this story by a first-time author available for everyone.

CHAPTER ONE

I ndiana summers were usually hot and muggy, but this weather was unseasonably mild for the month of August. Outside the car, the lights in her quaint town spoke of all things right in this world. She liked it that there were still places where people watched out for one another, and parents could rest easy that their kids would grow up safe. Police statistics were part of so many large towns, but violence rarely visited them here, and she was thankful for that.

Isabella rubbed her arm. She was cold from the chill that had settled in with the setting of the sun. She reached down to turn the knob controlling the temperature in her car. She looked down at her hand on the steering wheel. Her wedding ring was not on her finger, and every time she looked at her hand, it bothered her. Usually she wore it, but earlier she had taken it off to clean it. Her husband had come home from work a little later than expected, and in her haste to get out the door for her early dinner reservations, she had forgotten it.

She had been given a rare opportunity to have dinner with one of her close friends from college. They had gone to her favorite seafood restaurant in celebration of her approaching thirtieth birthday. Having enjoyed a little time unheeded by the trifling of a typical day, Isabella reflected on the evening's conversations and smiled. It had been a great evening. As the years had passed, inadvertently, their visits had gotten longer in between. She resolved to make more time for her close friends.

It was hard to believe that she was turning thirty. Her mind reflected back through her life. In spirit, she felt so young. Could it truly be ten years since she had married her high school sweetheart? Their two beautiful daughters were growing bigger each day. She smiled at the thought of Rebecca, who had turned seven in March. Everything about her was like her father. Even as a baby, she had been so similar to her husband's baby photos, right down to the little button nose. Her youngest daughter, Katherine, was more like herself. She was turning five in just a few months, and hardly a day passed without Isabella laughing at one of her funny antics or sweet little stories. Really, they both looked more like her husband. Occasionally, however, a stranger would comment that Katherine looked just like her. They were both their own individuals, and one of her greatest joys was watching their character form right in front of her eyes. The biggest surprise had been their blonde hair. Isabella's hair was red. All her life, she had imagined having a little girl with red hair, maybe even two. She shook her head and smiled, accepting that they were perfect just the way God had made them. Isabella was blessed to have such a beautiful family, and she was so thankful for the life she had been blessed with.

"Thank you," she whispered under her breath.

She pulled her car into the first available space at the local grocery store. She loved this part of town. Everything had recently been built, but the city had mandated that the architecture remained very classic in style. She lived in a small town just outside of Indianapolis, but even the greater metro area had always felt more like a big city with small-town character. She was only about ten minutes from home, so she called her husband to let him know that she was picking up a few items and then would be home.

She dialed the number as she forced open the door with her foot. She felt momentarily off balance as she tried to swing the door closed, balance the phone on her ear, and swing her purse on her shoulder. It wasn't uncommon for her to fall in these moments of distraction. She struggled to coordinate her thoughts and everything in her hands at the same time, and luckily, this time, she didn't fall as she headed into the store. She nearly giggled at her own clumsiness. She heard the rings continue in her earpiece. It appeared that her husband was not going to answer. After a few minutes, the answering machine picked up.

"Hello, honey. If you are home, pick up." She paused for a moment, hoping he would answer. When the silence remained, she decided to leave a message. "Sam, I am at the store. I should be home in about twenty or thirty minutes. Give me a call if you get this message before I get home."

Isabella wondered why he had not answered, but then he was notorious for falling asleep with the television on too loud. After getting the girls tucked into bed, he had probably dozed off and not heard the phone ring. She laughed aloud at the thought of him in his recliner with his head back, mouth open, and snores bellowing through the family room.

She checked her watch. It was just after 10:30 p.m. It did not feel that late, but the length of the summer days always made her internal clock feel inaccurate. She looked around her at the dark parking lot. It was very empty at this hour on a weeknight. In the sky, she noticed a distant flash of lightning. Traveling from the restaurant, she had noticed that imposing storm clouds were blowing in from the west. Within a few seconds, she heard the faint sound of thunder. She knew a storm was coming, but she hoped it would hold off until she reached home. Isabella clutched her purse close to her and hurried into the store. She only needed a few items. She wanted to make her purchase and get home. Being out late always disconcerted her. She had never experienced any specific danger at night, but she had heard too many formidable stories on the nightly news. Recalling them always made her senses prickle.

She was glad the store was nearly empty. She always enjoyed having a little time away, but she was anxious to get back home to her family. She quickly gathered the items she needed and headed to the checkout. The young girl behind the counter seemed as if she wished to be anywhere but here, and insolence was written on her face. She didn't even greet her while scanning her purchase. When Isabella offered her a smile, she pretended not to notice. Isabella grabbed her items and headed for the door, quietly humming her favorite song.

She reached the parking lot just as the rain began to blow in. The storm clouds made the sky darker than when she had arrived. Although it had started raining, it was not pouring. She was glad because she had forgotten to grab her umbrella from the trunk of her car. The clouds were ominously close to the ground. Isabella grabbed her two bags and left the cart near the door. Her hair whipped in her face, and the darkness pressed in around her. Isabella rushed to her car, searching in her purse for her keys. She reached the car and promptly started to open the trunk. A moment later, behind her, an oversized black SUV came to a stop. She noticed the movement, but dismissed it in her haste to deposit the groceries in the car. Just as she closed the trunk and started toward her car door, three men bounded from the SUV, cornered her, and grabbed each of her arms. She turned, feeling an instant surge of adrenaline.

"What are you doing?"

She heard one of the men laugh and struggled to see his face. He leaned up to her ear, speaking in hushed tones. "Come along with us, and don't make a scene."

Isabella started to scream but felt one of her assailants plant a crushing kiss on her mouth that silenced the sound. Isabella ripped her head away to make another attempt, but a hand covered her mouth as she was easily swept into the vehicle. When the door closed, she frantically tried to process the maddening situation.

"There must be some mistake! Who are you?"

Again, she heard a strained laugh from one of the strangers. She looked at his face, determined to end this escapade, but the stone-cold glare that met her eyes made her mind go blank in fear. For a brief moment she believed any attempt to escape was futile. Shaking off the hopelessness of the situation, her pulse raced as she sprang for the door in a definitive attempt to free herself. As they wrestled her back into the seat, she took another look at their faces. Two of them appeared to be foreign, possibly from the Middle East. The third appeared to be American. Her body began to give way to panic as she searched to grasp the implications of what was happening. One man sat in front of her, and the other two guarded from each side.

"What are you doing?" she demanded. "There must be some mistake. Tell me what you are doing!"

None of the men addressed her comments. Furious and aghast, she began to claw her way to the door in another attempt at escape. She knew she was strong for a woman. She had never been considered bantam and hoped that her hasty attempt to reach the door would catch them off guard. Immediately, all of the men hurdled her to her seat. Her body felt bruised all over from the struggle. She looked at the imposing face of the man that was restraining her against the seat. His eyes were black like flint, and his expression was acerbic. The dark look on his face revealed unspoken malicious evil. She glanced away from his penetrating stare to conceal her mounting fear. As this hateful man pulled away, the guard to her left threw her face down over his lap as one of the others ripped her purse from her arm and banded her hands together. Despair began to grip her as she felt bile rise in her throat. Her mind raced to comprehend the events unfolding. She refused to submit to this manacle and began to kick her legs. Hands shoved her to the floor. She could feel a knee in her back as the pain of his weight surged up her spine. Realizing she was in a perilous situation, her hope again began to flee. She stopped struggling. She needed to think. She was adept. There must be a way to escape. Her mind rushed to find a solution. She refused to concede, yet no viable option presented itself.

The vehicle was moving, yet she could not calculate how long or how far she had traveled. The pressure and pain of the knee in her back did not relent as time began to crawl by and hope began to wane. She could feel the abrasiveness of the carpet pushing against her cheek, and the smell of stale cigarette smoke filled her nostrils. Her mind raced through so many questions as time passed. She struggled against her mounting panic and began to think about her family. She pictured Sam asleep and unaware of the danger she was facing. She prayed for a way to alert him so he could save her from this nightmare. Then she thought of the girls. Tomorrow morning, Rebecca needed to practice her spelling words, and Katherine had swim lessons. Her family needed her to get home. They would be devastated if she did not come home. In that moment of reflection, Isabella resolved to do whatever she could to get home to her family again.

After what seemed like several minutes, she felt

one of the men cautiously lifting her from the floor. He pinned her to her seat. His menacing face was just inches from her own. She could smell a foul stench on his breath, the faint scent of alcohol.

"You can make this easy, or you can make it hard, but the inevitable will come. Do not doubt that my words are true, my little termagant. You are helpless. You are mine, and I will not relent. Accept this fate, or I will drug you."

Oh, how she wanted to spit in his face! This tyrant would not defeat her. His words were not true! She forced her body to relax in anticipation of the moment she would spring free. The car began to slow its momentum and made several sharp turns. She didn't know where she was or why she had been taken. The windows were very tinted, and there were few lights outside. Rain no longer pounded on the car as it had just moments before. She sensed they had taken her to some remote location outside of town. When the car stopped, the driver got out and opened the door. Her captors threw a jacket over her shoulders and began to move her from the car. Outside the door, she saw a small jet, the sound of the engine roaring in her ears. Frantically, she searched for a way to escape. No one was around in what appeared to be a small local airstrip. The darkness was suffocating and close as they exited the car. The sky was as black as ink, and the low, swirling clouds seemed to push in all around them. She could scream, but who would hear? Her composure began to crumble, and tears sprung to her eyes. She fought to resist the panic that seemed to enfold her. Hopelessness closed in, and the hum of the engine roared in her ears.

Her legs no longer felt strong enough to hold her. The words of her evil captor echoed through her mind. She stumbled and began to collapse. Effortlessly, two of her escorts lifted her just before she fell. She was overwrought with fear. Quickly, they supported her to the small jet and loaded her on the plane. She glanced around at the small cabin. There were only four large leather seats, two facing forward and two facing toward the rear. There were three small oval windows on each side. The pilot appeared ready to go as her Caucasian assailant seated himself in the copilot's seat. The other two forced Isabella to the right and into one of the rear seats. She watched the pilot, hoping he might be capable of rescuing her, but he never even turned around. Then, as quickly as the hatch closed, her spirit sank.

Each of the other two took the seats facing Isabella. She had already felt the malice of the one who seemed to be in control, but her hope waned as she searched the face of the other and found only indifference. He never even looked at her face. Her mind raced, desperately searching for any solution that would lead to escape. Almost as soon as they were seated, the plane began to move, and they were in the air. Isabella's hopes of escape were fleeting. She knew that as the plane carried her away from her home, her chances of returning were lessening. As nausea threatened to overtake her, she leaned her head against the seat, closed her eyes, and tried to take deep breaths.

"Are you going to be sick?" the evil one asked. Isabella could only shake her head as a small plastic bag was thrown at her. She watched helplessly as it landed on her lap.

"Turn around and I will untie you. I don't want you getting sick all over the place."

She continued to breathe deeply to gather her composure and turned around as her captor loosened her restraints. Fear of the unknown caused cold tentacles of dread to squeeze against her heart. Frantic thoughts and emotions were spiraling out of control. Silently and fervently, Isabella began to pray, and inch by inch her nausea subsided. Her breathing returned closer to normal. She was still petrified, but more than that she longed for escape.

She opened her eyes and tried again to question the one that had addressed her before the flight. Her voice, faint and trembling, begged, "Please, tell me where you are taking me. I do not understand. Can you please explain what is going on?"

Her pleas fell on deaf ears. They both refused to look at her or acknowledge her question. Again, she thought of her husband. How long had it been since the phone call she had made to him? Was he still sleeping or had he realized she was late? Would she ever see him again? Would her two young daughters grow up without a mother? Where was she going? Could she escape? What would these strange men do to her? Would her body be found dead somewhere? Despair started to creep in. She looked around her for her purse. She knew her phone was in it. But it was not visible. She realized she had not seen it since they had left the car, and she had not heard her phone ring since her abduction.

She tried to concentrate on how long they were in the air. She refocused her mind, reminding herself not be overcome and lose her head. Focus and awareness were her only friends, but her mounting fear would not subside. Moments continued to tick by as her mind reeled in and out of frightening scenarios. When her ears began to pop from the change in altitude, she realized the plane had started to descend. She tried to look at her watch to check the time and realized it was no longer on her arm. She had a long jagged scratch on the inside of her wrist. It must have been lost during her struggle in the car. What time had it been when she had entered the market? She tried to remember. From her calculations, it had to be after midnight. The captor she feared most reached in his pocket and pulled out a container of pills. He retrieved one and approached her. Before she could respond, he grabbed her jaw and shoved the pill in her mouth. She scratched at his face in defense as he reached for a bottle of water in his seat and poured it down Isabella's throat. She choked in surprise. He closed her mouth and held her nose. She struggled with all her strength against his viselike grip, but the hand behind her head tightened its grasp. She was suffocating. Her lungs burned for air. Moments passed. She continued to struggle, kicking and clawing him, but his grip never loosened. He was too strong, and his hold never waived. She started to see black spots. Instinctually, without thought, she swallowed. The realization of that unconscious moment seeped into her mind. The steel claws of hopelessness revealed that death was inescapable. It was only a matter of time now. In a few moments, the pills started to take effect. She tried hard to focus, but she only struggled against the inevitable.

CHAPTER TWO

A slow, gratifying smile spread across Hasam's face. She had been a tenacious woman. Capturing her had been an extemporaneous idea. There had been moments when he had doubted the sanity of this last-minute change. When she had not quickly relented her struggle, he had nearly beat her senseless. But he had reigned in his rage as this new plan had formulated in his mind. His original plan had been to capture the young checkout girl at the market. He had been following her for several days. She was not beautiful, but she was young, disenchanted, and living alone—a perfect target. He had casually chatted with her neighbor and learned that she appeared to have no family. She would have been a perfect servant and harlot for the illegitimate business trade to his country. Snatching young girls from the United States was not a regular occurrence. In fact, the risks nearly outweighed the profit. It was only his greed that had encouraged him to pursue the risk again. This had only been his second attempt in the U.S. The first had been pretty simple and rather uneventful, and the monetary reward had far exceeded his expectations. Abductions were easy in so many countries. Destitute parents in places like Malaysia and Indonesia would sell their children for a menial price, but this country was different. Here he had never heard of anyone selling their daughters. Plus, it was rumored that police protection in this country made it nearly impossible. But he knew that everyone had a price, nothing was impossible, and Western women brought a staggering price. They were a rare gem to the men in his business.

Hasam had carefully hunted this next victim, but only a few minutes before this kidnapping, he had learned that the clerk was working a double shift to cover for a co-worker. His plan was unraveling, and timing was so critical for success. Weeks of planning and arrangements had been made for this moment. Just as he was ready to abandon the arrangement, this curvaceous young redhead had walked into the store and rescued his tangled plan. He had instantly fashioned a new strategy and ignored the niggling anxiety and risk in favor of the potential fortune to be gained.

Feeding men's appetites was a lucrative business, and because of the isolation of women in his country, it was easy. His family was wealthy. In fact, he was independently wealthy. As the third son in his country, he was unimportant in the family business because his older brothers would always outrank him in birthright. But it was his zeal for success and control that had prompted him to search for lucrative business ideas, not to mention his craving for dominance over the weaker sex.

He had first been exposed to the culture of the United States in college. It was common for wealthy men in Saudi Arabia to travel for their education. His father had encouraged it. His older brothers had gone abroad, and their exposure had improved the family business when they returned home. Hasam had been appalled at the cultural differences of this strange land from his own. In his country, women and men were always separate. Women would never drive or even ride in a car with any man other than her driver or a close male family member. The religious laws were so strict about it that women could be beaten or arrested for this violation. Women were the reason for sexual temptation. They were always guarded and never left home without a chaperone. Hasam saw both of his wives for the first time on each of his wedding days. These rules of separation ensured that a woman wouldn't be tarnished before becoming a wife. But the U.S. did not live by the values of Islam. Because the United States had long abandoned moral values, all Western women were tramps.

His first day on the campus of UCLA, he had walked around in a daze. Women were scantily clothed with their hair uncovered. Men and women were openly affectionate in public places. On his first night, he had gone to a local bar with a few guys he had met on campus. That night, and several other times following, he had met a woman and on the same night had taken to her bed. Hasam had no respect for them. Actually, he had no respect for any women anywhere. To him, a woman's purpose was to serve a man in bed and bear children. There had only been one girl that had begun to change all of that. And just as she had started to convince him she might be different, he learned she had slept with one of his friends. He would never admit that he hated women because it was an emotion he would not waste on trash. He never felt guilt about the nature of his business. There was no reason for silly sentiment. Women were a valuable commodity, and he enjoyed exploiting them.

The plane began the landing approach at Washington Dulles International Airport, and Hasam had a few details to iron out in his plan. He scrutinized the young redhead in the seat in front of him. No woman in his country had hair like hers. He also knew that her green eyes would set her apart as well. She was an exceptional beauty. In his mind, she was clearly a woman made for a prince. He knew she would catch his eye. In fact, he knew she would become his instant obsession. Prince Latif was Hasam's childhood friend, and instinctually, he knew what interested him. The two had always had a close relationship even though they were very different from each other. Latif would never approve of the real nature of Hasam's business, so he never really disclosed the exact truth. His countrymen refused degrading jobs like cooks, housekeepers, or anything administrative. So they hired foreigners for this menial work. Saudi Arabia was full of foreign workers, and organizing and employing them was big business. As far as Latif knew organizing and employing foreigners was the extent of Hasam's enterprise.

Latif already had two Saudi wives, but Hasam knew

he had a secret desire for an American one. The question he could not answer was how strong was his desire. He was betting a lot on this one, and he was anticipating a big payoff. As a Saudi sponsor of this American woman, he knew he could claim a huge price for her marriage.

He took the black abaya out of his carry-on and slipped it over her head. He then carefully covered her hair with the matching khimar. He did not anticipate seeing any airport officials upon his arrival, but he prepared to take all precautions in case. Latif's private jet was known in the U.S. He was an important Saudi prince, and officials never questioned him. On the rare occasions where someone tried to overstep his bounds, the embassy was contacted and the flight schedule proceeded as planned. But those times were rare. Prince Latif was generous with his money, and airports learned quickly that it was advantageous to prevent delays.

"George, can you verify that the car is waiting on the ground for our arrival?" Hasam asked.

"Yes, sir."

Hasam listened as the copilot called his personal driver to check the arrangements.

"The car is ready, just as you instructed," George responded after ending his call. "Prince Latif will be arriving at his private jet in less than fifteen minutes. He anticipates the plane will be leaving on schedule."

George moved toward the door and opened the hatch as the plane was marshaled into place. The young woman began to stir as they assisted her out of the jet. Hasam had been careful with his dosage. He predicted she would be able to walk with assistance but would not remember any of the transfer. She would become cognizant later on the jet when she no longer posed a threat to his plan. They easily maneuvered her in the car for the drive to Latif's awaiting jet and then made the final transfer under the cover of darkness without any incident.

They escorted her to the bed in the private suite so that she could sleep off the drug-induced state. Hasam knew it would be a few hours before he would know if his plan would work as expected. Latif arrived about five minutes after Hasam had made the transfer and settled into his seat. He talked to the pilot about their flight plan home to Saudi Arabia, and less than a half an hour later they were in the air. Hasam sat back, stretched his legs, and relaxed.

CHAPTER THREE

Isabella opened her eyes, but the pain pounding in her head made her close them again. She tried desperately to get her bearings. In those few seconds, she realized she was not at home in her bed. Instantly, the night's events came flooding back to her as she rushed to sit up. The abrupt movement made the pain in her head scream, and her stomach lurched. Timidly, she lay back down as fear tightened in her stomach like a fist. She tried to focus her mind, brushing away the fogginess from the drugs. Could it all have been just a crazy dream? She knew it wasn't, but she tried to hold this realization at bay. The headache meant she was still alive. At least that was something to focus on for the moment. But she realized a lot of time had passed since she had made that phone call to Sam. Her family was certainly wondering where she was. She imagined Sam's frantic worried face, and she missed him; she missed them all.

She lay there on the bed with her eyes closed and tried to think of a plan. She was in a bed in a bedroom, that much she had discerned. She could feel movement and hear the slight rumble of an engine. It was not a car or a train. The movement was different than that. Understanding began to dawn; it was a plane, a different plane than the small jet she had been on the night before.

Blood pounded against her temples, affecting her concentration. First, she had to deal with the pain. She opened her eyes until they were mere slits and carefully sat up. The discomfort from this slight movement made her nauseated. She could see a door to a small bathroom. Slowly, she scooted to the side of the bed and draped her legs over the edge. She touched the short-napped carpet and realized her feet were bare. Gingerly, she lifted up off the bed. Her legs were unsteady as she stood and took a small step toward the bathroom door.

Just then, a different door to Isabella's left opened. The unexpected movement startled her, and she collapsed backward onto the bed. She grabbed her head in her hands and moaned out loud.

"You okay?" came a quiet woman's voice next to her.

"No. I have a splitting headache," Isabella responded.

Without lifting her head, she sensed the woman swiftly move to the bathroom. There was a rustling sound followed by the rattle of a container dispensing pills. The sink turned on and then off. In a matter of moments, the woman had returned to Isabella's side.

"Here something for pain."

"What is it?" Isabella asked.

"Trust me; it help pain. I work for Hasam for long time. This make you better. It not hurt you," she gently replied.

Isabella warily lifted her head from her hands and looked into the face of the young woman. She appeared to be foreign. Both her accented English and her face suggested that she was Asian.

Isabella got the impression that she was trustworthy, but she was hesitant to accept it. Even through the pain, she knew that any wrong decision on her part could be disastrous.

"My name is Mina." She smiled demurely, took Isabella's hand, and placed the pills into her open palm. "Take these; pain will stop."

"Okay."

Isabella dubiously lifted the pills to her mouth and swallowed them with the water from the glass she was offered. Then she carefully laid her head back on the pillow. This was wrong. Everything was all wrong! She should be waking up next to her husband in her own bed in her own house. She let out a long, slow exhale and prayed for the pain to pass. In that moment, she wanted to cry. No, she wanted to wail and scream. Again, she took a deep breath and tried to relax. She struggled to keep her sanity; she could not succumb to hysteria.

She sensed that Mina was moving about the room, but she let that pass from her mind. This was not a typical headache. It was so much worse. She suspected it was caused by whatever narcotic she had been given. Regardless, she needed the pain to pass so that her mind and body could function. For several minutes,

Isabella feared that the pills were not going to work. Then, gradually, the pain began to lessen. In her relaxed state, Isabella suspected she had momentarily dozed off. She sat up and looked around the room. Mina was still there in the bathroom. She carefully looked around the small room. There were several windows flanking it with opaque shades pulled down over them. She registered the sunlight outside.

"Mina, can you tell me what time it is?"

The young woman came to the bathroom door to answer. "No, Hasam say not to. You shower. I give you Hasam."

"Is Hasam the man that abducted me from the market?" Isabella asked.

Anxiety registered clearly on Mina's face in response to her questions. "I not know how you come on plane. Hasam and Najid bring you here. Hasam you sponsor."

"Hmmm." Isabella registered what Mina had said but could not grasp the implications of all that had not been said from Mina's veiled comments. She tried turning all the events over in her mind, but nothing really added up.

"What information *can* you tell me?" Isabella questioned.

"I not say more. I sorry. But I right about medicine. Your color better. You feel better. Is pain gone?"

"The pain is gone, but I cannot say that I feel better." Fear had become her silent consort in this demented scheme. It was a constant battle to harness it. Silently she prayed, "Lord, please help me." It was a simple and short petition, but it was all she could offer.

Mina came over to the side of the bed and knelt down in front of her. "You better if you take shower. I have clothes for you. Come with me; I prepare everything."

"I don't know. I don't know about any of this. I don't know what to do or where to go. All I want is to get off this plane and go home. This is a hopeless situation, and I don't want to take a shower."

"Hasam expect you shower. He tell me to get you dressed. He wait for you in main cabin. It easier if you obey. He come in here and force you in shower himself. He rough to many women. Please, I not want you get hurt," Mina pleaded.

Reluctantly, Isabella consented. She was beginning to feel an unusual companionship with this stranger. She had made a credible argument, and she believed it was sincere. She had also tasted enough of the acrimony of Hasam. Isabella made her way to the bathroom. Mina followed and pointed out the items available for her to use.

"Dry and fix you hair and use makeup I leave for you," she added encouragingly. "Hasam tell me you must look your best. I responsible. You understand?"

"I understand. Will you remain in this bedroom while I get ready?"

"I wait here for you. I help you. I serve you. I happy to serve."

"Thank you, Mina."

Isabella silently closed the door.

She hastily showered as commanded. Several times in the process, she had flinched at the slightest sound, but to her relief, no one had entered. Isabella stared in the mirror. The reflection she saw belied the fear in her heart. It was surreal. She had styled her hair simply, letting it curl around her face. It had grown long over the last couple of months. She had meant to get it cut, but time without the girls for a haircut was hard to come by. Now, she noticed that it had gotten long enough to fall several inches past her shoulders. Her face was showing a little strain from the lack of restful sleep and the stress from the night. She had applied a little makeup to cover the light gray smudges under her eyes.

She had been called beautiful a few times, but she knew that pretty was what most people would call her. She was not glamorous like an American movie star. Sam always called her a girl-next-door kind of beauty. However, Isabella did not know how men regarded her. Being married had changed her ability to be objective about her appearance. Over the years, she had really tried to focus on being internally beautiful. She recognized the truth of the Bible regarding external beauty. She truly believed it was fleeting. But it was easy to lose sight of that truth in the midst of life. She cared for her skin and exercised regularly. Even at thirty, she still looked much younger, and too often she had taken pride in that fact. She had learned at an early age that her hair was her signature feature. It was a vibrant lovely red, not auburn, but deep and rich. It was curly and long and nearly maintenance free. She had been fortunate to have such lovely hair, and she had been prideful about that too. Pride was a sin. Deep in her heart, she began to wonder if her pride had caused this all to happen.

Isabella's guilt and fear was leading her heart down a dangerous path. She needed to deal with this and then let it go, or it would lead her to self-pity and despair. She confessed her prideful sins, reminding herself that God was in control. It didn't erase her doubts, but it helped her gain composure.

"The Lord is a strong tower. The righteous run into it and are safe." Reciting the verse aloud gave her unexpected courage. She was never alone. Even now, God was with her. She could feel his presence. The quiet of the room enveloped her, and she began to hear the steady, even rhythm of her own heart. She took a deep breath, closed her eyes, and imagined the arms of her heavenly Father. They were strong enough to hold her through anything that happened and loving enough to trust. He was the daddy that mattered, the one that would never forsake her. She basked in that love for several minutes. The peace she felt was beyond belief, peace that passes understanding. The small room had become like a protective cocoon. If only she could use it to escape. She looked at her reflection again.

"It will be all right." She spoke her thoughts aloud to the young woman in the mirror. And for a brief second, she nearly believed it. Then she heard a faint knock at the door.

The peace splintered as fear surged through her veins, bringing her back to the moment.

"Yes?" Isabella responded as she partially opened the door.

"You ready?" Mina questioned in an amicable voice.

Isabella looked at her, and tears began to fill her eyes. Mina's obvious compassion fed her weakness. She was a cornered animal, and she knew her chances for escape were fleeting. The emotion she sensed in this young woman's demeanor declared that everything happening was out of their control.

"You be okay," Mina encouraged her.

Strangely, Isabella smiled at this simple comment. Hadn't she just said the same thing moments before? Maybe it would be okay. Maybe, just maybe, it would be okay.

"I tell Hasam you ready," she stated as she turned to leave the room.

"Wait! Can we just stay here a little longer? I'm not sure I am ready for whatever is about to happen."

"No, can't wait longer. I go now. Hasam not patient man. Mina be right back."

Isabella watched as Mina exited the room. Her heart began to race, and she could feel the blood drain from her face. She backed up against the bed, feeling her knees starting to give way. She had to sit down, or she would collapse. She was approaching hysteria when she heard the doorknob turn. She closed her eyes to ward off this inevitable moment. She jumped at the sound of Mina's voice.

"Hasam come soon. We wait here."

Mina leaned her back against the wall just inside the door and looked at the floor. They both waited in deafening silence.

CHAPTERFOUR

Latif had recognized the agitation in his friend as soon as he had boarded the plane. Hasam had been his friend longer than he could even recall. The two had shared so many childhood memories, and it had bonded them like brothers. Hasam could be malicious, and sometimes he worried about the repercussions of this evil in his friend. He objected to many of Hasam's extreme views of the world, and many times they had argued over their differences. But their friendship always superseded their disagreements.

Latif reclined in one of the large seats in the main room of the cabin. He was seated across from his friend. He casually browsed through several newspapers, updating himself on the current news from around the world. Hasam and Najid were watching a movie. There had been little conversation between any of them for the entire trip, but he had watched their body language. Several times, Hasam had walked to the end of the hall and listened at the door. He had prowled the aisleways more than he had been sitting. Each time he returned to his seat, he would give a knowing glance to Najid. He had even heard him talking to one of the servants in the hall only moments before. Latif knew something was brewing, and it was time to flush it out.

"Hasam, what are you scheming?"

"I thought you would never ask." A gratifying smile spread across his face.

"Oh, no, Hasam. What are you up to?"

"Latif, my friend, trust me. I have an extravagant idea. It is an idea that will appeal to even you."

"So, tell me this crazy idea, because I can't remember a time when that infamous smirk has ever been reassuring." Latif truly dreaded hearing what his friend was planning. Long ago, he had learned not be shocked by the crazy notions in his friend's tortured mind.

"I have a woman I would like for you to meet." Hasam held up his hand to silence the comment Latif was about to make. "Wait, I know you are going to argue, but give me a chance to tell you my little story. I have met a lovely American woman. She is on the plane with us right now, and I am her sponsor in Saudi Arabia. When I met her, I immediately thought of you. Don't shake your head, Latif. I promise she is just your type. Let me go get her. It is time the two of you met."

Hasam jumped to his feet before Latif could question him further. He stepped down the hallway in long quick strides and never even hesitated at the doorway.

He twisted the knob and pushed through the door. He quickly surveyed the room and noticed both of the women nearly bolted as he entered. He could smell their fear. Fear was an emotion he could exploit, and he was an expert at using it to his advantage. He turned to Mina first.

"Leave us. Now!"

Silently, she escaped through the open door.

Hasam slowly closed the door and turned to face Isabella. He took great satisfaction in watching her cower as he approached. She was seated on the bed, and her eyes were as large as saucers. Her fear was palpable. He stepped across the room, grabbed her by the arms, and hauled her to her feet. He stared directly into her eyes and gritted his teeth. He paused there for a moment. The fear and tension in the room was glacial, and he took satisfaction in knowing it.

"This is what you are going to do." He kept his voice just above a whisper, but the demanding tone was unmistakable. "Let me make this very clear. I will not tolerate any misbehavior. You are in a very precarious situation, but it can quickly become much worse. I am going to escort you from this room and introduce you to one of my friends. Do not say a word and do not struggle. If you speak, I will kill you. I know you think I am exaggerating, but I am not. You are in a plane flying over international waters. You are not in the United States anymore. I can kill you, and there is no one here to stop me. Is that clear?"

Timidly, she nodded her head to offer her agreement.

"When I introduce you to my friend, I expect you to smile and nod. It is that simple. After that, you are free to come back to this room for the rest of the flight. My instructions are explicit. I demand that they be obeyed. Do you agree to cooperate?"

"It appears I have no other choice."

Her reply was barely audible, but he detected the slightest insolence in her voice. Her subtle defiance infuriated him, but he knew Latif would appreciate the enduring spirit in her character. He was banking on Latif's response to this feisty woman, and for the first time since beginning this endeavor, he was certain this would work out exactly as he had planned. He had not met many impetuous young women, and he knew there were few in his home country. He was looking forward to seeing his friend's expression when he met her. He was already making plans for the money he would make from the transaction.

"In order to introduce you, I must know your name." His eyes were as hard as steel as they pierced through her resolve. "Tell me your name."

"My name is Isabella."

"Follow me." He turned and headed for the door.

Isabella followed him down the short hallway. There were a few other doorways on her left. One of the doors was slightly ajar and appeared to lead to another small room. She wasn't sure, but she thought she caught a glimpse of Mina. Another door was open and led into another small bathroom. The last door was closed. She looked out the row of small windows on the right side of the hallway. The sun was high in the sky, and there were only a few clouds. Below her, all she could see was water. She realized Hasam's words were correct. If they were over an ocean, then the laws of her country no longer protected her. Warily, she tried to make sense of what was happening. Her mind had endlessly batted around possible scenarios to explain all of this. Even now, she pushed away some of the more horrifying possibilities. She knew there were few possibilities that would not end in her demise. A tear streaked down her face as this realization sank in. Hasam was clearly an evil man. Did that mean death was imminent? Could the events she faced become so appalling that she would long for death? In those brief moments as she followed him, she realized she was in a dire situation.

Silently, she wiped the tear away. She was amazed that she could be so calm after truly comprehending the odds. Maybe the fear had finally dissolved into hopelessness. She wasn't sure. Over the past several hours, she had been consoled by the reality that she was alive and unharmed. She knew God was in control, but that did not mean nothing bad could happen to her. She tried to force the uncertainty from her mind to take in her surroundings.

The end of the hall had opened into another large room with several oversized seats arranged in small groups around the room. She also noticed a table surrounded by chairs on one end. On the far side of the room, Isabella recognized one of her other assailants. He did not even look in her direction as they walked down a narrow aisle and headed in his direction. There was a stranger sitting in one of the seats near him. She realized Hasam was leading her toward this other man. Her first impression of him was strange. She expected him to be like the other two, but he wasn't. Of course, she had to be mistaken. Wasn't she? There could not be a man on this plane that would look at her with kindness. It was not possible. She looked into his eyes again expecting to see indifference, spite, even hate; instead he gave her a sincere smile. She turned around and looked behind her, assuming someone else was in the room. But there was no one else. Puzzled, she turned back and looked again at his face as he addressed Hasam.

"So this is your friend?"

Isabella began to fume as she scrutinized the exchange. She bit her tongue to keep from speaking her rage. How dare he call her a friend? She had clearly mistaken his kindness. It was laughable that he would make light of her grave situation. Hasam turned a piercing stare in her direction to remind her of his previous instruction. As prescribed, she gave him a tight smile and nodded in acknowledgment of this stupid question.

Hasam responded to Latif. "This is Isabella. She is an American that desires to live in Saudi Arabia."

Isabella nearly choked at Hasam's comment and suppressed her desire to deny this blatant lie.

"Nice to meet you, Isabella. My name is Latif."

As understanding dawned in her mind, Isabella nearly spat in disgust. They were playing a cruel game, and she was the pawn. She could sense that Hasam was becoming very angry at her insolence. She attempted to reign in her anger and forced a cheerless smile.

Before Latif could question them further, Hasam turned her around and guided her from the room. She heard Latif say something, but in the haste to leave she did not understand what he had said.

Isabella could not sort through the tempest of

thoughts in her mind. Saudi Arabia? That was a lifetime away from her home and family. Her anger faded among scrambled thoughts as despair whispered in her ear.

Hasam turned and addressed him. "I promised I would only detain her for a moment. Isabella is not feeling well. She needs to return to the suite to rest." He continued to guide her back down the hallway. He deposited her back in the room and wheeled around to leave.

Isabella knew she had only a few moments to attempt to get information from him. She was desperate to know why he had referred to her as a friend going to Saudi Arabia. Her mind was swimming with questions only this hate-filled man could answer.

She swallowed hard and spoke. "Please tell me why I am going to Saudi Arabia." She hated that her voice faltered from fear. She instinctually knew that fear was a powerful tool to a man like Hasam, and she met his fierce expression with determination.

"Soon we will be landing in Saudi Arabia. My country is very different from the U.S, and women do not have any of the freedoms that you once possessed. You can only safely enter our country with my help. Without me, you have no representation and no money. You have no way to get back home. You must accept that I am your only hope. My government will acknowledge that you are my property, and they will not be interested in any far-fetched stories. The accusations of a woman are never accepted against the word of a man. If you try to make problems when we arrive, you will suffer the consequences. You are at my mercy."

He gave her a hard imposing stare and then added, "We still have several hours before we arrive. I will leave you to ponder your fate. Before we land, I will give you further instructions. Until then, I expect you to stay quiet until I return." He turned and marched from the room.

Isabella waited for the door to close and listened as he retreated down the hall. His words raced through her mind, searching for plausible options. When realization materialized, hope drained from her heart, leaving her empty and broken as she collapsed to her knees and bowed her face to the ground. She began to sob deep, convulsive, muffled cries. Grief racked every bone in her body. She covered her mouth to stifle the wails that escaped from deep within her soul. All the fear, the anger, the hopelessness came flooding to the surface. She had been keeping it bottled up for hours. Now it poured out of the deepest part of her soul. She could feel herself sinking into a deep dark pit, and for what seemed like hours, she gave into the release of her tears. She simply let the hopelessness swallow her up.

CHAPTERFIVE

L atif enjoyed watching Isabella leave the room. She was wearing an ill-fitting pair of jeans and t-shirt. Everything about her looked out of place here. But he had not missed assessing everything about her, from the soft pale skin on her face to the curved shapes of her body to her prominent jewel green eyes. Even at a modest distance, he had smelled the fresh, clean scent of her hair and skin. Her hair had been so unique. He had seen so few women with red hair. She intrigued him. There was something almost animalistic about his response to her. Something about her had touched deep in his soul. She had left the room, but the essence of her remained with him.

There was something unique about American women, and American women never came to Saudi Arabia. When he had been a young college student in California, he had dreamed of finding and marrying the perfect American woman. Foolishly, he had hoped that someone would fall in love with him, come to his home, and become his new wife. Of course, it had been nothing more than a dream. Latif had dated many women in the United States. He had enjoyed shaking off the antiquated ideas of women being separate from men for a while. Most American women lacked inhibition. They were fun and straightforward. Latif had also learned that American women liked him. While growing up, others had always commented on how attractive he was. But in America, women had been openly flattering. Women were drawn to him, and he enjoyed it.

Before going to the U.S. for school, Latif had already married his first wife. According to the Koran, a man could have four wives. It was an idea he embraced even knowing he was expected to treat them all the same. That meant being responsible for providing and caring for each of them equally. Polygamy was common practice among princes. Having more than one wife ensured he would have many children, and children were important in Saudi homes. To Latif having sons was an honor and blessing from Allah. He measured his worth by the number of sons he knew he would have.

Latif's first wife, Bahira, was incorrigible. He did not even like thinking about her. As an only daughter, her mother and father had spoiled her. In fact, she still acted like a child most of the time. Within the first week of their marriage, Latif had realized nothing would ever please her. He had quickly become indifferent. After they had been married about two years, she had given birth to a son. Youssef was his oldest son. He was twelve years old. His son had been the only blessing he had received from their marriage.

In college, he had quickly realized that American women would never accept being a second wife. And American women were not interested in relinquishing all their rights by moving to Saudi Arabia. So he had returned home after school with the hope of finding a second wife. Marriage in Saudi Arabia was simple. His mother had told him about a beautiful young girl, Dalia, she had met at her cousin's wedding. She was a distant relative of her family that lived in Jeddah. His father had contacted her father, and the arrangements had been made. He had seen her for the first time on their wedding day. Dalia had been very young and delicate. Latif had believed he would truly be happy with this new wife. But she had been so timorous. She never looked him in the face, and every time he touched her, she trembled. In the five years of their marriage, he had always been tender and patient with her, but she had never responded to him. Secretly, he believed she was disgusted by his touch, but he could not comprehend why. Shortly after they were married, he had learned from her maid that she cried every night for her family. After a while, he stopped trying to understand her. He had accepted that this marriage would never be anything more than a formal arrangement. She had easily become pregnant, and their first child had been a son. She had also given birth to a daughter just over a year ago. Latif had resolved that she would never be the companion he had hoped for.

Instinctually, his thoughts traveled back to Isabella. He said her name aloud. He felt Najid look his direction, but he ignored him. He was being senseless thinking about her this way. But she had been beautiful, and he savored these sensual thoughts of her. Her behavior had been strange during the encounter, but she was intelligent. He had seen her mind at work the moment she had come into the room. But the thing that had delighted him most of all was her vivaciousness. He had seen unbridled emotions brewing in her eyes. He had desired to know and understand the depths of that passion. His attraction to her had been immediate and powerful, and it grew even now as he remembered her. He knew he wanted her, and in Saudi Arabia, what he wanted, he got. He knew he should proceed cautiously with his desire for her, but he was too fascinated to be circumspect. His feelings were irrational, but he no longer cared. When Hasam returned, he intended to find out what it would take to possess her. Every time he thought about her, it energized him more, and not once did he consider that something could prevent him from obtaining her. In his mind, she was already his. He would have her no matter what it cost.

"So was I correct in assuming she would interest you, Latif? I persuaded her to make this journey to our land because I thought you might find her amusing," Hasam said.

Latif knew he must proceed cautiously. He was careful to control the expression on his face as he responded. "Hasam, why is she on this plane?"

Hasam shrugged. "I told you. She is coming with me to Saudi Arabia. When I met her, I knew you would find her appealing. I watched how you admired American women in college. You have always desired an American wife. Right now, I am all she has, and as one of my closest friends. I am offering her to you. So I'm asking, are you interested?"

"How do you know she will agree?"

"Latif…" Hasam chuckled at his comment and paused for effect. "Women do not always give consent in the arrangement of marriage. You know that as well as I do. I am sure you remember your sister Hafa's marriage. Even you commented that your father had intentionally ignored her appeals regarding her marriage. Women are too emotional to be trusted in such important decisions. Marriage is an arrangement to please the desires of a man. Forget about what she wants. I want to know. Do you like her?"

Latif turned the idea around in his mind. Of course he wanted her. His desire to possess her was so strong that he could nearly taste it. And he knew that in a way Hasam was right. Women were emotionally weak. Allah had given man the authority to care for them. It was not unusual for a man to choose a wife without her permission in Saudi Arabia. He knew she would be vulnerable and alone in his country. Really, she needed him. And the thought of how she could be treated by his friend repulsed him. They had often responded so differently to women during their time together at UCLA, and Latif had never approved of Hasam's hatred of women. He reluctantly recalled some of the appalling rumors he had heard about it. He had always chosen to ignore this side of Hasam, until now when Isabella's safety was in jeopardy.

He was fighting the inevitable. He knew what he wanted; there were few obstacles to prevent it. However, in the back of his mind was a niggling reminder that this was not right. He hesitated. Then with a definitive stroke, he pushed away his reservations. He realized he had already made up his mind before Hasam had even offered her.

"How much is this going to cost me, Hasam?"

"You are a wealthy man. Money is an insignificant matter. If you really want her, is there any price you would not be willing to pay? Trust me; I will be fair. But you must remember that someone like her is rarely, if ever, available to men like us. In our country, she is a rare and valuable gem. The bride price will not be cheap, but I am sure such an insignificant thing will hardly affect your bank account. We will complete the necessary paperwork as soon as we arrive. Then she will be off my hands."

The lovely face of Isabella flashed into his mind. The thought of her becoming his wife gave him great satisfaction. On some level, he knew it was wrong, but at this moment, he did not care. He believed marriage to this woman would be different, and he savored the thought of it.

"Okay, Hasam, name your price. I admit I am looking forward to completing this transaction when we get home. I assume you will take care of the necessary arrangements. I don't want any unexpected problems to hinder us. Is that agreed?"

Hasam nodded, as Latif noted the smug look on his face.

Isabella felt someone gently rubbing her back. She was groggy. She knew she had napped because she had been having a dream about Sam. He had been reaching for her and calling her name. His face had been so clear that even now she had to shake off the sense that he was with her.

Isabella turned to the voice she heard beside her. It was Mina.

"Are you okay?"

"No. I am not okay."

"What happened?"

"I am never going to get back home. I will never see my family again. My heart is aching. I think I am going to die." Isabella felt utterly helpless.

"You believe, and you have chance to see family. You not give up hope. We go to bathroom and wash your face. Then you feel better."

Isabella obeyed. She stood and walked into the bathroom, but she felt numb all over. Yet, amazingly, her body still functioned. She deeply grieved all her losses, and the pain was almost more than she could bear. She tried to pray, but she was sure that God could not hear her. He felt so far away.

Mina pulled out a clean washcloth and ran it under cool water. She wrung it out and handed it to Isabella. She just stood there looking at it. She had no desire to try anymore. She was ready to give up. Mina carefully took the washcloth from her hand and placed it over her tear-stained face.

"Breathe," Mina whispered.

Isabella took in a long deep breath. When she exhaled, it came out as a long, sad sigh.

"Tell Mina your name."

When she tried to speak it was barely a hoarse whisper. "Isabella."

"You strong. You going to be okay. Sometimes life is very hard. Mina understand this. You must not give up. You not let them win."

"I need to lie down on the bed." She felt the sting of unshed tears pressing behind her eyes as she looked into Mina's kind face. "Thank you for your help, Mina."

Isabella went to the bed and lay down. She placed the pillow over her face. She breathed in the soft, clean scent of the cotton. She wanted to cry, but she had no tears left. There was nothing to do now but wait. And waiting was something Isabella hated to do.

CHAPTER SIX

Their flight had continued for several more hours. Isabella guessed that they had been traveling for nearly a full day. She had watched the sun slowly fade from the sky, and eventually complete darkness had surrounded the plane. They had made a brief landing earlier in the afternoon. In those moments, hope of rescue had resurfaced in Isabella's heart. She had anxiously waited in the small bedroom, but no one had come to save her. As far as she could tell, no one had even entered the plane or asked for identification. The stop had been short and uneventful. When the plane took off again, her brief moments of hopefulness had slowly dripped away.

They had arrived in Saudi Arabia under the cover of darkness. Isabella had hoped that some government officials would question her identity upon arrival. But when Hasam had shown her the abaya, khimar, and niqab she must wear, she knew that no one would ever recognize her. When Mina had helped her put on the outlandish items, she had explained that the khimar must cover all of her hair. Not even a tiny wisp of hair could be visible. She had explained to Isabella that in Islam, a woman's hair was a sexual object used to entice men. The abaya had completely covered even her arms and legs. Her shoes and hands were barely visible. The dark black veil that covered her face had muted everything she saw around her. The gauzy chiffon material on her face annoyed her. Breathing into the cool desert air caused condensation on the niqab, and soon the wet cloth began to feel scratchy and damp on her face. Wearing these garments was unnerving to Isabella. She was sure that if she had been able to see her reflection, she would have looked like a black ghost. The garments totally wiped away her identity. In this strange country, she was no longer an American, and maybe she had ceased to be a person.

After the plane landed, Isabella had been ushered from the plane to an awaiting car and had traveled several miles outside the city. The moonlight had glowed on the surrounding area, vaguely illuminating what appeared to be a vast desert. Eventually, she had been brought to a large, walled compound. Upon entering the gate, the desert had changed into a lush garden with palm trees. The exact detail of the area had been obscured by the darkness of the veil covering her eyes, but she could make out some grass and other plants around the drive. Isabella could see one large main house and several smaller buildings intermingled on the grounds. The buildings and dwellings were white with simple basic geometric designs. Latif silently escorted her to one of the smaller adjacent buildings.

When he stopped just outside the door, she turned expectantly, waiting for the revelation of the next events that would challenge her life. He looked so different from the man she had met on the plane. When she had first seen him, he had been casually dressed in khaki dress pants and a simple, short-sleeved, oxford-style shirt. Now, he looked foreign. She had learned that Saudi men wear a thobe, a long robe similar to the ones women wear. His was white instead of black like Isabella's, and he had a red and white scarf over his head that was held in place by a black round band strapped around his forehead. The foreignness of his attire reminded her of just how far she had traveled in such a short amount of time.

"This will be your home. You are safe here. You have my word that no one will harm you." His voice was gentle and reassuring.

She had misgivings about entering, knowing there must be some mistake, but as she looked around in the darkness, she knew she had no other choice.

"I would like for Mina to stay with me. Is that possible?" Isabella questioned.

"Mina works for Hasam. I do not have the authority to bring her to you."

"Isn't this Hasam's home?" Isabella was puzzled. She could not comprehend where she was.

"Isabella, this is my home. I live in the main house over there. This building will be your home. Until I come for you, you must stay in your home or the adjacent garden. There are rules here about where a woman is permitted to go. You will have no contact with any men but a few servants and me. I will send over a maid to assist you in getting settled in."

Tears pooled in her eyes as she surveyed what must certainly become her prison.

"So I am to be your prisoner?"

"In time, I hope you will come to feel that this is home."

"This will never be my home, and I would feel much better if Mina were with me. She was very kind to me on the plane. When you are afraid and alone, it helps to have a friend." She looked up at him. She knew her black garments prevented him from seeing her face, but she sensed he knew she was watching him. She saw compassion in his eyes, and it confused her. It must be an act. There could not be any compassion in a man that stole women from their families, and anger hardened her resolve against him.

"I will send you a maid in a few moments. Please, go inside and wait." It was a polite command. Latif turned and walked away without looking back.

Isabella stepped through the doorway. The light inside the entryway was on. From the outside, the building had appeared to be one room, but upon further survey, she had realized she was in a small home. Just past the entry, there was a sitting room with cushioned seats around the perimeter. She saw another room that appeared to be a kitchen with an attached dining area. It had a pallet on the floor with cushions surrounding it. It reminded her of a table from a Moroccan restaurant near her home. There was a large bedroom and bath. The bedroom was very exotic. It almost looked like a tent. There were multicolored draperies over the walls and ceilings. In the middle of the room was a large canopy bed with mosquito netting draped over it. In any other place and time, it would have been very romantic. But here at this moment, it was foreign and imposing. Isabella sat on one of the chairs in the corner of the bedroom, pulled her scarf and veil from her face and hair, and waited with trepidation.

For the first time in as long as she could remember, her mind was completely void. She did not know where to direct her thoughts. Instead, she just sat silently, too afraid to contemplate the future. It was like attempting to focus in the midst of a dark void. The silence was deafening, except for the slight ringing in her ears.

After several minutes, a woman entered the room. She was completely covered from head to toe in black. Isabella wished she could see her face. Would the women in this land be as heartless as the men? She dreaded finding out the answer to that question. The woman quietly walked toward her and removed her niqab and khimar. The face before her was Mina's. Immediately, Isabella jumped to her feet and hugged her as tears began to slide down her face. She was overwhelmed. It was so foolish for a stranger to bring her such happiness. But this was an unusual time and place. And the familiarity she felt with this woman gave her just a moment of peace. For the first time in several hours, she felt the presence of her heavenly Father come flooding back to her. In response, she offered a simple prayer of thanks for this small, unexpected surprise.

For several moments, neither of the women said anything, but Isabella could sense that Mina was relieved to be with her as well. Friendship had never been so meaningful. It was like a simple ray of light in the midst of a dark, barren land.

"Now, Mina your maid. I no longer work for Hasam. I am relieved. Hasam very evil man. I live many days in fear. I doubt many times that I ever be free of him." Mina looked up at Isabella. She could see utter relief in her expression.

"You may be my maid, but I hope we can be friends. I will never survive this place without a friend. Please be my friend, Mina."

"We already friends. Mina very glad to be with you. Now, we get you out of abaya. You exhausted."

Mina helped her remove her abaya and began to search in a wardrobe for something to change into. Isabella could not wait to shed the restrictive garments. She shuddered at the obscurity of the clothing. She would not become a faceless soul in this endless sea of sand.

"I am very tired, but I am afraid that I will never be able to sleep," Isabella replied.

Mina brought her what appeared to be a long, loose-fitting nightgown. Isabella took it into the bathroom and prepared for bed. She found a washcloth and washed her face. There was also a new toothbrush on the sink. She used it to brush her teeth. It felt like it had been days since she had completed this simple action. She had completely lost track of the amount of time that had passed during her arduous journey. When she returned to the bedroom, Mina was waiting for her.

"What do you think will happen tomorrow, Mina?"

"I not know."

"Do you have any idea why I am here?"

"I not know. I told I no longer work for Hasam. Mina be your maid. That all I know." Mina's face seemed so sincere. She knew she was telling the truth.

"I cannot understand this. I know that women are abducted all the time. The news is always reporting them. But this is never what happens in a kidnapping in my country. Most kidnappings end in death or worse. How did Hasam and the others get me out of the U.S.? Were there no officials at the airport to ask for my passport? None of these events make any sense to me. How did this happen?" Isabella tried to grasp all the events that had transpired.

"Hasam know right people and have lots of money, Hasam remove many women from many places in world. Mina one of women taken from Indonesia. We once a family with some money. Mina and brother attend school. I learn to read and speak a little English. When tsunami hit our home, we lose everything. Family village destroyed. My family get very poor. When man offer money for me, they no choice but to take. Not much food left for my brother and sisters. Hasam money provide needs for several months. Mina want to go. I help my family. I not believe I would see so many bad things after leave my home. I have clean clothes to wear and food to eat. But being a slave..." Mina choked on the ponderous words and was unable to continue.

"Maybe you will be safe now." Isabella hoped this would be true. It felt good to worry about someone else for a few moments. She was tired of considering her own fate. Isabella thought about the gravity of Mina's words and even what she had not been able to say. She had been so sheltered in her safe little world back home. She was clueless of the atrocities that were happening halfway around the world. She had been completely self-absorbed in her own little universe. In just a few hours, everything had changed that, and she knew she would never be the same person she had once been. It was staggering and sad. The weight of it made her weary. She walked to the bed and sat down.

"I must leave now. I come in morning." Mina got up and started to leave.

"Mina, don't go. I want you to stay here with me."

"I must go. I have room I told to stay in. Servants have rooms near family." Mina walked toward the door and quietly left her sitting in this strange place, a prisoner utterly alone.

Isabella stared for several moments at the door that Mina had just exited through as emptiness crept in from every corner. The weight of the silence made her tense. She slowly shuffled to the bed, pulled back the blanket, and climbed in. The sheets were luxurious and so soft. The bed enveloped her like a gentle hug. She resisted giving in to the comforts of the room as she lay there thinking of Sam. When she closed her eyes, she could see his handsome face smiling at her. His dark hair was tousled. He looked so young. She pictured his soft, gentle, loving, blue eyes. He was such a great man. She ached for him, but she had no way to reach him. She knew he had to be overcome with fear over her disappearance. How would he ever find her now that she was halfway across the world? She tried to think of the girls and the pain that they were feeling, but it was more then she could bear. She pushed the thoughts away, letting the tears that fill her eyes wash away her last thread of hope.

She fell into a fitful sleep. That night, memories from her past were woven all through her dreams. She remembered the sweet laughter of her girls playing in their backyard. She could hear the gentle words of love whispered in her ear by the man she loved. Even in her sleep, she longed for home. A couple of times throughout the night, she had awakened to the sound of a lone howl in the desert. It was a disturbing reminder that she was far from home. But she was exhausted from the events surrounding her kidnapping, so she slept restlessly through most of the night.

Isabella opened her eyes to darkness. It was silent in the room. She sat up and looked around her. For several moments, she was disoriented and lost. Slowly, she grasped her surroundings. She threw herself back down in frustration and just lay there looking at the netting above the bed. She resisted the urge to cry again. Instead, she decided to find something to eat. She was starving. She wandered into the small kitchen and opened the refrigerator. It was empty. She closed it and looked out the window. The sun was up and pretty high in the sky. She realized it was very late in the morning. The curtains must have been pulled closed in her bedroom, causing it to be so dark. She wandered back into her bedroom, flipped the switch to the lamp on her bedside table, and looked around. The ill-fitting clothes from the previous day were draped across the chair. She had placed them there the night before after changing into her nightgown. She went into the bathroom and washed her face, brushed her teeth, and changed back into the clothes she had worn the previous day.

She opened the bathroom door and heard sounds coming from the other room. At first, she was startled by the idea that someone had arrived while she was changing. But curiosity took over when wonderful, enticing smells began floating from the other room. Her stomach began to growl. She made her way back through the rooms and found Mina in the kitchen preparing food.

"That smells wonderful. I am starving."

"You should be," Mina answered.

"What are you making?"

"I make fried rice, breakfast dish in my country. I hope you like it. I not know what to prepare. I go to market this morning to get few things for next few days," Mina replied gingerly.

"It smells wonderful, and I am so hungry. I have not eaten anything in … I have not eaten in more than a day."

"Go to dining room, and I bring you meal in few minute."

"Will you be eating with me?"

"No, I already eat. Isabella, eat; I straighten room. I already buy some clothes for you. I guess your size. I hope clothes fit you. I think. Mina get very good at guessing size when work for Hasam." Mina smiled and shooed her into the other room.

Isabella seated herself at the low table. It was so

alien sitting this way. As soon as she had arranged herself for the meal, Mina brought a plate of steaming food and placed it in front of her. Then she handed her a warm towel. Isabella wiped her hands. Then she searched around for a fork.

"Where is the fork?"

"No fork. Here, eat with hands. It good custom to eat with only right hand. After you finish, I bring water to rinse hands. Do not wait. I know you hungry. Eat." Mina turned and left the room. She reached for the plate to take a small portion in her hand. The food was very hot. She recoiled from the burning sensation in her fingers. She shook her head in annoyance. There were so many things for Isabella to become accustomed to. She drummed her fingers against the table as she sat in silence waiting for the meal to cool.

CHAPTER SEVEN

Isabella paced around the small apartment again. She was bored. After eating, she had showered and changed into one of the outfits Mina had purchased. The clothes were a pretty good fit. The jeans were fashionable but a little loose. She was wearing a stylish scoop-neck cotton shirt. It was very cute, but a little snug, and the green color matched perfectly with the color of her eyes. Mina had told her she was not required to wear the abaya and other coverings in her home or the adjoining garden. That was a relief. The memory of the concealing coverings was very unsettling. In the short time she had worn them, they had become a noose, choking away her individuality. In response, she had folded them and put them in the back of the large wardrobe in her room, hoping to never again have to look at them.

In the main sitting area, she had found a few shelves with some books. A couple of them were in English, but most were written in what appeared to be Arabic. She browsed over the English titles again, but they did not interest her. She wandered around aimlessly through the few rooms, aching for something to occupy the time. How many times had she circled these rooms in search of something to do? There was no television, no radio, and no phone. Isabella had never left the United States in her life; if there had been a phone, she would not have known how to dial home. She felt frustrated about her ignorance. She needed something to do. She was restless. Mina had left for the main house after she had showered and dressed. Isabella had begged for her to stay, but Mina had been commanded to work in other areas. She was forced to leave her alone.

Again, she walked around the rooms. The air was getting stuffy, and beads of perspiration formed on her upper lip. Her mind had gone around and around in circles, thinking, hoping, longing. The more she walked, the more hedged in she began to feel. She needed something to occupy her thoughts. Frantically, she searched around the rooms again. The walls were closing in on her, confining her. Her breathing was becoming erratic. How was she to pass the mind-numbing hours here? She needed somewhere to go, a way to escape. What had once been a reasonably sized apartment now seemed so small. Time and space with nothing but silence enveloped her as she scrambled to find an escape. She needed to get away. Isabella walked over to the door leading to the garden. She paused there, hesitantly holding the doorknob. She was apprehensive about leaving the safety of the house. There was something extrinsic about the outdoors, but she needed to get out of this place. She escaped out the side door onto a small terrace. She closed the door and leaned against the wall for support. She took several deep breaths to relax her body from the mania that nearly gripped her. The garden was stifling hot but shaded. This was not an escape; it was just a new enclosure. She looked around, appraising the comforts of her prison. She felt heat rush to her face from anger over her lack of control. She looked around, longing to get away.

The fresh, sweet scents of the garden intruded into her senses. Without conscious thought, she became aware of the beauty of the garden she had entered. She stomped to a small bush of globe-shaped purple flowers while effortlessly her anger began to fade. She paused in wonder. How unique they were. An indomitable desire to experience this lovely garden weakened her resolve. She quietly looked around, absorbing all the sights and smells. It was a lovely little oasis in the midst of this barren land. She walked around, touching and smelling all the unusual plants and trees. Without acknowledging it, she began to love this exotic example of creation. There was a small table with two chairs and an iron fence around the garden. From her garden, she could also see part of the extensive grounds of the property. The whole place was a paradise here in the midst of the desert. Everything was lush and green. Even in her longing for home, she was aware of the beauty of this land. This too was part of creation. It was evidence of the creative artist that had made it. She took a seat in one of the chairs and relaxed as she took in the landscape. She sat for several minutes, wondering at all the beauty around her. In this moment of

ete peace, she found a solace that offered her the
ity to pray. She gave all of her hopes and fears to
ner Lord. She released the anger and sought simple
guidance in the circumstance that she knew was out of
her control. She sought repose from her worries with
the only one that could bring her comfort.

Latif had noticed Isabella sitting in the garden. He
had not intentionally come out looking for her. He had
simply wanted to walk around the grounds to check
that everything had been cared for while he had been
away. Yet, he had been drawn to her. He had not dared
to approach her. Instead, he had made sure to conceal
himself behind a cluster of date palm trees. He wondered what she was doing. At first he had thought she
was dozing in the chair. But several times he had seen
her shift in the seat. It looked as if she might be meditating, but he could not tell for sure.

He stayed for a long time watching her. She was
beautiful to him. He loved her hair and her smooth
skin. He was curious to know how it felt. He could only
imagine. The shirt she was wearing was tight and left
little to the imagination about the curves beneath. Her
face was elegant and lovely. Latif could hardly wait for
her to be his wife, but he must be patient. The month
of Ramadan would begin in just two days. He knew it
was not advised by Muslim scholars to marry during
this month of fasting and self-discipline. Ramadan is
a blessed month. It is the month Muslims spend their
days reflecting over their sins and seeking forgiveness.
Reading the Koran was required. The fast begins each

day of this month at the first hint of dawn and continues until dusk. He knew he was required to refrain from all evil thoughts and deeds, purifying himself with self-restraint and acts of kindness. It was not a month to marry Isabella. So he was prepared to wait until the end of the month to have her.

He had talked briefly with his father about his impending marriage. His father had not been happy. He had reminded him that Americans do not easily acclimate to this restrictive way of life. He advised Latif to reconsider the foolishness of this marriage, assuring him it would only end in disaster. Latif had patiently listened to his father's advice. He knew it was not wise to proceed against his father's wishes, but in the end, he had not been persuaded by his arguments. Latif had called his mother and told her that she must plan the wedding party for the seventh day of Shawwal, the month following Ramadan. He knew Allah would reward him for his patience, because waiting to possess Isabella was the biggest sacrifice he had ever made.

Hasam and Latif had completed the paperwork for the marriage with the local authorities earlier that morning. It had been a simple process requiring only Hasam and Latif's signatures to make it legal. Marriage in Saudi Arabia was simply a civil agreement. There was nothing sacred about it. And divorce was easy for a man. It only required that a man repeat, "I divorce you" three times in front of a witness. A mehr was agreed upon at the time of marriage. This was an amount to be paid to the wife at the time of divorce. While divorce was a simple process for a man, it was not so easy for a woman, and for Isabella, divorce would never be an option.

Latif watched as Isabella stood and walked serenely around the small, walled garden. Reluctantly, he pulled himself back toward the main house. He had spent too much time admiring her. He knew it was time to get back to work.

Isabella was growing restless. It had been nearly a week since she had arrived here to serve her prison sentence, and she was going crazy. A few days before, Mina had arrived before dawn to prepare her breakfast. She had wakened her and instructed her to eat. Patiently, Mina had explained the requirements for the month of Ramadan. Isabella had been frustrated by this imposed fast. She had repeatedly told Mina that she was a Christian. Christians do not follow the laws of Ramadan. But Mina had stated that Islam was not just a religion in Saudi Arabia; it was the law. There was no separation from Islamic laws and the government. Even the king of Saudi Arabia was advised by the Ulema, the religious leaders, so that the laws of the Koran were upheld in everything. Isabella was baffled. She could not wrap her mind around a country that imposed the laws of the Koran, even for people that did not practice the religion. She tried to imagine the outrage of Americans if our government mandated Christian laws for those who were not Christians. She was certain that even the Muslims in the U.S would express outrage at any laws like that. Yet it was openly accepted in most of the Middle East. Even worse was the fact that Saudi Arabia was the most stringent of all the Middle Eastern countries.

Following breakfast, Mina had left. For the rest of the month, Isabella would not see Mina during the day, nor would she be allowed to eat until dusk. She was completely alone for all the daylight hours. The forced solitude was excruciating. Most of the time, she was insane with boredom. Other times, she was distraught thinking of her family. She missed them. She had never gone this long without seeing or talking to Sam and the children, and she struggled not to think of the grief they were feeling. She knew that they could not comprehend where she had gone. She was certain Sam was out of his mind with worry. There were even moments throughout the day when she would grow so angry at the fateful events happening against her will that she would scream out loud. Her days became monotonous, slowly crawling by as she wrestled with surging, uncontrolled emotions ready to sweep her away.

Again, her mind relived the events that had transpired, but none of it made sense. On the plane, she had tried to think through possible scenarios for her abduction. She wondered if she would be sold into some kind of sex trade. She had also considered that she might be forced into another type of slavery. She had even wrestled with the possibility that she would be forced to become someone's wife. But why would she be stolen from her home, taken to a strange land, and then held captive in confinement? She repeatedly rearranged everything in her mind, but none of the pieces fit together. In the end, her thoughts always came to a dead end. She was not sure how much longer she could take the isolation, even as she accepted the fact that her mind was becoming unbalanced.

The night before when Mina had come to fix dinner, allowing her to break her fast, she had pleaded with her to stay a little longer. Mina had calmly explained that she was not allowed to stay and visit with her. Isabella had started crying like a child. Mina had been kind in consoling her, but she knew Mina was becoming frustrated with her arguing. Isabella knew Mina would be disciplined if she did not obey the specific instructions she had been given. She was trying not to be selfish, but she was losing her mind. Isabella asked if she could have some books to help pass the time and a Bible. Mina had promised to see what she could provide but made no promises.

Mina had arrived that morning just before dawn. She had been able to bring a few American novels for Isabella to read. Isabella lay in bed looking over the covers and titles of the books while Mina was in the kitchen making her breakfast. None of the books interested her, so she carelessly tossed them all aside. Normally in the morning, she got up and showered while she was waiting, but today she stayed in bed. Depression was setting in. She did not have the energy to get out of bed. Mina came to her room to summon her for breakfast.

"Isabella, breakfast ready. I make scramble eggs, just way you like."

"Thank you, Mina, but I am not hungry this morning. Leave them. I will eat them later."

"I not leave them. You eat now, or I throw out." Mina was exasperated.

Isabella was feeling agitated. "Are you a Muslim?"

"Why you ask?"

"Just answer me! Are you a practicing Muslim?" Isabella nearly screamed at her.

"No, I not. Why matter?"

"If you are not Muslim, then why must you impose these rules on me? There is no one here to determine when I eat my breakfast. No one will know if I eat it now or later. Why must you insist? I will not hold you responsible if I am caught. No one will punish you if I do not eat as you have informed me that I must do. I do not mean to be insolent, but I am no longer willing to cooperate with this foolishness! I am not hungry. If you must throw the eggs away, I will not complain. I just think all of this is stupid!" Isabella struggled to hold her temper.

"As you wish," Mina quietly responded. Isabella heard her go into the dining area, pick up the plate, and throw the contents in the trash. Then Mina left out the front door.

Isabella spent the entire day in bed. She read one of the books, and she took short catnaps throughout the day. She refused to shower, nor did she go out in the garden. Isabella was depressed, and she was angry. She was mad at Latif for making her a prisoner in his home. She was agitated with Mina for not being her ally. But most of all, she knew that she was mad at God. She could no longer pray, and if she tried, she only questioned where he had been in the midst of this pain and injustice. This was more than she could bear. She was nearly at the end of her rope.

That night, Mina came to make her dinner. She came into her room surprised that she was still in bed.

"You been in bed all day?" she asked.

"Yes. I have no reason to get out of bed. I am still not hungry. There is no need for you to fix dinner for me."

"Isabella, you must eat."

"Mina, please do not argue with me. If you make something, I won't eat it. I don't want to waste your time. If anything, I need a friend. Please come and tell me about your day."

"Okay. I only stay a short visit. I must tell Chen you not eating. You not want to hear about my day. It very boring."

"I do. Please tell me. I am so lonely. I miss my family. And I think I am losing my mind," Isabella gently implored.

For about twenty minutes, Mina rattled on about the mundane jobs she performed throughout the day. She talked a little about some of the other servants in the house and the places they were from. She talked most about Chen, the director of the servants. Isabella began to wonder if Mina was beginning to have romantic feelings about her boss. But she did not question her about it. She just liked hearing Mina talk, and the sound of her voice gently eased away a few of the rough edges on her frayed nerves. She needed this companionship. All too quickly, Mina had to rush off to help clean up from the meal in the main house, and Isabella was alone again.

CHAPTER EIGHT

Chen approached Latif to voice the concerns that Mina had brought to his attention. Latif immediately registered the distress on Chen's face.

"What has happened now, Chen?"

"I receive disturbing report from Mina about Isabella," he solemnly replied.

"Proceed."

"Isabella not want to eat today. She not shower or get up from bed. Mina said that she worried about her. She afraid to leave her alone. She say that every day Isabella cry when she leaves and question why she being held like prisoner."

Latif silently considered Chen's words. He realized he had been a fool. Without thinking, he had made Isabella a prisoner in his home. He had left her completely alone. She was probably homesick, and she had no friends to visit her. He tried to imagine how she was feeling. She must be desperate, confused, and alone. He knew he must make up for his foolishness.

"I will call my sister, Hafa, and have her come and visit her tomorrow. If there is anything that Isabella is asking for, please give it to her."

"Anything she wants, you want me to give her?" Chen questioned.

"Yes, anything. It will be several more weeks before our wedding ceremony. I do not want her to get sick. Do anything you can think of to make her happy."

Latif was still considering Isabella's condition after Chen left with his instructions. For the first time, he was concerned for her well-being. He knew he was being selfish by taking her as his wife, but there was little that he could do now. He could not return her to the United States. He had not questioned Hasam about how he had acquired her, but he suspected that everything had not been completely legitimate. He had noticed immediately that even the picture in the passport Hasam had produced for the marriage certificate had not been Isabella. He had not talked it over with Hasam, knowing that he would give a fabricated story instead of the real events that had transpired.

Latif contemplated having a short visit with Isabella. He desperately wanted to see her. But he was not sure if it would be wise to go to her yet. He decided to think on the matter a little longer before making a decision. He would have a better idea about her condition tomorrow after his sister's visit.

The next morning, Mina entered to make breakfast for Isabella. Chen had surprised her by being so agreeable about the requests Isabella had made. He had provided a very modern stack of American best-selling novels for Isabella to read. In all the time Mina had been in Saudi Arabia, she had never seen any books like this. She even suspected that some of them were illegal. She also had a Bible for Isabella. But she was very afraid of what her reaction to this book would be. The book was written in Arabic, and Mina was very certain she could not read it.

She had also been surprised when Chen had instructed her to have Isabella ready for a visitor. He had not told her who would be visiting, and she had been afraid to ask. Mina felt sorry for Isabella. She knew from their brief visits that she was distraught over her family. She also knew that the isolation was making her crazy. Lately, she had been emotional and argumentative about everything. Mina constantly reminded herself that it was Isabella's bizarre circumstances that brought out her insolent behavior. Isabella had a true, honest heart, and even when she was difficult, Mina could see it.

Mina owed a great debt to Isabella for providing an escape from Hasam, and it was more than she would ever be able to repay. Within the first few moments of meeting Isabella, she had sensed her kind and gentle heart. Because of circumstances and need, they had formed an instant bond. Mina had frequently lost her patience with Isabella over the last couple weeks, and she regretted it. She tried to be sympathetic, but at times she truly tired of her complaining. Of course, she knew she would probably act the same or worse if she were in Isabella's shoes, and she resolved to be more tolerant of her mood swings.

Mina peeked into Isabella's dimly lit bedroom. A soft light from the hall slightly illuminated the pre-dawn darkness. Mina could see that she was awake as she quietly approached the bed. When she reached Isabella's side, she saw tears swimming in her eyes. Mina knelt beside the bed and gently stroked her hair. Her pain was raw and open. Looking into her eyes, she saw into the depths of her soul, and the vision made her heart bleed.

"Isabella, you okay?"

She did not respond. Mina wondered if she even knew she was there and desperately searched for a way to rescue her drowning friend. She hoped that some of the gifts and maybe even the impending visit would cheer Isabella. She needed it. She had never heard of someone dying from a broken heart, but she wondered if it were possible. Isabella truly looked broken and on the edge.

Mina softly sang a song she had heard her mother sing to her baby sister. She knew Isabella could not understand the words to the song, but she hoped the melodic sound would speak comfort to her hurting soul. She used the lullaby to draw her out of her stupor. As she sang, she began to see a spark of life return to her eyes.

"That was lovely, Mina. What did the words mean?"

"The song called 'Suliram.' It mean go to sleep, go to

sleep; you protected by my love. It a song my *ibu* ... um, mother, sing to sister to help feel better."

"Thank you, Mina."

"I have gifts for you. Here a couple new books. I have Bible for you. Please not get excited. It written in Arabic. I think you not able to read it." For an instant, Mina saw her face awaken from the depression only to see the spark quickly extinguish. "Mina learn that you have visitor today."

Isabella did not even lift her head from the bed. "Who is coming to visit me?"

"I not know, but you get out of bed. Take shower, and I make something very special for breakfast." Mina gently pulled on Isabella's arm to encourage her out of bed. Reluctantly, Isabella sat up. Mina went into the bathroom to start the shower. She came back and gently pushed her into the other room. Mina looked closely at Isabella and realized she had lost several pounds in the short time since her abduction.

"I get clothes for you to change to after shower. I leave them on bed. Then I go to kitchen to fix breakfast. Come to dining room when you finished."

Isabella obeyed but gave no response to her comments. Mina was desperate knowing that she needed to help her distraught friend.

Mina went into the kitchen to begin preparing pancakes for Isabella's breakfast. She had purchased an American cookbook at the market. Hoping to cheer her friend, she had searched for the perfect meal. Now, she hoped it would help. Mina had truly considered Isabella her friend. In a way, she had become her family since she knew she would never get a chance to see her real one again.

Isabella had truly been grateful to Mina for making her a special American breakfast, but she knew her response to it had disappointed her. She had tried to show her appreciation, but the few bites she had eaten had been tasteless in her mouth. It was not because Mina was not a good cook. At any other time and place, she would have loved the pancakes. Isabella had simply lost the desire to eat. She had even wondered if she had lost the desire to live. Isabella sensed that Mina was deeply concerned but found no encouragement in it.

She had showered and dressed to appease Mina. Her reflection in the mirror had revealed a sallow-faced stranger. She looked terrible. Dark circles had formed under her eyes from the many restless nights. She was sleeping all the time, but her sleep was often troubled and riddled with dreams. She slept to forget where she was and to remember where she longed to be. This morning after breakfast, she had taken a short nap, and she had dreamed the sweetest dream. She and her family had gone on a fall camping trip in southern Indiana. In that short time, she had been transported over the miles of ocean to her home. Sam had been cooking breakfast over the fire. Rebecca had been riding her bike around the campgrounds. And Katherine had made friends with a young girl from the campsite across the road. The two girls were sitting together in lawn chairs playing with Katherine's doll, taking turns rocking the baby to sleep. She could feel the cool, crisp wind on her face, and the smell of bacon mixed with campfire smoke filled the air. But the little respite had been short, and waking always brought Isabella back to this tortured nightmare.

After she had awakened, she had looked through the new books that Mina had brought for her to read. She was searching for something to occupy her mind. She had sifted through the entire stack. The Bible was lying at the bottom. Isabella carefully picked it up. Even though she could not read it, the feel of the smooth leather in her hands was soothing. She rubbed the cover and thought of the God of the ages, her God. She longed to open this book and read the pages. Her heart ached for a few words from him. She even opened it and looked inside. Her heart had become as parched and barren as the desert around her. She was thirsty for his words, but the strange characters were so foreign looking. It was another reminder of how far she was from her home. She gently caressed the pages, hoping the words would transfer their meaning and silently praying for courage to face this new day. She closed the book and held it to her heart. This book with the words of life written in it was valuable to her even though she could not read it. She longed for word from her Savior. She slipped the book under her pillow, hung her head, and silently wept.

After several moments of emotional release, she had gone to the sink and washed her face. She walked out to the garden and took a long, deep breath. It was the first time she had been able to come out here in several days. The smells of the desert were so different from Indiana, as unusual spices and fragrances wafted in the warm breeze. It was a very hot day, as many of the days had been since she had arrived, but the humidity was low. The house shaded the garden at this hour of the morning. She sat for a few moments, fighting against her restlessness. Giving up, she soon wandered back into the house but resisted going into the bedroom and sleeping. Instead, she grabbed the stack of books and went in the sitting room.

She had just settled into one of the sofas to get lost in some new novel when Mina came in to tell her that her visitor had arrived and would be coming in just a few moments.

"Who is coming to visit, Mina?"

"Hafa, Latif's sister, come to visit. Latif invite her," Mina replied.

"Does she seem nice?"

"Yes, I think so. She has very nice smile."

Isabella was overwrought with emotion. She was excited and afraid, hopeful and discouraged. She just could not decide if this was a good thing or something to dread.

Just as she was ready to tell Mina she was not up for a visitor, a young, exuberant-looking lady stepped through the doorway. Mina was right; she did have a nice smile, but she was cautious and suspicious of this young woman.

"You must be Isabella. My name is Hafa. I am Latif's sister," Hafa offered in a sweet-sounding voice.

"Yes, I am Isabella." Isabella awkwardly looked at the mysterious woman that had entered her home. It was rude not to invite her to sit, but she was not interested in being kind. She watched as Hafa stiffly waited for an invitation.

A few awkward moments passed before Isabella finally offered. "Hafa, you may have a seat. Mina, would you please bring us some coffee?" Isabella requested.

"Isabella, you must not break fast," Mina hesitantly reminded her.

"Oh, you are right. Please forgive me." Her voice was laced with sarcasm in response to the frustration she felt at obeying this absurd ritual. "This fasting, Ramadan, whatever ... all this is foreign to me." Isabella carelessly brushed away the mistake with a wave of her hand.

Hafa smiled at her. "All this must be so strange to you. Do not apologize; I am not offended. I am sure I made silly mistakes like that when I was living in the United States."

"You lived in the United States? Was it recently? Where did you live?"

"I lived in Brooklyn, New York. My uncle lives there with his family. My mother persuaded my father to send me to live with them and attend boarding school. Educational opportunities are limited for women here. I would never have been offered the chance if I had not had family already living there."

"Did you like our country? How long did you live there?"

Hafa smiled again and then patiently answered. "I lived and attended school for two years before I came home to be married. And I really enjoyed living in America. There are so many great things about the U.S., but there were also things that I missed about

Saudi Arabia while I was there. I was happy and sad when I left."

Isabella was intrigued. She could not fathom how someone from this country would ever want to willingly return here, especially a woman. Why would she want to give up her freedom? She longed to understand more about this woman. She was apprehensive to accept this delightful woman even though her manner was open and friendly. Yet Isabella somehow knew that she was sincere. Hafa was beautiful. Her skin was a deep, rich brown, and her golden caramel eyes sparkled when she talked. Her hair was black, straight, and long. Regardless of her mistrust, she was drawn to Hafa, sensing a kindred bond to her that she could not explain.

Isabella had not realized the true extent of her loneliness. At home, she had Sam and the girls to keep her company. She enjoyed when he came home from work or when the girls came home from school so that she could hear about their day. Plus, she had some really great friends she regularly talked to. She was a social person, loved people, and even enjoyed interacting with people in the grocery store. There had been times that she had delighted in spending some time alone with a book or studying her Bible. But even then, the study had sometimes correlated with friends at a weekly Bible study. She knew it was okay to be alone; solitude was important for reflecting and contemplating. But the solitude here had become imposing. Mina was here every day, and Isabella enjoyed building a friendship with her. But Mina was only able to have short visits because of her other responsibilities. Sometimes in the morning she came by just to make breakfast and then left. It was hard being so isolated with only her thoughts for company.

Isabella visited with Hafa for over an hour without noticing how quickly the time was passing. Hafa was like her in so many ways. Even though they had grown up so far apart, already they shared similar thoughts and feelings. Yet, in a lot of other ways, they were so different. Isabella wondered if having any conversation for such an extended period of time had ever felt quite so enjoyable. The conversation, even though it was very superficial, was like rain on her barren soul. And for this brief respite, she reveled in the delight their camaraderie brought her.

"Isabella, I should be getting home. I have really enjoyed visiting with you. Sometimes I miss America, and visiting with you takes me back there for just a little while. Would you mind if I come back in a couple of days for another visit?" Hafa started to get up to leave.

Isabella longed to extend the visit just a little longer while hoping that Hafa truly would come for another visit. "I would love for you to come anytime. I am very lonely here. There are so many long days, days to think, even grieve. I really miss my..." Isabella's eyes filled with tears as she choked on the words.

Instinctually, Hafa moved next to her and took her hand. "You are homesick?"

"Homesick? I do not think that is a strong enough word to explain how I feel," Isabella sadly replied.

"But I assumed that you wanted to come to Saudi Arabia. What were you hoping to find by coming here? Or were you running away from something?"

Isabella nearly gasped out loud at this strange comment. Slowly and quietly, she answered. "Hafa, I did not choose to come to Saudi Arabia. I was taken by force from my home and family. I would never have chosen to leave my life in America to come here. Never, ever would I have chosen this."

Hafa stared at Isabella for several minutes. She seemed too dumbfounded to speak. "I want to hear your story. Please start at the very beginning and tell me everything. Do not leave out any details."

Isabella told her in great detail about her husband and her girls. Isabella related all the details of her abduction story to Hafa. She even honestly explained her emotional trials here in captivity. Throughout the entire story, Hafa was speechless and completely engrossed in the story. Isabella sensed that she empathized with her plight. On several occasions throughout the story, Hafa even seemed close to tears. Once Isabella finished disclosing every last detail, they stared at each other in silence. Isabella was unsure of what to do. So she just waited, and in a strange way, she felt a little better. The sorrow over all that she had lost was still there, and her anger over the injustice did not diminish. But in sharing her burden, she had somehow lessened the load in her heart.

Eventually when Hafa spoke, disgust dripped from each word. "You have been through an amazing and horrifying nightmare. I am ashamed that any man in my country would do this. But I am flabbergasted that my brother would ever be involved in this disgusting plot! What is worse, I must add to your pain with something that should not be said to you. But I must, if only to prepare you for what is to come."

Isabella sank back in her seat as dread captured her breath. She was not sure she could handle anymore bad news. Her pulse pounded in her ears as she waited.

Hafa's eyes filled with tears as she spoke. "Latif is your husband. Several days ago, the papers were signed. It has been made official by the minister of state, a personal friend of Latif's. According to the laws of this land, you are married to my brother."

And now, all the pieces crashed down around her and fell into place as the events of the last several days became as clear as crystal in her mind. The intense pain was like a gavel in her heart. Fate had spoken in the voice of her new friend, and it had destroyed every last shred of hope within her. She folded over onto herself and held her legs in a hopeless hug. Tears dripped from her eyes and fell to the floor. All she could think was, *My life is over.*

Hafa's expression was filled with turmoil. "I am so sorry, Isabella. I must talk to my brother and see if I can change this. From the short conversation I had with him, I am certain that he does not know that you are married. I do not know what he will do when he finds out. Please do not give up hope. You have a family that needs you. Maybe this can be undone. Maybe, just maybe, Latif will let you go home.

Isabella tried to muster a little of her hope back, but even while speaking the words of encouragement, Hafa had sounded unsure. In that instant, she feared all hope was lost. How would Latif ever return her home? If he did, wouldn't he face criminal prosecution for his involvement in this plot to bring her here? He would never expose himself to that. She was almost certain.

Isabella turned to Hafa with a few questions she just had to ask. "How can I be married to him if I did not give my consent?"

Hafa took a deep breath before responding. "According to Sharia law, women are subject to the authority of a man. You are not supposed to be married against your will, but there is little to prevent it from happening. As a foreign woman, you needed a male guardian to sign the marriage contract. Hasam was your guardian and spokesperson; he signed for you in your place."

"But I have not seen Latif since we arrived. Are you sure there is not a mistake?"

"Latif has chosen to postpone the wedding celebrations until after the month of Ramadan. There are strict rules about this sacred month. I think Latif has only waited for you because of that."

Isabella refused to allow Hafa's haunting words to penetrate her consciousness as she proceeded to question. She must no longer remain in the dark about her future. "He is legally my husband, but he is waiting until after Ramadan to take me as his wife. Is that what you are saying?"

"Yes. But it is possible he will seek a divorce once he realizes you are already married."

"I am married to Sam in my heart. I have pledged my heart to him in an oath to God. Plus, I am legally married to him in the eyes of the law. Those things cannot be undone. How can I be married to Latif?"

"Isabella, you may think marriage is a sacred oath,

but our law only views it as a contract. And I am not sure, but I do not even know if our government would consider a U.S. marriage contract binding here. This is a very unusual situation. I am not sure what will happen. All I can do is offer to help make this right. Again, I am sorry. What has been done is wrong."

Hafa reached out and took Isabella's hand. Isabella looked at her with a blank stare. This woman was her only hope, and she longed to believe that she would have some influence over her brother. Hafa reached out and gave her a slight hug for encouragement and then stood to leave.

"Isabella, I have to go to my brother right now and explain everything. Are you going to be okay? Would you like me to find Mina and send her to you?"

"Yes, I would. And if somehow your brother does not agree to send me home, would you please let him know I need to talk to him? I cannot marry him. I simply cannot. I must make that clear to him if he will not listen to your reasoning. Please promise me you will give him that message."

"I will." Hafa turned and walked toward the door. She could see the defeated change in her demeanor. Isabella knew that Hafa was sincere. She would plead her case, and certainly she could convince her brother to change his mind. With a tiny ray of hope in her heart, that is exactly what she prayed for.

A few minutes later, Mina came to her. "What has happened?"

"Latif and I are married."

"I heard many rumors from some servants, but I unsure if they were true. I sorry I not tell you. I afraid you be more upset. I not want you to worry, especially if it not be true."

"I am not angry, Mina. I understand. I just don't know what to do. This really can't be happening. I want to run and hide, but there is nowhere to go. Can you stay with me for just a little while?"

"Yes. Hafa tell me to stay with you rest of day. She said that she tell Latif and Chen her instructions."

At least she would not be alone. Mina walked with her back to her bedroom. They quietly talked a little about trivial things because neither of them wanted to bring up their unspoken thoughts. When Isabella became very groggy and struggled to stay awake, Mina left her alone to sleep.

CHAPTER NINE

Mina had just come and awakened Isabella from another restless sleep. Latif was coming to talk to her. She checked the clock. It was nearly 7:00 p.m. It had only been a few hours since she had met with Hafa, but it felt as if it had been yesterday. Days had begun to run together in this timeless existence. Isabella got up and went to the bathroom. She washed her face and smoothed down her hair. She did not apply any fresh makeup. There was no need to look appealing to Latif. Silently, she prayed he would bring her good news while trying to hold her hopes in check. She knew she was at the mercy of this stranger.

Mina came into the room. "Isabella, he is here."

Isabella felt her heart skip several beats. She was so frightened; her feet felt frozen to the floor. Everything was riding on this conversation. Her stomach was in turmoil. She wanted to know what he would say, but she dreaded that he would bring frightful news.

Hesitantly, she followed Mina to the sitting room. She glanced up and saw that he was seated on one of the sofas. Isabella sat in one of the chairs nearby. Mina disappeared from the doorway. She did not know what to say to this stranger who was supposedly her husband. She was afraid to look at him, so she just stared at the floor in front of her feet.

Finally, after a brief moment, he addressed her. "I hope my staff is treating you well, Isabella. I know I should have come to you sooner, but things are very complicated. Hafa has explained the entire situation to me. And I want to start by saying that I am sorry. I did not know you were abducted, nor did I know you were married. What Hasam did to you was wrong."

Latif hesitated for several moments. Isabella looked up at him. She hoped his silence would mean he was willing to send her home. She hoped.

Latif was looking at her. With his gaze locked on hers, he continued. "Isabella, I cannot send you back home."

It was the last straw. Isabella was furious. She wanted to gouge out his eyes. She wanted to scream and make him feel her pain. Forcefully, against all odds, she reigned in her fierce emotion. She would refrain, holding her temper in check. She needed to make a viable argument, and no man would listen to the ranting and raving of a madwoman. For all that she held dear, she must not lose her head. She took a very long deep breath while never breaking from his gaze. She was sure her anger was readable, but she proceeded as calmly as possible.

"Let me make this really clear. I want to go home.

My heart, my soul, and my body all long for my husband and my children." Latif started to comment. She stopped him with a fierce gaze. "I want to make this very clear to you. I am not your wife. I will never be your wife. My family is in Indiana. You are not my family. I have not, will never, consent to becoming your wife. I am not sure what you hope will happen, but I will not agree. I am a free woman. I want to return home. I appeal to you in the name of all things right and true. Please send me home to my family."

For a moment, she saw a strong flash of anger in his face. It had passed so quickly that she questioned if she had actually seen it. When he spoke, his voice was even and calm. "Isabella, I assure you, you are my wife. As my wife, you are now a citizen of Saudi Arabia, bound by all the laws of this country. You do not have a way to return home without my written permission. You have no right to file a legal grievance against me in court. You have no way to divorce me. So I repeat, you are my wife. We will have a marriage ceremony in just a few weeks. After the ceremony, we will be traveling to Jeddah for a short honeymoon. I have made up my mind. Nothing you say will change it."

Isabella jumped to her feet. She was just short of hysterical, and she nearly screamed, "Why? I deserve to know why."

"There are a couple reasons why. Isabella, please sit down, and I will explain them to you." Isabella refused and remained on her feet. His calm control of the situation angered her further. When he realized she would not obey, he continued. "I cannot send you home. If you report this incident to the police or FBI, I would never be able to return to the U.S without being arrested. My family has several company investments in your country. Any scandal would sever our ties with those companies and prevent me from ever forging new ones. Hasam would also be questioned, if he were caught. He has been my friend for years, but I do not trust him in this. He would not hesitate to pin this entire thing on me to save himself. Also, the political upheaval that this would cause between Saudi Arabia and the U.S. would have global ramifications. The king would hold me responsible and possibly call for my death. Even if I wanted to divorce you and send you home, I cannot do it. I simply cannot send you home. You must resign yourself to this. I am your husband now, and this is your home."

"What if I promise I will never say anything to anyone?" Isabella's voice was nearly a whine.

"I want to believe you, Isabella, but there is too much at stake. I cannot risk it. I'm sorry."

She saw remorse in his eyes, but even more clearly, she detected a strong resolve. She was ready to beg and plead, to scream and fight, but she knew it would not help her. Instead she turned and ran from the room. She never wanted to see his despicable face again. As soon as she left the room, the floodgates opened. She fought to keep from wailing out loud. She did not want to give him the satisfaction of knowing that he had broken her. She fell on the bed and grabbed the Bible out from under her pillow. She held it against her chest, hoping that it would help her shattered heart, and for hours she did not move.

Latif left out the front door. His mind and body were full of conflicting emotions. The strongest emotion he was feeling was desire. She had angered him as no woman had ever angered him. But in his anger, he had felt an overwhelming desire to have her, to hold her, to love her. She had expressed more passion than any woman had ever expressed to him before. He was determined to take that passion and watch it melt into desire and maybe even love. He earnestly wanted to make her love him. On impulse, he had nearly gone in her room. He had wanted to hold her, to make her understand. He had longed for it. But instinctually he knew that she needed time. She needed to be alone with her thoughts. Eventually reason would win out. It was only a few short weeks until he would claim her, only a little while until the ceremony. It would not be long until Ramadan would be past. He could wait for just a little longer, but waiting would be the hardest thing he had ever done.

Isabella had given up. Latif's words had destroyed her. She tried to think of home, but her mind was empty. She tried to pray, but God was nowhere to be found. She knew that Mina was here; unfortunately, she no longer cared. If she could, she would shrivel up and die, sad and alone. Already something inside her had. She clutched onto the Bible in her hands as if it were a life preserver preventing her from drowning in the deep, dark, endless ocean. She choked out loud at the strange analogy as it passed through her mind. This place was the deep, dark, endless ocean, if only it would swallow her whole. She waited in anticipation of it, but her heart kept beating, her lungs still took in breath, and her blood was still flowing through her veins. Her heart and soul may have died, but her body stubbornly did not. What could she do? A lone tear ran down the side of her cheek into her hair. She had cried so many tears that her face felt dry and taut from the moisture and salt. Her throat was parched and sore, but she had no desire to drink. She had no desire to move. She caressed the cover of the Bible. One last time, she tried to pray. It was a simple request. "Help. Lord, please help me."

She lifted the book and gazed at it. If only she could read the words, if only, if only. She turned on her side and laid the book on the bed. Randomly, she opened to a page. She just sat there looking at the words. She began to look at the calligraphic style of the letters. They were beautiful in an unfamiliar way, but she could get no meaning from these timeless words. She just sat there for several minutes. Then she closed her eyes and began to pray for guidance. She felt forsaken and knew only God could help. When she opened her eyes, she began to look at the text again. She slowly leaned in closer to the text, blinking her eyes several times. Since she had finished her prayer, she had started to sense something about the text. Could God speak his words to her just while she looked at the text? She did not think that was how God worked. Again she looked closer to the text. The words did not change, but somehow as she looked at the foreign language, it started to make sense.

Quietly, she said aloud one of her very favorite passages in Isaiah. "But those who hope in the Lord will renew their strength."

Was it possible that God had come to her in this strange and foreboding country to bring her a special message in this strange language? She thought it just might be a miracle, because somehow she had understood what the words meant. She looked at the passage again, but it was just an unknown script. The recognition was gone. Isabella was confused. Maybe she had just imagined it. She did not know. But Isabella could not shake the sensation that God had done something very incredible. It had been a small personal gift to her in this very dark hour, like an Old Testament story. She could not fathom the profound wonders of her God. Instead she just reflected on his love. She began to go through and recall all the stories and verses she had heard and read and memorized over the years. In this land so close to the land of Abraham, God was offering something very personal just for her. He was Yahweh. It was silly, but the encounter was so amazing; she thought maybe God might even change her name. She nearly smiled at the absurdness of it. This revelation did not remove Isabella from the grave situation she faced. She still wanted to go home. She still needed her family, but somehow for the first time she felt at peace in this place. She knew God was with her in this land. He was her God, and he would walk with her through it all. He could arrange for her rescue, but he didn't. Instead he had bent down so low to reach her that he had nearly whispered in her ear. It was unfathomable, but it was something tangible that she could hold on to. She knew for certain that her God would never leave her or forsake her, and for the moment, that was enough. She would face this indomitable mountain. She did not like it; she prayed for God to change it. But for the first time, she was willing to accept it. She suspected God had a plan, a plan for her future. And in her heart, a small ray of hope began to grow.

Isabella woke the next morning. It had been the most restful night since she had arrived, and this morning she had a plan. She hoped that it would work. It had been on her mind the moment she had awakened. She needed to talk this over with Mina to think it through out loud and get her advice. She was hesitantly optimistic. She dressed and showered and met Mina in the kitchen a little while later.

"Good morning, Mina. Can you stay with me just a little while? I would like to talk something over with you."

"I stay just a little while. I have things I required to do in other places. But I like to stay for little visit."

"Mina, I know this may sound crazy, but I want to try to escape. I am so clueless about so many things in this country, but I am certain there must be a way that I can get away from here before, before—"

"I not know, Isabella. I think escape not possible." The look on Mina's face clearly registered her apprehension about the suggestion.

"There has to be a way. There must be a way to

escape. I have been trying to formulate a plan, but there are so many uncertainties here. Can you help me think through some ideas? What about a disguise? In the black abaya, no one would know who I am."

"Mina explain how travel work for women in this country. You used to way things work in America. You think you take ideas you know and make plan to leave, but it not work. Everything here different from your country. Women have no freedom. They not drive. They not go anywhere without man. They not travel without permission from men. You have no way get papers or money to travel. No one travel in this country without papers. It too dangerous to leave home alone. If Isabella try to leave, mutawa, religious police, would make you have papers. No identification, and you go jail or bring back here. Punishment be very bad for you. You put idea out of your mind."

Isabella was shocked by Mina's words. Regretfully, she was beginning to understand a little of the culture of this country, but she was determined to find a way to escape. "I understand why you are concerned, but there must be a way. There must. Is there no one in this country that could assist me in returning home?"

"Isabella, I am servant. No one here help me or you escape. I no friends to ask for help. I not speak to any men from this country, and women are mean and ignore me until they make me do hard work for them. Sometime they hurt me. I not know anyone to help you. To try escape could be bad. You help me escape from Hasam, but I not know way to help you. I am sorry. Please, you must not think about it."

"I do not want to give up. I want to believe that

there is a way to keep all this from happening. I want to go home. I am certain there has to be a way to escape." Isabella was desperate to hold on to this idea.

"I see you pray to your God. I watch you feel safe with help from him. Pray. Maybe he give you way to escape. That all you can do. Pray new plan not make you go in jail. You must be patient."

"Being patient means that I will have to marry Latif. I do not want to accept that option. The idea is repulsive to me. I cannot promise that I will not search for a way to get away. Will you try to think about it? Maybe you can think of something."

Isabella was desperate to find an escape. When she had been most discouraged after finding out that she was to marry Latif, she had found comfort from her Lord. But she had been unwilling to accept this fate. She needed to hope for another solution. Mina was right; she needed to pray and watch for an opportunity to escape. If God did not provide an escape, she would be forced to become Latif's wife. Certainly God would provide an escape. She did not even want to think of the alternative.

The days and weeks continued to crawl by in Isabella's enslaved existence. She was still bored, and most days she thought she would go insane from it. As her despair had lessened, she had resolved to occupy her mind with something productive. She passed the days reading through some of the books that Mina had provided. She still slept too much due to the monotony of the long days, but she had found a notebook to use as a diary to record her thoughts. She needed things to keep her mind active and alert while continuing her search for a plausible plan that would lead to escape.

Within the last two weeks, Hafa had visited a few more times. She had hoped for a way to petition her into becoming a collaborator in her plan for escape, but she had not felt right about bringing up the topic. They had talked about a lot of things. Isabella had talked about her family back home while Hafa had entertained her with funny stories from her childhood, as well as her time in the United States. Isabella looked forward to each of her visits. They had become precious respites from the tedium of her days. She sensed that Hafa was dissatisfied with her life here in Saudi Arabia, but she had shared very little about why. Hafa was married and had two sons. Her sons had never come with her for a visit, but Isabella hoped she would one day meet them. Her oldest son, Ali, was eight, and her youngest son, Jalil, was six. Listening to her talk about them made her desperate for any news from home about her own daughters. Isabella felt Hafa's love for her children, and as a mother, she could relate. But Hafa never talked about her husband, and Isabella suspected that they did not have a happy marriage. Hafa had briefly shared the arrangements of their marriage. Isabella had been so shocked that Hafa had married a complete stranger. Hafa had explained that it was the custom in her country for the husband and wife to never meet before the wedding ceremony. Because men and women are always separate, she had to trust in her father's decision. A woman rarely talks to or sees her husband before the ceremony. Sometimes a young girl will even be forced to become the third or fourth wife of a man in his fifties or older. Hafa was privileged to be the first and only wife of her husband. But women were expected to follow the wishes of their fathers in marriage, regardless of their own feelings. Often, when a wife was asked for her approval during the ceremony, she remained silent. According to custom, this is a sign of her humble acceptance of her fate. It was too amazing to consider. She thought about Latif, remembering that she might have to marry a complete stranger as well. It was not right. It was really more than she could comprehend. Women had a right to be human, to make their own decisions. Women had a right to freedom. She posed the question to Hafa after they had been visiting for a while that afternoon.

"Hafa, why do women accept the control of men over every aspect of their lives?"

"It is hard to explain and complicated. Some of the time, I can understand it, and other times I cannot. Women in your country have nearly all of the same freedoms as men. I know you think it is a good thing. Sometimes even I long for some of those freedoms. But other times, I am afraid of that kind of freedom. Unlimited freedom leaves a woman unprotected and vulnerable. Women are emotional and easily deceived by promises from men. When I lived in the U.S., I saw many girls at my school used by boys. One of my friends even got pregnant. When she told the boy about the pregnancy, he just laughed in her face. It made me very angry that any man would treat a woman like that. Here, in my country, women are protected from that kind of disgrace. Girls and boys do not go alone in cars to dark movie theaters. They are not given an opportunity to commit the sins that are so frequently ignored in your country."

Isabella silently considered her words. In some ways she was right. "I guess I can see your point. Dating and relationships are complicated. It is safer to control all the decisions of children so they do not make these mistakes. But women have the right to be individuals. Everything in your life is dictated by a man. I refuse to believe that if given the choice, you would chose to live your life that way. I do not believe God created women to be the property of men."

"I told you it was complicated." Hafa smiled at her. "I am not sure I can explain it to you. Most of the time it makes sense to me. But just like most young women in my country, I sometimes hope for a few of the freedoms that other women have. I also believe Allah did not create women to be the property of men, but I am not sure we should get into a philosophical discussion about religion."

Hafa was silent for several moments. Isabella could read conflicting emotions on her face. She seemed to be carefully formulating her thoughts before she spoke. "Isabella, I really like you. I enjoy our visits. And I am glad that you are my new sister. For this reason, I want to say this: you must be careful when you talk about your God here. Some people in this country are not tolerant of Christians. Most are not tolerant of any religion except Islam. If the mutawa were to hear you make a religious comment… Oh, Isabella, I don't want to scare you. Just remember that you live in a Muslim country. All of the laws of this land are dictated by what the

Koran teaches. I am not offended, and I understand that you are used to having the freedom to speak about your God. I do not want to hurt your feelings. I just want you to be aware that you must be careful."

"Are you saying I could get into a lot of trouble if someone overheard me talking about my God?"

"That is exactly what I am saying. And I don't want that kind of trouble for you." Kindness and compassion were evident on Hafa's face.

"Thank you for your concern. I will try to be careful. But you must also understand that I love my God very much. Being a Christian is not my religion; it is who I am. Anyone I befriend will certainly know that. If someday that gets me into trouble, then I will just have to face it. I cannot change who I am just because I am in a country that forbids it. Does that make sense?"

"I do not totally understand or agree, but I respect your conviction about your beliefs. We will just leave it at that."

Isabella regretted not having the chance to talk more to her about this. She would be patient and wait for the opportunity to talk more to Hafa, and she would pray that God would prepare her heart for the truth. For now, she would have to leave it at that. Patience. Patience was not one of Isabella's virtues, but everything in her life right now required her to be patient. Sometimes it was more than she could bear. She thought about the words that Hafa had spoken and remembered her Bible. She must try to keep it hidden at all times. She did not want it to be taken away. For the first time, she realized that it was probably illegal as she wondered exactly how Mina had gotten it.

Later that week, she woke counting the days she had left before the impending marriage. Time was running out. She lay in bed just watching the digital clock on the side table slowly change with each passing minute. She looked around at her bedroom. She had become so familiar with this place in the weeks she had been here. When she had arrived, it had been foreign and foreboding. She looked out the window near her bed. The sun was shining, and a few wispy clouds were floating by. There had been no rain in all the weeks she had been here. At home, rain was such a part of her life. She did not always like rain, but it was essential. Here in the desert, she longed for rain. She missed the clean smell of the air following a thunderstorm and the soothing sound of rain on the roof. And that was not all she missed. There were so many little things she missed every day. She had missed so many smiles and belly laughs. She had missed appointments and bedtime stories. The sight, the smell, the taste of home, she missed it all.

Hafa had visited the day before, and Isabella had been bold enough to hint about her desire to escape. She had tried to be subtle but clear. She was certain Hafa had understood the meaning of her hints. She had visibly seen the consternation on her face when she had said it, but Hafa had ignored the comment and moved onto another topic. In a last-ditch effort, she had even brought the subject up to Mina the night before in the kitchen, but she was still adamant there was not a safe way to escape. The month of Ramadan had just ended. She knew the date of the ceremony was getting too close. Panic was closing in on her. Where was God, and why had he not provided a way of escape? What did his silence mean?

The Bible that Mina had provided still administered small moments of encouragement. Even though she could not read any of the words, she treasured it because it held a precious message. She could not read the Arabic words, but often after meditating on the text, she would clearly be able to understand the meaning. She still did not understand how or why, but she always looked forward to these moments of complete comfort from God. Sometimes she thought she was really reading the text in Arabic; other times she wondered if she was only remembering other verses she had memorized or heard in the past. Just today, she had read passages from Psalms written by David while he was fleeing from Saul. Although these passages had spoken to the pain in her heart, there had been no miraculous rescue attempts or plans for an easy escape. She did not want to admit it, but it seemed she would be forced to become Latif's wife. And she just could not conceive how she would do it. She knew she had no choice, but what should she do? She got up out of bed and went to the kitchen to brew a cup of tea. She sat down at the table with her Bible and opened to a random page, silently praying for God's guidance in the days to come. She asked for a way to escape and hoped that today she would come up with a possible plan. As she looked over the text in front of her, the foreign words became clear.

I lift my eyes to the hills, where does my help
come from? My help comes from the Lord, the
Maker of heaven and earth. He will not let your
foot slip; he who watches over you will not slumber; indeed he who watches over Israel will never
slumber nor sleep. The Lord watches over you, the
Lord is your shade at your right hand; the sun will
not harm you by day, nor the moon by night. The
Lord will keep you from all harm, he will watch
over your life; the Lord will watch over your coming and going both now and forever more.

Psalm 121

She opened her notebook and wrote down the words,
and then Isabella began to pray for help. Most of all,
her heart longed for deliverance, but she knew this was
not the kind of help this passage was promising. God
was promising to help her through anything, even this.
God was promising he would be her guard and protector, not her rescuer. She wanted to hope for a way out,
but the more she prayed, the more she felt that God
had a plan for her here. She began to pray for Hafa
and Mina. She even reluctantly gave a small prayer
for Latif. In those moments of prayer with these wonderful words of promise fresh in her mind, she began
to see the people of this land and the darkness they
lived in. She knew there must be few, if any, Christians
allowed to come here. Most of all, she began to really
see the hearts of these people that God loved, a people
that he had created, children of Abraham that were
deceived by the teachings of Islam. She didn't like it.
She even questioned how or why he would ask it of her.

However, she knew that God had a plan for his glory even through the sins of the men that had brought her here. She wanted to resist. She longed to run from this strange revelation, but for now she tried to be willing. She prayed for strength to endure it and peace to accept it. And for a little while, she rested in him.

CHAPTERTEN

Isabella was leaving the confinement of her little home. Hafa was coming to take Isabella shopping. For the first time in over a month, she was leaving this place. The idea was more then a little exciting. Latif had given Hafa money so Isabella could purchase new clothes and a dress. She did not like the idea of buying a dress because she knew what it was for, but she pushed those thoughts from her mind. Today, she was going to enjoy this small reprieve from her isolation. She was going to see a little of this strange land. Mina had helped her get back into the abaya, khimar, and niqab. She let the veil fall over her face as it again wiped away her identity. She did not like putting on these items, but she knew it was required.

She waited as Hafa climbed into the backseat of the black Range Rover. Then she climbed in beside her. The hint of freedom made her feel strange and a little nervous. She had been confined so long and was happy to have a chance to get out for a short trip.

She still longed for a way to escape. She even hoped that her rescue would happen today. But as time passed, she feared there was not a plausible way to get out of this country alone. Instead, she took one day at a time, waiting and hoping in the Lord. So today she would enjoy this little adventure. Hafa had told her they would be going into Riyadh, the capital city of Saudi Arabia. They would shop at the Kingdom Centre, a large skyscraper with a three-story mall in one of the wings. Isabella was shocked to learn that Riyadh was a very large city with skyscrapers and shopping malls. She was quickly becoming aware of her ignorance of the world outside the U.S. After they were settled into their seats, the driver took them down a long, straight highway where Isabella saw vast amounts of the desert for the first time. It was desolate. It was a clear day, and Isabella could see for miles and miles across the landscape. Much of the great expanses of sand were interspersed with small green plants while other areas were just desert sand and rocks.

"Hafa, I have never been to the desert. It is so different from my home, but it is beautiful."

"Yes, but so different from the lush green land you come from."

"It is," Isabella replied reflectively.

"Are you excited about shopping today?"

"I am excited to make a trip into the city. I want to be excited about shopping, but I am very anxious as well. Buying a dress makes the inevitable seem much more real." Isabella had shared with her on multiple occasions her reservations about the wedding. She suspected Hafa understood and maybe even agreed. She just never voiced her opinion about it. Instead she took Isabella's hand and gave it a little squeeze. Isabella was glad to have her friend with her for encouragement.

The stores sold all of the trendiest clothes from all of the top designers. During their shopping adventure, Isabella could not always read the labels or understand the prices, but she suspected they were spending an exorbitant amount of money. When Isabella questioned Hafa about spending too much, Hafa told her they had not come close to spending the money her brother had given them. Isabella was shocked. She had never spent this much money on clothes in her life. Isabella was having a lot of fun and was amazed at the choices. She had purchased several new outfits. She had tried on a few dresses throughout the day upon Hafa's urging, but she had not purchased anything. To be honest, she did not want to purchase anything. She was procrastinating, and Hafa knew it. Hafa guided her into a store specializing in evening gowns. Isabella was amazed at the selection of colors and styles. She tried on several dresses. None of the dresses were white, because women did not usually wear white for their wedding in the kingdom. A couple of the dresses she tried on were perfect, but she refused to select one of the beautiful gowns for the ceremony.

"Isabella, you must purchase a dress," Hafa urged.

"I can't. Hafa, will you please choose one for me? I don't want to do it."

"I wish you would choose one. It might be a step toward accepting what is to come."

"I can't. I don't want to think about it. I will trust you to choose one. Please." Isabella nearly pleaded for Hafa to understand.

"I will choose two; then we can decide on the day."

"Whatever you think is best." Isabella finished getting her abaya on to prepare to leave the store while Hafa made the necessary purchases for her.

After shopping, the two of them went to a restaurant for dinner. They were seated in a section for women so that they could take off their veils to eat at a small table in the corner with comfortable cushions on the floor. She looked around at the exotic plush restaurant. It was cozy with the dim lighting from the ornately punched pewter hanging fixtures. Isabella enjoyed sampling a couple of the traditional Saudi dishes. It had been such a long time since she had eaten in a restaurant. The food was delicious. Isabella had eaten more in this meal than she had in several days. She was full and content.

It had been a very tiring day, but the trip had been more fun than Isabella had expected. It had briefly taken her mind off the days to come. But now that she arrived back to her new home, she felt guilty for enjoying this short respite from her isolation. Thoughts of Sam and the girls, her parents, everyone back home were always with her. But today in the busyness, they had slipped to a hidden recess in the back of her mind. She quickly put away the new purchases and quietly dressed for bed. It was a little early to retire, but Isabella was feeling very reflective. She curled up in the soft, luxurious sheets and blankets on her bed and said a heartfelt prayer for the new friends in her life. She also asked the Lord to take away her thoughts of what was to come. She did not want to accept her fate, and thinking about it made it all too real.

As she lay in bed looking up at the canopy over her head, she reflected on the days leading up to her marriage to Sam. She had been overflowing with excitement. All her hopes and dreams had been fulfilled in becoming his wife. They had both been so young and in love. She remembered the nervous look on Sam's face as she joyfully walked up the aisle to meet him. He had been so handsome dressed in his black tux and white vest that they had picked out together. When Isabella repeated her vows to the man she loved, tears of happiness had filled her eyes. During the minister's prayer, Sam had whispered to her that she was beautiful. Love was shining in his eyes. The memory of his handsome, loving face made Isabella's heart squeeze. The whole day had been like a dream, like being the princess in her own fairy tale. She would always love him, even if she never got the chance to see him or tell him again. He was and always would be her husband. That marriage was the marriage God had ordained for her. In light of that, the upcoming ceremony would be nothing more than an abomination.

"I miss you, Sam, my love." Isabella's eyes were full of unshed tears. Her heart yearned for him. She thought of the heartache he was feeling as she accepted he would never find her. How would he ever know she had been taken to the other side of the world? He had no idea of the events that were to come. He probably thought she was dead, and maybe that was better than the truth. She never wanted him to know the truth of what was to come. She knew it would break his heart. She cried herself to sleep, praying for the man she loved so dearly.

Today was the day. She had awakened with nausea and a strong feeling of dread. Hafa had come to greet her early that morning and had gone right to work arranging for everything. She had instructed Mina to pack Isabella's clothes and personal items for the coming journey to Jeddah that would follow the ceremony. Isabella had hidden in the garden while her suitcase had been packed. Hafa had remained in her room for over an hour giving Mina specific instructions.

There had been moments that morning she had contemplated running away into the desert. Even in October, the days were still around ninety degrees Fahrenheit at the heat of the day. She knew she would die out there all alone, but she was not sure that she cared. Mina had been with her the entire morning before Hafa had arrived, so there had really been no chance to try to get away. Truth be told, she was unsure that she could have truly summoned the courage to run. She suspected death in the stark, dry desert would be slow and painful, but so were the events that were unfolding before her.

The party was going to be held in the gardens of Latif's parents' house. Most wedding ceremonies in Saudi Arabia lasted for several days, but theirs would only be today. Hafa had informed her that Latif hoped to spare her the discomfort of playing hostess to so many strangers for such an extended period of time. There would really be two parties. Because the men and women always remained separate, there would be a men's party and a separate women's party. Hafa had tried to prepare her for the ritual aspects of the day. She was not looking forward to any of it. She knew she would not see Latif until he was ready to take her away with him. Because the legal aspects of the wedding had already taken place, there would be no official ceremony. Isabella would be dressed in her gown with a slight veil over her face. Latif would come and remove it as foot stamping and applause would be given by the women in attendance to show their approval of the union.

Hafa arranged for several servants to load her luggage in the car as they prepared to go to Hafa's parents' house. The car ride was as silent as death. Isabella still had not seen the dress Hafa had selected, and she did not care. Isabella knew that a few female members of the groom's family would arrive before the ceremony to perform the *halawa*. The Koran stated that all body hair except on the face and head was to be removed every forty days. For a new bride, this ritual was performed on the wedding day. A paste would be made by boiling sugar, rosewater, and lemon juice. Then two of the oldest family members would painfully remove the hair from her body. It was a very ancient custom. Isabella had adamantly protested, but Hafa had told her that she could not persuade her mother to make an exception in her situation. The whole idea was bizarre and beyond believable.

Isabella usually never drank, and in Saudi Arabia, it

was illegal. But while the family prepared and during the party, everyone consumed a large variety of alcoholic drinks. She had been given a glass of wine. In her nervousness, she slowly sipped it. It was a bitter, dry red wine, and she did not like the taste of it. But the alcohol eased her nerves and took the edge off of her emotions. Latif's mother had made all the arrangements for the day. There was a hairdresser to fix her hair and someone to artfully apply her makeup. Kohl was applied to her eyes. When she looked at her reflection, she almost did not recognize the beautiful, exotic stranger in the mirror. Her hair had been very loosely arranged in the back of her head, and curls cascaded down her neck and over one shoulder. Isabella watched as Hafa brought her the gown that she had chosen. She had selected one of her favorites. It was a deep mocha color that was completely strapless. It fit her waist and hips like a glove. It was not tight, but it was more flattering than she liked. The bottom flared out just above the knees in a mermaid style. After she had finished getting dressed, Hafa approached her. She could see a hint of tears in her eyes as she approached. She handed Isabella a box.

"Isabella, you look stunning. I know Latif will be shocked when he sees how beautiful you are. I hope you will begin to love him one day. He truly is a kind and generous man. I know you are unhappy and that our ways seem strange to you. But remember, marriages have been arranged like this for centuries. Your customs are really new and strange, not ours. Also, I am truly glad we have become friends." Hafa hugged her. "This is a wedding gift from Latif. Open it."

Isabella noticed her hands were trembling as she opened the box. Her nerves were in frazzles. She looked at the gift and gasped with shock. Inside was the most beautiful necklace Isabella had ever seen. She ran her fingers over all of the jewels. There were three large, teardrop-shaped emeralds surrounded by clear sparkling diamonds. She guessed that each of the emeralds was over two karats, and the diamonds were too plentiful to count. She also noticed there were earrings that matched. This was a gift for a princess or a movie star. She was just an ordinary person. She was so shocked by the outrageous gift that she just stared at it.

Hafa broke the silence. "Let's put it on you and see how it looks." Isabella just stood dumbfounded, looking at her.

Hafa took the box and removed the necklace, placing it around Isabella's neck. It felt heavy and unnatural. Then she gently placed the earrings into Isabella's hand. Isabella carefully removed the backs and placed them in her ears.

Hafa admired them on her. "What do you think of the gift, Isabella?"

"I don't know what to think. They are too much. A gift like this is meant for a princess, not an ordinary woman."

"Isabella, it is an appropriate gift for him to give you. Latif is a prince. He can afford to give you these and many more. Don't you realize he is a very wealthy and important man?"

Isabella was stunned. The gift had been shocking, but now she had learned she was marrying a prince. She tried to search back through all the conversations

of the last month. Had she truly missed hearing someone tell her that Latif was a Saudi Arabian prince? It
was all beyond considering. Isabella's eyes were swimming with tears. She was trying to sort it all out in
her mind, but the wine had gone to her head, and she
was beginning to feel numb. When Hafa handed her
another glass of wine, she eagerly took it. She regretted
drinking to anesthetize her fears and emotions, but the
numbing effects of the wine helped keep the turbu-
lence in check. After a few sips from the second glass,
she was beginning to relax. The rest of the afternoon
was mostly a blur of introductions and superficial conversations with strangers.

Latif had been anxious to complete his duties as the
groom at the party so he could go to Isabella. As he
made his way through the courtyard to the garden
where the women's party was taking place, he quietly slipped in without anyone noticing. He wanted
to watch her unobserved. Just inside the gate, he hid
behind a young acacia tree and carefully scanned the
crowd for Isabella. She was not hard to miss. She was
facing away from him, listening to chatter from one of
his aunts. Then he saw Hafa walking toward him. He
was surprised that his sister had noticed him arrive.
She slipped behind the tree to his hiding place.

"I suspected you would be coming a little sooner
than expected for Isabella. I want to talk to you quickly
before we are noticed. I must warn you Isabella is very
troubled by all the events that are happening today. She
is extremely emotional. Please be patient with her. She

is not young the way a wife normally is, but she is still very innocent. She is a special woman. She is open and honest. She trusts me, and I have come to value that trust. Latif, my brother, you know I love you, but you have lost your head when it comes to her. Marrying Isabella was not the best idea, but you would not be persuaded to change your mind. So listen to my advice. If you push her too fast, I am not sure what she will do."

"I understand, Hafa." Latif was watching Isabella. He was hoping she would turn around. He knew that the veil covered her face. But he was anxious to see her. "Please bring her to me."

Both Latif and Hafa stepped out onto the lawn of the garden. A couple women began to ululate in response to his arrival. As Hafa made her way to a surprised Isabella, the sound of all the ululating voices culminated into a loud chorus of sound. He watched as Hafa whispered a few words to Isabella and then proceeded to lead her to him. Even though he could not see her face, she was beautiful. The dark brown of her dress made her fair skin seem like smooth porcelain, and his fingers ached to caress it. The dress was perfect for her in every way. It was sexy enough to accentuate every part of her body, but tasteful and flattering. He yearned to know everything about this rare and valuable creature, his wife.

When they approached, Hafa softly offered, "My dear brother, here is your new wife."

He gently reached out and held Isabella's arms. Her warm skin was as soft as silk under his touch. He could just make out the silhouette of her face under the veil.

He effortlessly removed the covering over her face, feeling a tightening of his chest when he looked at her. Her large eyes showed innocence and fear as her emotions visibly wavered under the scrutiny of his gaze. In the background, he could hear the applause of approval from his family and close friends. In that moment, she was more breathtaking than he could have imagined. His pulse quickened at the realization that Isabella was his, and he cherished this very precious gift. He tried to speak these emotions to her, but the words caught in his throat.

"Isabella, you look so beautiful. I am honored that you are my wife." Their gazes locked for several minutes. He could see the reservation in her eyes. Her fears and so much more were visible in those expressive eyes. In time, he would wipe all that fear and uncertainty away. "Isabella, it is time for us to leave. Hafa will show you where to change into your traveling clothes." He turned to Hafa. "Send one of the servants to alert me when she is ready." He gently squeezed her arms to try to reassure her, wanting her to know he cared for her. Then he turned and left the garden. His mind and body were filled with longing and anticipation. He knew they should stay and greet the guests at the party and even say good-bye to his mother, but he was anxious for them to be on their way.

Latif attempted to hide the gratifying smile on his face. He was relieved that the weeks of waiting were nearly over. Isabella was his. But he tried to damper his joy for Isabella's sake. He knew she was afraid and even a little angry. But he was happy, and it was hard to hide. The day had gone very smoothly. His mother had met him in the house as they had prepared to leave. She had announced the praises of all the women. They had all unanimously agreed that Isabella was a beauty, but his mother had not been happy that he was leaving so quickly. He had apologized to her and then said good-bye. His father had only chuckled at his eagerness to get Isabella alone.

Once the plane had taken off, Isabella had fallen asleep. She looked exhausted from the events of the day. He could smell just a hint of alcohol on her breath. He silently wondered if the effects of it had made her drowsy. She was seated beside him in a small jet that would fly them to Jeddah. They had been in the air for about an hour, and Latif expected to land within the next twenty to thirty minutes. He would have loved to have taken Isabella to Cairo for their honeymoon but had not wanted to risk taking her out of the country. He had intentionally stayed away from her until the ceremony, but the lack of contact made him a little unsure of Isabella's mental state. Hafa had shared openly about their visits. From all that she had shared, he was looking forward to getting to know her. But he knew she was upset about the marriage.

He had spent time with both of his wives before leaving. They seemed indifferent to sharing his time with another wife. Women were raised in his world to understand their purpose and place within the harem. That is why Latif had longed for more. He wanted a wife that could be a friend and companion, not just a lover. But it seemed that the years of separation between women and men had strained the marital relationships of most people in his country. He had even heard rumors of intimate female relationships within harems to make up for the lack of male companionship. He was appalled at the idea and refused to think about such things.

Isabella wiggled a little in her seat as she slept. Latif enjoyed watching her. She looked as peaceful as a child. His hands longed to stroke the smooth skin on her face, but he did not want to risk waking her. Watching her this way touched something within him. She was his, and he intended to protect her and make her happy. He never thought he would have an opportunity like this. He could not blow this one chance. Latif had given Isabella permission to remove the khimar and niqab while they were alone on the plane. Her hair was still arranged as it had been for the party. He carefully lifted one of the loose curls around his finger. He was fascinated. He rubbed the strands between his thumb and fingers. It was fine and soft. He was looking forward to feeling more of her over the next few days.

Latif pulled his eyes away from her. Watching her while she was so near evoked sensual emotions within him. Latif looked out the window to the desert below. They had dropped in altitude, and he could begin to make out the sea on the horizon. The rich red sunset bathed the sky and sand in rich, colorful hues. He tried to contemplate the beauty of it, but he was distracted by the woman beside him. He had booked the royal suite at the top of the Rosewood Cornice Hotel with beautiful views of the Red Sea. He had stayed in the suite a couple of times for business travel. The suite was a beautiful, large, modern suite with flanking window views that were breathtaking. He hoped Isabella would be impressed.

He heard Isabella let out a soft moan. He turned to look at her and realized she was awake. "Did you have a nice nap?"

"Not really. I have a bit of a headache. I had a couple of glasses of wine. I do not usually drink, but at the time it relaxed me. Now, I have a headache."

"I can get you something for the pain."

"I think you can probably find something for my headache, but I don't think you can give me anything to take away the pain in my heart." Isabella's eyes watered as she spoke.

"Maybe in time I can help the pain. I really do want to make you happy, Isabella. You are my wife. I am responsible for you now."

"If you really wanted to make me happy, you would send me home to my family." A lone tear streaked down her cheek.

"Isabella, we have already discussed this, and I had hoped you had moved past it. I am very happy you are my wife. You seem so sweet. Plus, you are so beautiful."

Isabella just looked at him but did not respond. He could read sadness in her eyes. He also saw a depth, a wisdom, which intrigued him. He reassured himself that he could make her forget her home. Why would she not grow to love him? He was handsome, young, fit, and wealthier than nearly every person in the U.S. Maybe he was overconfident, but he did not think so.

He picked up his ghutra and agal and positioned

them back on his head. He turned back to Isabella and casually commented, "We will be landing very soon. You should put on your khimar. You will find Jeddah is a little more relaxed than other areas of the kingdom. When we are out in public, you can go without your veil, but I would still recommend that you cover your hair. And you must always wear your abaya in public. If you do not, you will be at risk of attracting the scorn and possible flogging of the mutawa." Latif noticed a disdain in Isabella's expression and wondered if it was in response to his traditional Saudi clothing.

He watched as she averted her eyes away from him before she spoke. "Hafa said that Jeddah is sort of a resort area for people in Saudi Arabia. She said there are gorgeous beaches all along the Red Sea. But how do you enjoy the sun and water when you must always wear an abaya?"

Latif shrugged. "Men and children can wear swimsuits and swim in the sea at the beach, but women must always be careful to keep their hair and body covered. There are a few private beaches in Jeddah where Western men and women can wear swimsuits and enjoy swimming together, but you can't at any of the public beaches."

"You must be kidding! Saudi men and children can swim in the sea to cool off from the hot desert heat while their wives sit in their stifling black clothing and watch! Do you know how preposterous that sounds?"

"It is our custom. I know it does not make sense to you, but most Saudi women know and accept these laws."

"As a Western woman, I am used to all the freedoms

of a man. How do you think I will ever be happy here when all that and more have been brutally stripped away from me?" Tears started flowing down Isabella's face as she spoke. She turned away from him, desperately trying not to give him the satisfaction of seeing her cry.

When she jumped from her chair, went into the small bathroom, and closed the door, Latif rested his forehead on his fist. Well, he had known she was a passionate woman. He had also known the adjustment would not be easy. He took a deep breath to get his anger under control. After a few minutes, he snickered. He could not believe their first conversation had been an argument. Maybe this would be harder than he thought.

Isabella's composure was nearly in shreds. The limousine had dropped them off at the front door of the hotel. Outside the car, she could just make out the sea. It was nearly dark outside; only a slight glow at the horizon made anything beyond the lights of the hotel visible. She knew what was coming, and she was desperate to get away. An attendant met them at the lobby doors and escorted them to a private elevator and entrance into their suite. She wanted to run and hide, but there was nowhere to go. Desperately, she had searched for anyone to help her, but there had been no one on the way to the elevator. Inside, the elevator felt like a tomb. She began to feel the walls closing in on her as they ascended to the top of the building. She could feel her pulse quicken, and her breath came out in shallow gulping breaths. When the elevator opened, Isabella struggled to regain her balance to exit. The attendant opened the door to the suite and handed the key to Latif. He stepped aside and motioned for them to enter. Latif walked ahead of her, but Isabella did not move. Her feet were rooted to the ground. She could not go in. She would not go in. The attendant and Latif both looked at her expectantly. Isabella just looked at Latif and shook her head.

Latif turned to the assistant. "Please excuse us. My new wife appears to have a little honeymoon jitters." He smiled and winked at the attendant, motioning him back into the elevator. When the elevator doors closed, Latif addressed Isabella again. "What are you doing? Do you plan to sleep in the hall?"

"I will if it means I do not have to sleep with you."

"Isabella, please be reasonable. Besides, we will have separate bedrooms. I am used to sleeping alone. Come into the suite. I want to show you around. You will see it is luxurious. Then I will show you to your room."

"You are telling me that I will not have to sleep with you? We are married, but we will have separate bedrooms?"

"That is correct."

"You expect me to believe you have married me, but you will not … touch me?"

"I did not mean to imply we would not be intimate as husband and wife. I only mean that you will not have to sleep with me."

Isabella sat on the floor and defiantly replied, "I will not go in there."

Isabella could tell he was becoming angry, but she

did not care. She had resolved to fight with everything inside her to keep this from happening.

Latif clenched his teeth and spoke. "You will come into our suite, even if I have to throw you over my shoulder and carry you. But if you make me resort to force, then I will not stop there. I will take you directly into the bedroom and have my way with you right now. I had not intended for our first night to be like this, but you are leaving me little choice."

Isabella remained seated and did not move as she pondered her options and clearly realized that she had none. He was much larger than her and could easily overpower her. The idea of being hauled into his bed and raped was appalling. It was actually worse than anything else she could imagine happening inside that suite.

Latif started toward her. She could read fierce anger in his face. His eyes were as black as flint, and she knew he intended to carry through with his threat. Isabella sprang to her feet and sprinted past him into the suite. Fear ran through her veins and made her pulse race. She was in a perilous position. She needed to defuse the situation to buy a little time.

She whirled around and faced him just inside the door. She braced herself as he came toward her; then she muttered, "Okay, okay. I will cooperate. Please do not carry me to your room. I am sorry; I did not mean to make you angry. I will try to stop being difficult."

Latif stopped and planted his fists on his hips. She could see the rushing emotions surge across his face. Then slowly she saw his anger begin to fade. They faced each other for several minutes. When Latif addressed her, he shook his head and gave her a choleric smile. "You are going to make me crazy. From the first moment I saw you, I knew that you would be a spitfire."

Isabella was relieved and shocked that Latif could change so quickly in front of her eyes. She knew it might be a mistake to cooperate, but she must. For the first time, she really looked at this man that considered her his wife. She tried to read anything about his character that he would reveal. He was arrogant and spoiled and that made her angry. Too many times he had received what he wanted, but she did not intend to be included in that list. Reluctantly, though, she admitted that he was trying to be congenial. As she studied him, she also noticed he was striking, and she did not like it. She supposed it had always registered in her subconscious, but until now she had not allowed herself to admit it. Would it be harder or easier if he were old or ugly? She could not decide. Then she thought of Hasam. Suppose he had been like Hasam. She shuddered to think of it and conceded that things could be worse. That was enough to encourage her to cooperate for the moment.

The smile disappeared, and his expression grew intense. "I am warning you now; I will not tolerate any more of your defiance. I am a patient man, but my patience can only last so long. We need to come to an understanding about that."

Isabella bit her tongue and nodded. She wanted to combat against his dominance. Her heart screamed for a fight. Instead, she was biding her time. She hoped she could outwit him in this game they were playing, but she had her doubts.

"Would you please show me to my room?"

"I will show you around; then I will show you where your room is." He began to lead her around the suite. Reluctantly, she followed.

Isabella could not help being in awe. The suite was amazing, nicer and more opulent than anything she had ever seen. The huge salon could easily seat several people comfortably. Each room had large windows facing the sea, and every room had a television. There was a private dining room with a large table that would have seated at least ten people. There was a hot tub with a floor-to-ceiling window displaying a breathtaking view of the Red Sea. All the rooms and bathrooms were large and extravagant. This suite made her apartment at the compound seem shabby and small. It was truly the most amazing place she had ever seen. She regretted that she was impressed. This place, this life, could be seductive; she needed a firm resolve against the lure of this luxury. This place was like a fairy tale, but she must remember that she was not the princess. She tried to remember all the things she loved about Sam and the girls. She must not forget all the precious things in her life. She must not lose sight of home and the hope that she would soon return. Even as she thought it, she was believing a lie. But she wanted to keep believing it.

At the end of the tour, Latif led her to her bedroom. While they had been looking around, several bellhops had brought their luggage and deposited them into their rooms. A maid was unpacking her clothes and placing them in the closet. Isabella realized that it was not Mina. "Why is Mina not here? She is my maid. I want her here."

"She has other responsibilities while we are away and could not make the trip."

"Can you please send for her?"

"No." She heard the finality in his tone. "Now, I will show you to the master suite. Please follow me."

Isabella's heart skipped several beats. She was afraid she was going to hyperventilate. She tried to reassure herself. Hadn't he said he would not rush things? She prayed that he only wanted to talk.

When they arrived at his door, he opened it and motioned for her to enter ahead of him. Cautiously, she complied. The room was lavishly decorated in cool blues and golds. It looked like a room for a prince. From the king-sized bed to the furniture in the sitting area, no expense had been spared. Latif directed her to have a seat on the plush sofa. After she was seated, he took a seat beside her. Without asking permission, he reached up and started removing the pins from her hair. Isabella tensed at his touch, but he continued until all her hair fell loose around her shoulders. He paused with his hands in her hair and looked deep into her eyes. The raw desire she saw scared her. Involuntarily, she pulled away and got up to move. Latif gently grabbed her arm.

"Isabella, please sit. I will not touch you. I just want to talk."

She was suspicious of him but decided to relent for the moment. Slowly, she sat back down on the couch as far away from him as she could get.

"Isabella, look at me."

He looked at her openly and affectionately. His eyes no longer revealed passion and desire. Instead they seemed earnest and kind. She could feel him carefully pull back the curtain that safely covered his emotions. He was letting her peek at his heart. Isabella closed her eyes and took a deep breath. She opened her eyes as he began to speak. Confidentially, Latif began to tell her about his life. He related funny stories from his childhood, even ones that included Hafa. He shared with her his desires for his business and his future. He shared his love for the U.S. and about his time at UCLA. He shared intimate lessons he had learned from his father and even special moments they had shared on their way home from the mosque. He told her about his love of his country, the desert, and Western art. He even told her about a special camel he had considered a pet when he was five. With words, he was giving her a little piece of his heart. While he talked, his face was animated with the stories he told, and his eyes sparkled when he spoke of the things that he loved. She resisted being drawn in by him. He was seducing her. She felt it. He was not touching her with his hands; instead he was speaking to her heart and caressing her with his words. She steeled her heart against feeling emotion toward this stranger, but he continued. Unexpectedly, she found herself laughing as he related a crazy tale from college. It felt good to laugh, and for a moment, to let go, even relax. She still longed for home, but the intimacy of his words spoke to her heart. She wanted to resist him, but she needed this companionship. She had been lonely, and his words were an elixir for the emptiness. Unwittingly, she began to let down her guard. She began to really see him. He was passionate and spirited but also loving and kind. Yet she must not lose sight of who he really was. She had seen that side of him as well.

There was a light knock at the door. Latif got up to answer it. Isabella looked at the clock on the stand beside the bed. She was shocked to realize they had been talking for a couple hours. Latif came in pushing a large room service tray with a satisfied grin on his face. He carefully began to lift all the silver plate covers to reveal a delightful smorgasbord of food. Her stomach rumbled at the enticing sight and smell. She realized she had only nibbled the entire day. Now, she was hungry.

Latif seated himself beside her again and scooted the tray in front of them. He motioned for her to take anything she wanted. When she had finished, he filled a plate of his own. His conversation had broken the ice. Isabella was surprised that some of her fear had abated even as she remained cautious. They continued to talk throughout the meal. Isabella even began to share a few of her own stories, but she was still reserved about giving too much to this strange man.

After they had finished eating, Latif took both of their plates and replaced them on the tray. He turned toward her, reached up, and drew her face toward him. She started to pull away, but he gently held fast. When he looked into her eyes, he began to open his soul. "Isabella, in your country, when a man marries a woman, he gives her a vow. That is not our custom, but I don't care. I want to tell you my vow to you. Know that I am speaking straight from my heart when I say I am very happy to be your husband. Marriages in Saudi Arabia are often distant and unloving. But I want ours to be open and loving. I want to be your companion and your friend. I have longed for an American wife that could be open and passionate like you are. And I vow that although I cannot send you home, I will make up for all you have lost. I will care for you, and in time, I hope we can find love. These are not mere words; I offer you my heart. It is yours."

Latif's eyes were misty from the emotion he had poured out. He held her there for several moments. She tried to look away, but he turned her face back to his. His eyes were the color of milk chocolate. His skin was dark and smooth. He was exotic and enticing. He was impressive. He was a prince in every sense of the word—in mind, body, and spirit. Whether she liked it or not, he was using all that charm to weaken her. She needed Sam, but he was too far away to help her. At any other time, she would have run away from this, but there was nowhere to go.

"I want to make love to you, Isabella. I promise that I will not force you, but I want to make you my wife." Isabella started to shake her head and pull away. But he refused to let her go. "Please, do not resist what is inevitable. I could never hurt you, not ever."

She must not panic. She had to rationalize with him before she truly lost this battle. "Latif, I am not your wife. Don't be angry. I am not trying to hurt you. I am just trying to make you understand. How can I be your wife when I am married to someone else?"

"He is not here. You will never see him again. We

have been legally married. Why can you not accept that you are my wife?"

"Latif, I am a Christian. I took a vow to my God when I married Sam. That cannot be broken."

"So your God must also realize that we are married as well. One marriage does not make a second less binding. If I do not release you, then you are my wife."

Isabella's eyes filled with tears. "But it is wrong to have more than one husband."

"But you already have two husbands. You cannot change that. Do not fight what you cannot control." His hands tightened to suggest the tension that her resistance evoked in him. She was trapped with nowhere else to go. She felt the tears as they pooled in her eyes. When his lips moved toward hers, she panicked. She jerked free of his hands and started to jump from the couch, but his response was too quick. He grabbed her, crushing her body against him. She was helpless to free herself. When his lips came down hard and unyielding against her mouth, cold claws of steel began to clench her heart. This was her life. Like a trapped animal, she had hoped for escape. Now it all looked bleak.

She was nearly sitting on his lap, and her labored breathing made her feel faint. His mouth was next to her ear when he quietly spoke. "Where do you think you can go? There is no place you can hide that I cannot find you. Stop fighting the inevitable." There was a hard edge to his voice, but he remained calm.

Isabella was going numb. She was defenseless against this powerful man. She knew he intended to take her and felt her will beginning to concede. "You might take my body, but you will never truly have me."

CHAPTER ELEVEN

The room was shadowy when Isabella opened her eyes the next morning. A blinding strip of light came through a slight opening between the curtains in the hotel room. It was the only light in the room, and it caused everything to appear in dark shadows, but it did not hide the luxury of this room. She lifted the covers up over her head. She wanted to cry. She really needed to cry, but something hard and unyielding locked her tears away inside her. This was not a day she ever wanted to face. She closed her eyes tightly, trying to force the images of the previous night from her memory. But she could not forget; she would never forget. Now, whether she liked it or not, she had two husbands, one that she loved and one that she did not. Where was her God? Why had he not saved her? This could not be the life she was required to live. She wanted to scream at the top of her lungs, but she feared Latif would come looking for her. She needed to disappear.

With a sweeping motion, she swept the covers away. She swung to her feet and tramped to the bathroom. She was angry; no, she was furious. What had she done? How she longed to turn back time and erase those intimate moments. If only she could make this nightmare disappear. She promptly undressed and got into the shower. As she touched her skin, she felt the disgusting grime from the actions of the night before. She lathered the soap and began to scrub her skin with a washcloth. Even after several attempts, she could not remove it. Frantically, she tried again, but nothing helped. She knew that the soap would not clean her, but she was desperate to try. She still felt the soil of regret, but now her skin was red and raw from scrubbing. Reluctantly, she got out of the shower. She dried off with one of the fluffy white towels and then got dressed. She needed to rub lotion into her inflamed skin, but she did not want to. She wanted the soreness to be a reminder, a punishment.

She went back into the bedroom and sat on the bed. The room was still gloomy from the lack of light. She liked it that way. The bright light made everything come into crisp focus. Focusing was painful. She thought about Latif. She remembered the feel of his touch, and the memory was repulsive. She wanted to get away. She never wanted to see his face again. But she was also disgusted with herself. He had gambled and won. She was sure that he was enjoying the satisfaction of it and that made her even more enraged. She wanted to yell and scream, to vent her anger and pain. Instead, she threw the entire stack of pillows from the bed across the room, but she did not feel any better. She needed to do something to release the ache in her heart. Impulsively, she picked up a vase from the side table filled with lovely fresh flowers. She was ready to sling it across the room when she heard a soft rap on the door. Realization awakened her to the moment. Isabella painstakingly returned the vase to the table without making a sound. She sat motionless without answering as the seconds ticked by. She knew it was Latif. She waited in the tingling tension that filled the silence, afraid he would open her door. She hoped he would assume she was still sleeping. She inhaled sharply, noticing a slight turn on the doorknob. Moisture formed on her upper lip as she held her breath. Frozen. Several minutes passed. Then she heard footsteps move away from the door. She exhaled in a long, relieving sigh. She looked around the room for a place to hide. Maybe she could hide for hours or even days in the closet like a child. If only life could be that simple. She looked at the clock. It was only 9:00 a.m., and the coming week seemed to stretch out in front of her like an eternity.

Latif wondered about Isabella. He had awakened early that first morning, disappointed she had left his bed. He could still feel her skin and smell her intoxicating scent. He simply smiled. She was amazing, just as he had suspected. For weeks, reservations about making her his wife had crept into the corners of his mind, but now they were gone. Isabella belonged to him, and he savored that thought.

He had a few business items to take care of and wanted to have them completed before she woke up. So he quickly showered and prepared for his day. He paused to reflect on the beauty outside his window as he took a sip of his morning coffee. The sun was powerful. The reflection of it on the deep blue of the sea was breathtaking. Today, everything seemed a little brighter. For the first time in weeks, everything looked clear and reassuring. He was glad he had made the sacrifice with Isabella. He sensed time had eased the transition for her. Plus, in the one month of Ramadan, he had atoned for all the sins of the year. Allah was appeased, and he was absolved. It was a great feeling.

The butler came into the room to inform him his breakfast was waiting in the dining room. On the way, he stopped at Isabella's room to wake her for breakfast. He was anxious to see her. He quietly knocked but heard no answer. He waited, listening for sounds of stirring from her room, but he heard none. He started to enter but paused. He leaned his forehead against the door. He wanted to see her, to reassure her. Hesitantly, he stepped away from the door. It was better to let her sleep this morning.

Latif looked at the clock. It was after 1:00 p.m. Breakfast had been finished hours ago. That morning, he had been detained much longer than expected on a business call. Then he had lost himself to all the details of setting the day right. He had lost track of time.

Outside the window, the day was sunny and inviting. He needed to set business aside and find Isabella. He was surprised he had not heard her this morning. Certainly she was not still sleeping. He rearranged the piles on his desk for later and set off looking for his wife. He smiled every time he thought of her. It was silly; he was acting like a young schoolboy. But he knew she was a dream come true, and he aspired to convince her.

He passed the butler on the way to her room. He momentarily paused as the butler addressed him.

"Sir, your lunch is ready and waiting for you and your wife in the dining room. Would you like for me to summon her?"

"No, I will let her know that lunch is ready. Do you know, is she still in her room?"

"According to her maid, she has not left her room all morning."

Latif was puzzled. "Is she still sleeping?"

"The maid said she is awake and dressed."

The butler bowed and went toward the dining room, and Latif turned to go to her room. This was unusual. He had hoped that she would come to him this morning. Had she come out and decided not to disturb him? He chastised himself for getting too absorbed in his work, wishing he had sought her out sooner. He hoped she was not angry with him. He approached the door and knocked. After several minutes when he did not hear a reply, he called her name. "Isabella."

When she still did not answer, he quietly opened the door. He immediately noticed the room was dark. He looked around the room, letting his eyes adjust to the darkness. She was seated in one of the side chairs that she had scooted around to face the partially open window. The only light in the room shined onto her. She looked tousled and young, almost like a child. At first she seemed to be looking out the window, but then he noticed that her eyes never moved. Was she unwell? Why had she not answered him? He felt a moment of slight panic. "Isabella." He spoke lovingly just above a whisper.

She turned to him, but her face was blank. No emotion registered. Her green eyes looked dark and empty. It was as if she was a ghost, and for a moment, she frightened him. He was frozen inside the doorway, uncertain what to do. She just turned her head back to the window. This was not the reaction he had expected.

Gently, reassuringly, he attempted to draw her out. "Isabella, please come to the dining room with me and have lunch."

This time she completely ignored him, and it frustrated him, but he held his anger in check. He quickly crossed the space of the room to stand in front of her. "Isabella, look at me."

She looked into his face. Then he saw it—anger. She was angry with him. He was unsure exactly what he had done, but he intended to get to the bottom of the situation. He bent over and grabbed the arms of the chair and looked directly into her eyes. He knew this intimate closeness was making her uncomfortable, and instinctually she wrapped her arms across her chest.

"Isabella, I can see that you are angry. What is wrong?"

Her face was a mask of cold stone. Minutes passed in silence, but Isabella's glare did not soften.

Latif tried to push away his irritation. "Lunch is ready in the dining room. Make yourself presentable and come eat with me. After we have lunch, we will go and see the town and do a little shopping. The fresh air will do you good."

Again, he lost her gaze outside the window. Unsure what to do, moments passed as he patiently waited for her response. "Isabella, look at me."

Reluctantly, she looked up at his face. This time her eyes looked misty with unshed tears. Then he saw pain. He could not understand all of these emotions. He knelt beside her. "Tell me what is going on in that head of yours."

She just shook her head. The distance between them was greater at that moment than it had ever been. He struggled to comprehend it. "Will you have lunch with me?"

Finally, she spoke. "I am not feeling well. Can I just remain here for a little while?"

"No, you must try to eat. You might even feel better if you come out of this dark room."

He grabbed her hand and attempted to pull her to her feet. She tried to resist for a few moments, then she relented. Latif led her to the bathroom. He reached for a clip to arrange her hair. Artfully, he pulled the mass of curls and arranged them away from her face. He sensed she was recoiling from his touch, but she did not pull away. Turning on the water at the sink, he grabbed a washcloth. Once the water was hot, he squeezed out the excess water and handed it to her. The kindness of his gestures seemed to give her a little strength. She wiped her face. When she was finished, Latif led her to the dining room and helped her take a seat. She ate small bites of the meal, refusing to make any eye contact with him. Latif attempted to make small talk, but she only shrugged at his questions. In just a few hours, something had happened. He tried to understand what had caused this change, but he could not. Instead he decided he would give her a little time to warm up to him again. He knew that somehow he could make the situation right between them.

The souk market was bustling with people. Isabella looked around at the faces. With nearly everyone wearing either a thobe or an abaya, the crowd appeared to be a mass of faces. Some women still wore veils, but many only covered their clothes and hair. For the first time, Isabella could see the people of this country, and she found herself searching for someone to rescue her. In this crowd, most were native to this land, but she noticed a few were not. She searched for a friendly, familiar face to take her home, but in the end, all were strangers making their way to some unknown destination.

Isabella had been unenthusiastic about shopping with Latif, but he had insisted. Everywhere there were vendors selling their wares for a bargain price. If she could have shared an exotic trip like this with Sam and the girls, she would have been fascinated. The gold jewelry alone was awe inspiring. This country so full of wealth had so much gold to offer to all that would come and buy. Latif even commented that gold prices in this country were much lower than most places in the world. She passed several booths with tables and walls completely covered in gold. Necklaces, bracelets, earrings, rings—it was beyond anything she had ever experienced. She browsed the shops without a desire to purchase anything. Normally she loved beautiful things, but today she had no interest. Latif had offered several times to purchase anything she desired, but she did not want anything from him. The thought of accepting a gift, any gift, was unappealing. She refused to be bought and used by this arrogant, selfish man.

As they made their way through the shops, she enjoyed being rude to him and even felt a smug satisfaction by his puzzled expression when she brushed aside his graciousness. Because she could not overpower him, she had resolved to be cold and compliant while her anger and hatred burned inside her like a smoldering coal. It gave her something to savor on this most unsavory day. She plotted ways to become a master at turning his affection into a game. He might have control over her in many ways, but she could manipulate him emotionally. She did not understand what he felt toward her. They had barely known each other, but she sensed his attachment to her was not as superficial as it might seem. She could not wait to wield it like a weapon against him. The thought of it gave her a little satisfaction. She squared her shoulders, taking back some of the dignity that had been stolen from her the night before. She was forced to be compliant, and she did not like it, but manipulating his emotions was a game she could play and win.

"After dinner, Isabella, please come to my room."

He sensed her tension in response to his suggestion. Isabella and Latif had finished their shopping trip just in time for a late dinner. She had barely touched what he had ordered to be served in the private dining room, and she had rigidly refused to engage with him in conversation while he had eaten. In fact, she had been cold and distant the entire day. This had not been the way he had imagined their first day together. He was concerned with her attitude but confident in his ability to change it. He had secretly made a purchase at the market for her. He had watched her admire one of the beautiful gold necklaces, and when she was not looking, he had purchased it for her. He was planning to give it to her that night. Wives in Saudi Arabia were slow to warm up to the marriage bed, but he convinced himself Isabella would be different. There had been no time to woo her like a traditional marriage in America, so he would cultivate their relationship over this week and the coming ones. Soon she would desire him the same way he wanted her. Their relationship would not be based on control and manipulation; instead they would share mutual affection. It would take time and effort, but the effects would be worth it. Already he was anticipating the evening and all that this marriage promised for his future.

He even began to wonder if she would give him a son. He imagined the lovely child they would create together. Maybe the child would even have her bewitching green eyes. He appealed to Allah for a son to be born of their union during this special week. A child would strengthen their bond together. It would make everything between them perfect. He lingered at the table a few more minutes, savoring this wonderful thought, not wanting the idea to subside.

Lightning flashed through the sky. The curtains were only open a small amount, but the flash was unmistakable. A few seconds later, she heard a low rumble of thunder in the distance. She sat up in bed. She must have been mistaken. She had been in this country for nearly six weeks and knew that rain was a foreigner in this dry and wasteless desert. She waited expectantly. There was another flash. Isabella jumped out of her bed and ran to the window, ripping back the curtains. Now she was certain it was lightning. Just as she reached the window, rain began to pour out of the sky. Rain, pouring rain. She giggled. How silly she felt, almost giddy. It was raining in the desert. She wanted to run outside in her nightgown and just soak it in. She thought maybe the rain would wash away the pain and anger, the helplessness. She wanted to water her soul with the tears of her God. He was crying with her over all she had lost. It was a simple, childlike thought, but it resonated deep in her soul. She thought back to the Bible she had left under her pillow. She remembered the promises she had received so many days ago. She hungered for more. She thirsted for more. In a moment, she understood all of Jesus' references to living water. It made perfect sense. In the desert, water is always in short supply. Without it, nothing can survive. Just like

Christ, just like Christ. Tears of love and understanding coursed down her cheeks. This rain was a reminder she had been given that precious gift of living water. The moment was surreal. She stood there watching, wondering. Any other time, she had hardly regarded the rain. Now it was valuable, beautiful, refreshing.

She lost track of time just standing there watching the rain. She watched the plethora of drops trickling down the window. She followed the trails of raindrops with the end of her finger against the glass. The lightning and thunder intensified. It was stunning watching the magnificent power of the storm. She was conscious of time passing but also unaware. The moment transcended time. If only prayer and the presence of God could always be just like this. Maybe this was a little like heaven—being, but not really being aware. She shook her head. Thinking messed up the feeling. For now, she would not try to understand. She would just rest in the moment.

The rain started to dissipate as the storm had nearly passed. As the rain lessened, the feeling of foreboding returned. She tried to hold on to the peace, but slowly hopelessness began to return.

"Isabella." The gentle plea was imposing in the silent room. She swung around and staggered back against the window. She had not heard anyone enter. She was startled and irritated by the interruption. He had come into her room and destroyed her moment, and any residual peace fled with his arrival.

"What do you want?" Irritation registered in her voice.

"After lunch, I want to show you something. Be ready to go on a short trip."

"Where are we going?" She was still frustrated, but curious.

"It is a surprise. You will love it; trust me." She realized that she was a little intrigued, even in her frustration. He looked like a young boy with a secret as he left her room. Where could he be taking her now?

The rented four-wheel drive vehicle sped smoothly across the endless sea of sand. Just outside of town, they had left the road to make their own trail through the desert. After the rain, the temperature had risen from the heat of the day, and the humidity was higher from the moisture in the ground. The air conditioning in the vehicle kept them comfortable. Even in the few hours since the rain, the desert had started to turn green with grasses and plants sprouting in small patches around them. Isabella reluctantly realized the adventure had caused some of her anger to disperse. The anticipation was making her feel audacious. She watched the changing landscape in silence, occupied by her own thoughts. Even Latif seemed quietly reflective as they trekked to some secret destination. It was only the second full day they had been in Jeddah, and she still did not feel at ease in his presence. She asked Latif again where they were going, but he only smiled a devilish smile and shrugged. This was unlike any road trip she had ever embarked on.

Latif had given her permission to wear only her abaya and a loose scarf. It did not conceal all her hair like the khimar she normally wore in public. Under her abaya she wore a pair of shorts and a cotton T-shirt. He had dressed in khaki pants and a light, long-sleeved cotton shirt. He was relaxed and confident as he casually drove on, blazing an imaginary trail.

The desert was more delightful than ever. All around her, everything was changing from the rain. They drove only a few miles before everything transformed dramatically. Isabella rolled down the window to get a better view. The stifling heat nearly stole her breath, but the beauty of the desert floor was amazing. All around her, flowers had bloomed like a carpet on the desert floor. In only a few hours, the entire area had transformed from sparse desert to resplendent garden. In the visible distance, she could see a small creek flowing with acacia trees and other larger flowering plants growing nearby. The view was marvelous and lush. In record time, these plants had raced to reach maturity to store up their seeds for days, months, even years until another rain gave them life again. Never had nature spoken to Isabella as it did in this country. The desert was strangely fascinating. Again, Isabella felt a tug on her heart for this country and people that God had created. In the allure of all that she could see, her heart opened and sang praise to the great creator of this place. She had not been in church for many weeks, but she knew she was in her Father's sanctuary, and her heart rejoiced with praise.

Latif stopped the vehicle and encouraged her to get out. As they made their way to the water, he reached for her hand. Hours before, she would have jerked her hand free, but now she let him hold it lightly in his own.

She looked up at him and realized he was watching her with an amused smile. His face registered contentment and pure happiness. This place had aroused an agreeable response in her soul as well. She realized she too felt happiness in reaction to this loveliness. As they walked through the carpet of color, she could smell the aroma of all the blooms. The smell was intoxicating.

Latif turned to face her. "How do you feel?"

"I don't know. I am in awe of this beautiful place and the God that created it. May he be praised."

Latif smiled down at her. "I am glad that you are happy. Rain comes so rarely to the desert. But when it does, the transformation is awe inspiring. I am glad I have the opportunity to share it with you. I enjoy seeing the pure joy on your face as you experience the beauty of my homeland." He reached up and brushed a stray hair from her cheek.

She turned away. The intensity of his gaze frightened her a little, and she pulled away from his hand, exploring deeper into the valley. He followed a short distance behind her. When she reached the creek, she turned back to him.

"Would it be appropriate for me to take off my shoes and wade in the water?"

"Yes, but please be careful. There is a Bedouin camp just beyond the trees over there. I do not want one of the men to try to take my new wife." Latif chuckled at the shock that registered on her face.

"What do you mean?"

"You are a rare beauty, Isabella. Any Saudi man would pay a lot of camels to take you as a wife."

"I don't like the sound of that. I have already experienced something like that once."

"Please don't look so startled. I would never give you up." Latif considered her his possession, and the fierceness of those feelings flashed across his face. In a strange way, this thought made her relax. She sat and removed her shoes. The water was warm and refreshing. She lifted her abaya just above her knees to keep it from getting wet. Her feet made little ripples in the clear, ankle-deep water. She looked around, wanting to experience every part of this remote oasis. The whole experience made her feel carefree and young, and some of the tension of the last few days lifted. She could feel the weight of Latif's gaze as she made her way a few yards up the stream. When she turned to look at him, she offered a shy, sincere smile.

"Isabella, I think we should make our way back to the vehicle. I see movement from our neighbors. I believe that they may be coming toward us."

Isabella obeyed. Quickly, she bent down and replaced her shoes. When she stood, she reached up to tuck all her hair under her scarf and held it tightly under her chin. Latif's warning had frightened her. In the distance, two men were coming toward them on camels. Once they reached them, Isabella looked at the ground and ducked behind Latif. One of the men spoke to Latif in a foreign tongue she could not understand. As they conversed, she turned her back to them, gazing out over the desert landscape.

When their conversation ended and the men on camels rode away, they reluctantly made their way back. She hated to leave this place. The peace and beauty of this sanctuary had temporarily driven away the dark, haunting shadows of the past weeks, and Isabella longed to hold on to the feeling of it. She needed to keep this treasure for the many dark days to come, and she hoped this memory would stay alive to help her through.

Isabella looked at the fresh flowers in the vase beside her bed as she contemplated the events of her day in the desert. The room was quiet and dark. The solitude helped her collect her thoughts and calmed her unstable nerves. Latif had still expected her to come to him that night even though she had tried to discourage him. Tears streamed from her eyes as she remembered his unwanted touch. He was gentle, just as he promised that first night, but his tenderness only fed her guilt about the encounter. His desire was fighting for her response, but she refused to give in. She was desperate to protect her heart from this stranger. He was determined to keep her against her will, determined to transform her into a Saudi wife. When she closed her eyes, she could see the sadness in Sam's eyes. If he knew … She had tried to push all thoughts of home from her mind over the last several days. However, they had a mind of their own. No matter how hard she tried, she could not stop the longing, love, and hope that called to her day and night. Sometimes the intensity of her aching heart overwhelmed her.

No matter how kind and loving Latif tried to be, he could not compare to Sam. In ten years of marriage, they had experienced a lifetime of love. God had

blessed her. Her husband had always loved her uncon-
ditionally. When she lost her cool or messed up, he
was always there to help. Of course, they had experienced hard times. They were both quick-tempered,
so their fights had often been intense. But never had
she doubted his love. Physically, her arms ached for
him and the girls. She longed to hear their voices. She
needed to give them her love. While they were so far
away, she would store it all away for a future time. Even
though it was an impossibility, she could not extinguish
the simple hope that they would soon be reunited.

She prayed again for strength to endure. She needed
a hope for tomorrow to make it through this long, dark
night. Again she was reminded of the beauty of this
incredible place. In a few weeks, this foreign land had
shown her its hidden beauty, and she could not fathom
how she had adapted to this new place. The difference
in her two worlds was incomparable. At home, she
lived in a plush green land. Even in the heat of summer, it was lush compared to this strange place. She
missed the trees and flowers, the beauty of the seasons.
At home, the leaves would be changing, and fall was
Sam's favorite season. Her long lost home called to her,
making her heart ache for it all.

But today she had experienced something unexpected. Even in this desolate place, she had seen life.
The simple beauty of God's creation had spoken to her
heart and confused her feelings while this small sign
had given her hope. She had been reminded that all the
world belonged to the Lord. He loved these Arabs just
as he loved the entire world. She could not grasp it. To
her, Latif was not worthy of her love; he was not wor-

thy of her Father's love. Her feelings were wrong, and she knew it. How would she ever love him that way? To consider it felt like a betrayal of all she held dear, but God had asked her to do it. How many times had she reminded her daughters of the two greatest commandments? Love the Lord your God and your neighbor as yourself. Latif, Mina, Hafa—they were her neighbors, and she was convicted of this truth.

Again, she prayed for strength. God was asking for the impossible. Without help, she would never be able to live out what God had commanded. So she simply promised to try and asked God to help her see these people as he saw them.

"With God all things are possible," she whispered. It was a prayer and a claim to the age-old promise. She wondered if her love could ever be like this land. In the most surprising ways, like the rain, could it bring forth the beauty of Christ's love within her heart? She doubted it. Instead she begged for supernatural help as she drifted off to sleep.

CHAPTER TWELVE

Darkness had settled over everything in the room. Only the light from the full moon filtered in from the windows. Isabella was waiting as she always did for Latif to drift off into deep sleep. He was a pretty light sleeper. Once, in her haste to escape his bed for the night, she had awakened him, and he had called her back to him. Since that time, she always waited until she was sure she could leave undetected. Latif was lying on his side, facing her. His face was peaceful. From comments he had made, she guessed he was near her age. But in the shadows of this room, in the peacefulness of sleep, he looked so young. His lips formed into a pout. She looked away from them. The thought of his lips unnerved her.

It had been a week since that first night. She shivered. In her mind, she knew she could not have avoided what had happened between them, even as her heart accused her of betraying all that she loved. She tried to reason through the myriad of emotions, but could not come to a clear resolution. Intimacy with a man was a complicated thing. When her heart longed for Sam, how could she ever really be Latif's wife?

It was a painful situation to be in. Yet in this week with him, there had been brief moments where she had been able to relax. There had even been moments, like the one in the desert, where she had felt kindness toward him. She tried to see him as a spoiled, rich prince. It was true in a sense, but her assessment was stereotypical and shallow. In this week, he had been a dichotomy. On several occasions throughout the week, he had been obstinant and selfish, demanding and overbearing. That part of Latif was easy to hate, and often that is what she felt toward him. Still, other times he had surprised her with gifts and words of kindness. In those moments, he was open and amiable. Without warning, her heart would be drawn to him. She was lonely and that made her vulnerable. When she was with him, she was careful to guard her heart. But often she found herself wondering what God expected from her. Did he require her to honor and love this man who claimed her? Was she required to submit to him in the way the Bible insisted? These were questions she could not answer, and there was no pastor or counselor to ask. Instead she wrestled with these conflicting emotions. In the end, she just submitted to her heavenly Father and asked him again and again to help her love this man as he loved him.

Again, her gaze drifted to Latif. His skin was so dark in comparison to hers, which was so pale. They were opposites on every level and should never have been brought together. Now that this little rendezvous in Jeddah was ending, what would their relationship be like? Would she see him more or less? She resolved to ask him in the morning on the trip back to Riyadh. Silently, she slipped from the bed and headed for the door. It was time to move to the safety of her room.

Latif turned off his alarm and climbed out of bed. It was just before dawn. He turned toward Isabella's side of the bed, but she was not there. He focused instead on performing complete ablution, or ritual cleansing, before his Salaah, prayer time. This complete cleansing required him to shower. Then he would arrange his prayer rug and face Mecca. Prayer five times a day was a requirement by the Koran, and each day his prayer was always the same. For his noontime prayer, he would go to the local mosque. When he was at home, he frequently attended the noon prayer with some of his brothers and his father. These rituals had been a part of his daily routine for as long as he could remember. Because he had been born in Saudi Arabia, he was a Muslim, and all Muslims followed the laws of the Koran. This was the same for every man, woman, and child born in his country. He never questioned or doubted these written laws; he just accepted and followed them.

After he had completed the recitation of his prayers, he flipped through the morning paper, disappointed that today would be their last day in Jeddah. He was not ready to go back. He was enjoying this time alone with Isabella. There had been rocky moments between them, but he was certain things were progressing well. Yesterday, he had even contacted his father to let him know he was planning to stay an additional week with Isabella. Unfortunately, his father required him to return as scheduled. An unforeseen business problem had arisen, and his father expected him to come home to resolve it. Reluctantly, he had agreed. His father counted on him. He was expected to take his father's position of leadership in the family business in the future, and he did not dare jeopardize that position. Family responsibilities were more important than his personal desires, so he had agreed to adhere to the original schedule.

It was strange to realize they were returning to Latif's home as a married couple. The plane had just lifted off the ground, flying toward Riyadh. Latif was sitting beside her, but his presence filled the cabin. She tried to ignore him and the conflicting emotions she felt when she was near him. She looked out the small window beside her seat at the breathtaking view of the sea. The sun was high in the sky, and it reflected off the water like glistening jewels. Jeddah was such a beautiful city, and she was a little sad to leave it. But she was looking forward to seeing Mina and Hafa again. She missed them.

"Isabella, I think we need to talk about something." When she turned to Latif, his expression was rather grim. Suddenly, she felt apprehensive.

"I should have told you this a long time ago, but I didn't. I guess it just never seemed to be the right time.

Now, there will probably never be a good time, but it needs to be said before we return home." Latif paused. It seemed like several minutes before he spoke again. "Isabella, you are not my only wife. I have two other wives living at home in Riyadh."

Latif was silent. She sensed he was watching her. She stared at her hands folded in her lap. Several emotions surged around inside her, but she could not grasp what she really felt. She was a little shocked. She had never even considered he would have another wife, let alone two wives. But as she thought about it, she realized she was also angry. If he already had two other wives, then why did he insist on having her as a wife as well? How ridiculous. She looked back out the window. She was too busy mulling over what Latif had said to focus on the view. She should have felt jealousy, but she didn't. If he was really her husband, then why did she not feel she had a claim on him? Instead, under all the strange emotions that she felt, she was relieved. She could not explain it or understand it.

"Isabella, are you angry?" She looked back at him. The timid look on his face amused her. It was so uncharacteristic for him to ever appear vulnerable. Instead she concentrated on keeping her face emotionless.

"I am a little angry. If you have two wives, then why did you insist on having me as your wife as well?"

Latif seemed to relax a little at her question. "In the Koran, a man is permitted to take four wives if he can treat them all the same. I wanted another wife, and when you came along, it seemed to be the will of Allah."

Isabella closed her eyes. Would she ever grow

accustomed to these strange teachings of the Koran? Everything about Latif's beliefs seemed in contrast to the things she believed. "So when we return, what should I expect?"

Latif seemed surprised by her matter-of-fact reaction. "In many ways it will be the same as it was before the wedding party. The main house in the compound is the main residence. My rooms are there. My wives have there own areas somewhat like yours. My first wife, Bahira, lives in her own wing in the main house. My second wife, Dalia, has a small house similar to yours." Latif looked at her. He appeared to be attempting to read how she felt. "I will share my time with you when we return."

"Will I still see you?" Everything about this conversation felt strained to Isabella, but she wanted to understand what she should expect from him.

"Often, I will come to you in your home. We will spend time together just as we did in Jeddah, but I am also required to spend time with Bahira and Dalia."

"Will I meet your other wives, or will we just live as neighbors and strangers?"

Latif smiled. "When we return, you will be introduced to both of them. Time can be very boring for women in Saudi Arabia. As I am sure you know, there are not many things for women to do to occupy their time. Often the women have parties with each other to ease the solitude. During the day, they will probably invite you to join them at their parties in the main house."

"How will your wives feel about me?"

Latif chuckled at this innocent question. "Are you asking if they will be jealous?"

"I suppose."

"No, they will not be jealous. Women in the kingdom are not raised like women in the West. Both of my wives have always known they would likely share their husband with other women. It is an accepted way of life."

Isabella was skeptical. She knew the nature of women, and this did not fit her expectation. "So they will become my friends?" The idea was preposterous.

"In a way, that is what they will be. Hafa and other women you will meet will also be your friends. Men and women that are not related are always separated, but solitude can be hard. The word *harem* actually means to have pity or sympathy. Women spend time together to help deal with the isolation and boredom. In Bedouin families, the women work together to share responsibilities. But wealthy women have servants to take care of that, so they are free to socialize together. It works to everyone's benefit to get along."

"Like one big happy family." Isabella could not resist the hint of sarcasm in her comment.

"In time you will understand and accept it."

"You said you will come and visit me in my house. Will I ever be required to come to you in your house?"

"No, and you will never meet my friends. In fact, you are never permitted to come into the men's quarters in the main house for any reason."

"Will I have any say in when or how often you come to visit me?"

"No." Latif answered quickly and firmly. She noticed

the characteristic firmness in his gaze. It was the look that refused to be challenged. She had seen it too many times since meeting him, and it was a look she was beginning to hate.

"I have to admit there are not very many things about this life I am going to like." Isabella shook her head as she spoke. "This is all a little too bizarre."

She turned back to the window, wanting this conversation to be over. Everything familiar about her previous life was gone. In its place were isolation, boredom, and loneliness with little to look forward to. She had realized over the week that any hope of returning home was impossible, but the monotony of the bleak, empty existence that would be her life was suffocating. There was nothing left to hope for, and she no longer felt the will to fight or escape. In this short time, she had slowly acquiesced to the inevitable. Anything more was futile.

CHAPTERTHIRTEEN

Isabella was feeling a little forlorn about returning. She had never been such a moody person, but now conflicting emotions were always stirring within her. Most of the time, she could not determine what her true feelings were. The only feeling she could truly identify with and understand was the longing for home.

She had been happy to see Mina. The two had even embraced upon her arrival home, and Isabella sensed that Mina had missed and worried about her while she was gone. But since her return, Mina was a little reserved around Isabella. She knew that Mina considered her a friend and was fond of her. But Mina was awkward at times, as if she did not know how to handle their developing friendship. Isabella often tried to draw Mina's feelings and desires out, but she sensed reluctance. She was certain that the difficulties of the life she had lived had hardened her somewhat to true kindness. The injustice of the things Mina had faced through the years angered Isabella, and she resolved to be a trustworthy friend to this sweet, loving woman. Mina deserved more than she had received.

Most of all, Mina needed the hope and love of a Savior. From the brief conversations over the last several weeks, Isabella had learned Mina did not believe in any God. The cruelty and injustices of her life had convinced her that no God could exist. No just God would allow all the things Mina had seen in her life. She had even commented that if there was a God, then he was definitely not loving. The couple times Isabella had tried to explain, Mina had closed up. She did not want to hear any words from Isabella about hope and love. Pain had become a welcome protector in Mina's heart. Expecting pain and hardship prevented her from futile hope. Hope in a hopeless situation was dangerous to a person as loving and kind as Mina.

Prayer was her only weapon against Mina's cold, wounded heart. In the days and weeks to come, instead of boredom, Isabella resolved to pray. There were so many promises about prayer in the Bible, and she planned to claim them. She wanted to be useful, and her life needed a purpose. She thought of Hafa's advice about sharing her faith. It was risky to be bold about her God in this dark, sinful place, but she resolved to make a difference, and prayer was the first place to start. Then maybe the Holy Spirit would open their hearts to truth. Isabella knew she was a small, insignificant person in the scheme of God's plan, but God had used plenty of simple people. This thought gave her heart something to look forward to. It gave her just a little hope.

That night, as Isabella lay in her bed, she had trouble falling asleep. She feared that Latif might come to her tonight, and she could not relax. Over the last week in Jeddah, sleep had come to her rather easily. She was always awake late waiting for Latif to fall asleep so that she returned to her own bed exhausted. Tonight, she was restless, and insomnia always made her long for the safety and security of home.

From her estimation, Katherine's birthday was just a few weeks away. The Islamic calendar does not follow the same calendar as the United States, so her days were not regularly updated by that calendar. But in her notebook, Isabella was trying to keep track. If she were at home, she would already be planning the party. Planning parties for the girls was always fun, and she enjoyed sharing the excitement with them. Months before, Katherine had already shared all her ideas for her birthday. Turning five was a big deal to her little Katherine. In less than a year, she would be going to kindergarten. Thinking about missing these things grieved her heart. Isabella wiped away a stray tear.

Her sweet, beautiful girls. Where were they? Did they still lie in bed at night and cry for her? Did they wonder if she was dead? Sam was a great father, but he was not their mother, and they needed her. Little girls need their mothers. In her heart, she prayed for them, but it was of little comfort. She prayed again, as she often did, that God would arrange for her rescue. She longed to hold her babies in her arms again.

She got out of bed and went outside to the garden. The moonlight was bright, illuminating much of what was around her in a soft, white glow. It was chilly, so she hugged herself for warmth. The feel of the cool air cleared her head. Weariness consumed her body and brought her to her knees. The stone patio was cold on her legs. Above her, the sky was filled with an abundance of twinkling stars. She was disheartened with the weight of this life that lay before her and tired of this feeling of helplessness. There on the patio, shivering from the cool night, she gave her life to her Lord. She wanted relief from the weight of her worries. She was tired of wallowing in the sadness and self-pity of the life she could not go back to. She resolved to move forward and be useful from this day forward. In her prayer, she also begged to be spared from having a child. She did not think she was pregnant, but she knew that in time she might be, so she asked God to close her womb. If she ever got a chance to return to her home, she knew having a child would make it more complicated. Then she began to pray for the people in her life here in this new home. First, she prayed for Latif. She did not know exactly what to pray for as she imagined his face and her desire to be free of him. This too she gave to the Lord. She thought of the two wives she would meet. All the fears and concerns over these unknown relationships, she gave the burden of carrying them as well. Then, in earnest, she prayed for Mina and Hafa. She prayed God would work in their hearts and give her an opportunity to share with them about him. After a long time of crying and pain, she gave her husband and children to God. Releasing them was the most difficult. She knew they needed her prayers now more than they needed her. She petitioned the sovereign of the universe to care for her family. She gave over all the lost hopes and dreams, all the missed smiles and tears. She gave it all to the one who could restore it. So many times she had sought to return. Now she asked only for fortitude to withstand, letting go of all that was most dear to her. In a gesture to the openness of her heart, she lifted her hands above her. She offered this life, and the life she longed for, to the one who expected her to give him everything. She stayed with her arms and face raised for as long as she could. She offered him what little praise she could muster, and in those long moments she began to feel a new strength replenish a small token of what she had given up. Bowing her head, she made her way back to the warmth of her bed. Overcome with exhaustion, she drifted into a deep restful sleep.

Latif made his way from the main house through the extensive gardens to Isabella's private residence. He was excited to see her again. The night before, according to custom, he had spent with Bahira. She was his first wife and therefore deserved some privilege with that position, but he missed being with his new wife. He knocked lightly at her door and then entered.

"Isabella?"

She came in from the other room, her face registering a slight concern over his arrival. She came and stood in front of him but did not say anything.

"Are you okay?" He asked her.

"Why are you here in the middle of the afternoon?"

"I was just taking a little break from work after my prayers and lunch. Most businesses close for a few hours during this time.

"Oh."

"I have some news I want to share with you. I have contacted an interior designer to help you with remodeling your home. He has been instructed to provide anything you wish. You can even order furniture and accessories from the U.S. You have freedom to decorate in any style you like, sparing no expense. There is an additional guesthouse on the property you can move to if you are uncomfortable living here during the remodeling process. I want you to make this place into a home, a place where you feel comfortable."

"When should I expect the designer?"

"I have scheduled an appointment with him tomorrow morning." Latif searched her face to see if she approved. Her faced registered little emotion. "Isabella, let's sit down and visit for a while. I have missed you."

"Hafa will be arriving soon. She is planning to take me to a party with the women in your home later this afternoon. I think she is going to introduce me to your other wives."

"Good." Latif was a little worried about the introductions, but he tried not to let it show. "But we can still visit until she arrives. I wish we could have spent more time in Jeddah."

"It has been quiet here since our return. Being in Jeddah was so much different than my life here."

"In time, I do hope you will miss me when we are apart. I am willing to patiently wait for that day." Latif walked into her small sitting area and took a seat on the sofa. Isabella followed and moved toward the chair to have a seat. "Please come sit next to me, Isabella."

Reluctantly, she complied with his request. Once she was seated a safe distance from him, she turned toward him and said, "I am just unsure about the nature of our relationship. Marriage here is very different than I am used to. I am trying to learn what is appropriate. Can you tell me, how will I know when to expect your visits?"

"Most days, I will come and visit you. It might be in the afternoon or at night. Of course, I am also required to visit my other wives, so I will not be able to come everyday. Today, I just really missed you and wanted to talk. Last week, we were busy seeing the sights and shopping. I do not feel we had a lot of time to get to know each other."

Latif paused as he slid so close to her his leg lightly brushed her thigh. "I miss you, Isabella." Being close to her was enticing, and he could not help but notice everything about her. He tried to restrain his desire when he turned to speak. "Yesterday, I went to visit one of my brothers. He said I looked very happy. He thinks my new marriage has been good for me, and I agree with him. Being with you has given me a youthful energy. You are a special woman, Isabella. That is why I want you to redecorate your home. I want to give you back a little of the happiness you have given me."

Latif stroked the side of her soft cheek and then gently kissed her lips. Isabella tensed from his forward advance, but she did not pull away. He desperately wanted her to respond to his kiss. Imagining that, she had made him eager for more, so he kissed her again, this time more deeply. He wondered if he would ever tire of her. She was so refreshing. He was quickly losing control of his desire as he drew her into his arms.

Again, Isabella froze, pulling away, she asked, "Latif, I thought you wanted to talk."

Unwilling to ignore the passion growing within him, he again pulled her into his arms. This time when he felt her stiffen and push away, he reluctantly released her. Passion pumped through his body. He wanted her, needed her, but he did not want to push her away again. He took a deep breath, gathering control of his desire.

Teasingly he smiled. "Isabella, you distract me. I only wanted to talk, and yet I find myself completely unable to focus."

"Maybe I should move to another seat." He reached for her hand, urging her to stay near him.

"Stay. I will behave." Again Latif smiled. He would win her heart without her even knowing it was gone, but to do it would take time and patience. "I want to know more about you, to understand who my new wife really is."

She was slow to share about her life, but he was learning the nuances that helped Isabella relax and open up to him. Latif eased into light conversation about his day, and reluctantly she relaxed into easy conversation. He learned she loved to read as he questioned her about some of her favorite books. She also shared some about her faith. When Isabella talked about her God, her conviction was evident. He loved her passionate nature, and talking about things she loved made her eyes dance with delight. Latif had always known she was a Christian. Hafa had shared this with him right away, but it had never bothered him. It was acceptable for a man in his country to marry a woman that was not Muslim, but it was inexcusable for a woman to marry outside her faith. When Isabella had children, they would be Muslim, just like he was. It was an accepted part of life, so he did not worry about it.

He also shared some stories from childhood about Hafa. They had always been very close. They shared the same mother, but were also very similar in many other ways as well. It was not common for brothers and sisters to get along, making their relationship different from most. Her friendship to his new wife delighted him, and he hoped they would become very close in the years to come. Their new friendship was very different than the relationship Hafa had with his other two wives. She never spoke negatively about them. To insult them would have been unacceptable, but he had known that Hafa did not like them. Truth be told, he did not blame her. Marriage was complicated, and for this reason, he was prepared to work hard at his marriage to Isabella.

His visit was cut short by the arrival of his sister. Latif excused himself after reminding Isabella that he would be returning later that night. He walked back to the main house. It was time to get back to work, but while he walked, he savored the thought of the night to come.

"I know I am being silly, but I'm nervous about the party. Hafa, what should I expect?"

Hafa giggled at Isabella's uneasiness about the party because her nervousness seemed a little out of character. Under other circumstances, Isabella was a very strong woman, and it was funny that meeting Latif's wives and other friends and family unnerved her.

"It is just a party, Isabella. Relax. I will introduce you to everyone. You won't be alone, and no one has any expectations of you. By the way, you look lovely today. I think the weather in Jeddah was good for you. Maybe you enjoyed the attention of my brother more than you want to let on?" Hafa winked and smiled at Isabella.

She smiled at her friend's teasing and just shrugged. Her improved appearance was probably more a response of her prayers the night before, but she decided to save that discussion for another time. She followed Hafa to the party in the main house, trying to remember what her friend had said.

As they entered, Isabella looked around. The décor in the foyer was dated. There was too much color, and everything was overdone. Isabella was no decorator, but she knew someone with little taste had furnished this room. They made their way down a short hallway where she could hear voices just ahead of them. The room they entered was decorated similarly to the entry. She ignored the décor and looked around at all the faces in the room. Nearly every conversation had stopped as all eyes turned on her. Maybe it was just her imagination, but she felt assessment from every one of them. Isabella would have preferred to crawl into a hole. Instead, she bravely waited to be introduced by her friend. She looked back over the small group, trying to guess which two were Latif's wives. Her curiosity surprised her. Before arriving, she had told herself that meeting them was unimportant. Hafa hesitated for a moment and then deliberately walked across the room. Isabella took a deep breath and followed. When they stopped, a woman Isabella guessed to be close to her age stood and kissed Hafa on the cheek and then turned an appraising eye toward her. In an instant, Isabella knew this was one of Latif's wives. She looked into her eyes, hoping to meet a gracious host, but her gaze was met with hostility. The woman was lovely, but as different from Isabella as night and day. She had very short, dark brown hair and dark brown, almost black, eyes. Isabella guessed that she was at least an inch or two taller than her. Her face was round, and she had applied a lot of kohl to her small eyes to make them appear larger.

"Bahira, please meet my friend Isabella." Hafa turned toward Isabella to address her. "Isabella, this is Bahira, Latif's first wife."

Isabella nodded and smiled at Bahira. "I am very glad to meet you." Bahira smiled tightly in response, but the smile never reached her eyes.

"*Ahlan feeki.*" She turned to her guests and announced, "Please meet Isabella; she is new to our family."

Hafa turned and began making her way to the opposite side of the room. As Isabella followed, she noticed a few familiar faces from the wedding party.

"Dalia, I want to introduce you to Isabella."

Isabella knew that this was Latif's other wife. As Dalia stood in response to Hafa's introduction, Isabella noticed she was a rare beauty. She was very petite, at least three or four inches shorter than Isabella's average height, and everything about her was delicate. She had lovely dark brown hair and bewitching hazel eyes. Compared to all the other women in the room, Dalia was undoubtedly the most beautiful. She was exactly the wife she expected for a Saudi Arabian prince.

Isabella puzzled over the idea that Latif would desire her when he already had two very lovely wives. Isabella felt very out of place in this group of dark exotic women, and she wondered if she would ever fit in.

"Nice to meet you, Isabella." Dalia's voice was dripping with sweetness, but no kindness registered on her face. Dalia carefully appraised Isabella from head to toe, jealousy clearly evident on her face.

Isabella replied, offering her a generous smile, "Pleased to meet you as well, Dalia." Dalia did not return the smile. She quickly turned back to her seat and resumed talking with her friends.

Hafa led Isabella to a small group of women on the edge of the large room and introduced them all as her close friends. Isabella noted that one of them was even Hafa's father's young wife, Uzma. She appeared to be only a few years older than Isabella. All of Hafa's friends seemed very intrigued by her. She spent much of the afternoon and early evening talking with each of them as they questioned her mostly about life in the U.S. A couple had spent some time there on trips, but none had lived there like Hafa. She slowly began to relax in response to the friendliness of Hafa's friends. A couple of times during the party, Isabella noticed Dalia watching her from across the room. She could not help but wonder about Latif's wives and the relationships they shared with him.

Just before dinner, she told Hafa that she was ready to go. Before leaving the party, Isabella went to Bahira and thanked her for inviting her to the party. Bahira seemed surprised by this kind gesture and even graced her with a slight, sincere smile. When she turned to leave, Hafa walked with her across the beautifully manicured lawn.

"So, Isabella, was that as scary as you thought it would be?"

Isabella paused reflectively before she responded. "I suppose it was not worse than I expected. How do you think it went?"

"Well, I think Dalia does not like for her beauty to be outshone by another of Latif's wives. She takes great pride in her reputation as Latif's delicate and beautiful wife."

Isabella was shocked that Hafa would consider her beauty comparable to Dalia's. "Hafa, how could I ever outshine Dalia? She is one of the most beautiful women I have ever met. No one in that room would find me more beautiful than her."

Hafa shook her head in wonder while bestowing an affectionate and loving smile as she spoke. "Isabella, you are very sweet and humble. I am always surprised by your genuine innocence and sweet spirit. You are a rare jewel, just as Latif has affirmed. You underesti-mate your own beauty, my friend, but what makes you shine above all others is the light that shines within you. You are open and kind, even to those who do not deserve your kindness, and so few possess a gift like that. When you combine that light from within with your graceful beauty, unique hair color, and eyes, you outshine even Dalia."

The sincere affection in Hafa's comment touched Isabella deeply. She still did not believe she was as beautiful as Dalia, nor did she care, but she appreciated the compliment from her friend. "Thank you, Hafa."

"Now, how do you think the party went?" Hafa seemed completely intrigued.

"Well, I was surprised your friends were so interested in the United States. And I did not know what to expect from Latif's wives. I am not sure either one of them liked me very much, but then I am not sure they could ever honestly see me as a friend. Won't they always see me as a rival?"

"Marriage is not like that here. Women all expect to share the affections of their husbands, and do not judge Bahira too soon. She is a cold and skeptical woman and slow to trust anyone. I could be wrong about this, but I think she is very intrigued by you. She has never liked me, but she might surprise you. We will see in time what she thinks."

"I will try to be open minded with both of them. I know I am the stranger. I must prove myself to them. Neither may ever come to be my friend, but I will always try to show them respect. Of course, I will continue to pray for them."

"It is always funny to hear you make reference to your prayers. Sometimes I even think you truly believe you are having a conversation with God. What do you do when you do not hear his answers?"

"Hafa, my friend, prayer is a conversation with God. He loves me and enjoys when I come to him with my petitions. I always know he will answer my prayers. Sometimes I do not like the answers he gives, like not providing a way of escape from my marriage to your brother. It is hard to explain, but I know God hears and answers my prayers. He is faithful to listen, and that is what makes all that has happened bearable. Without help from my God, I am not sure I would have survived this. If prayer is not a conversation with God, then why do you do it each day?"

"I do it because the Koran commands it. That is why I pray. I must follow all that the Koran dictates. To do otherwise is *haraam*, sin."

"Then prayer is very different for me than it is for you. When you pray, what do you pray for?"

"Each prayer is specific to the time of day. It is always the same prayer everyday. I give praise to Allah several times, ask for forgiveness for my sins, and ask him to give me guidance. Praying brings me closer to Allah in this life and the next."

Hafa's fervent expression of faith was compelling to Isabella. She admired Hafa's simple acceptance of these commands to obey but was sad that her faith was not relational. Religion like this was empty. It was nothing more then an exercise she was required to perform. The realization made Isabella sad, but she resolved anew to pray for her lost friend.

"Hafa, I am glad you are my friend. Can you stay and have dinner with me?"

"I can't. I need to get home to my children and my husband. But I will come by again in a few days to visit. Peace be with you, my friend."

"And to you, Hafa. I look forward to seeing you soon."

It made Isabella sad to watch her friend leave. Latif would be coming to her again tonight, but before then she hoped to distract her thoughts with an extended visit with Mina. When the uneasiness started to surface in her heart, she simply asked for help from God, her faithful friend.

CHAPTER FOURTEEN

The next morning, Isabella got up as usual, but this time when she looked around the rooms of her home, she saw it with fresh eyes. Since last night, she had been trying to decide what she liked about her home and what she wanted to change. The remodeling project gave her something fun and different to focus on. It would be a lot of work, but the more she considered it, the more she liked the idea. This remodel would be different than anything she had ever done because it would be the first time she had been given the opportunity to redecorate without money being an issue.

She was reminded of all the decorating projects she had completed in the little home she shared with Sam and the girls. They were certainly not poor, but they had always been careful with their money. Often, she had searched at garage sales and thrift stores for items to use in her decorating projects. She had not minded the frugalness; instead she had enjoyed the thrill of the hunt. She thought of that little house and missed the hominess of the place she loved. It had been so many days and nights since she had been there, yet she remembered every detail of it as if she were there. She could even imagine little Rebecca rushing in after school from the bus stop and Katherine meeting her at the door just as she did everyday. These emotional memories were always with her, but for now she brushed them off to focus on the tasks at hand.

As she considered the remodel, so many thoughts and ideas were swimming around in her head. Should she decorate this place with American designs and furnishings or stay with a more exotic style from the region? Maybe she would do a little of both. She wondered what the decorator would be like as she walked around the small home, looking carefully at the dimensions of each of the rooms. She thought about the styles she loved, like colonial American and French country, but somehow neither of those styles fit. Her favorite room in the house was the bedroom. It looked like an exotic wealthy Bedouin tent. She just could not decide. Maybe she would wait and bounce her ideas off the decorator, hoping he could make some sense out of her eclectic style ideas.

She heard Mina come in the front door and go into the kitchen. Since she had returned from Jeddah with Latif, she had sensed a growing distance with Mina. She wanted things to be the way they had been when she first arrived, but she was unsure what had caused the change in their relationship.

Isabella made her way into the kitchen and noticed

Mina putting items away in the small kitchen refrigerator. Isabella missed doing her own cooking but enjoyed all the things Mina cooked for her. Mina made an art out of cooking and was always experimenting with new dishes to try out on Isabella. It was nice to be pampered, but cooking was something she had done for her family for years, and sometimes she missed some of the most basic things from her old life.

"Good morning, Mina."

"Good morning. You up early this morning. You hungry?"

"I am always hungry when you start cooking. If you are not careful, you will make me fat," Isabella said, teasing her friend.

"You lose much weight. I glad you putting on weight." Mina gave Isabella a gentle smile. "When you arrive, I afraid you starve to death."

"Without your friendship, I am sure I would not have survived. Some days, I still would choose anything over this life, even death. When I feel that distraught, I can only seek refuge in my God and Savior. And often, I thank him for giving me a selfless friend like you." Isabella's voice echoed the emotion of her words.

Mina reached over and touched her hand. Isabella could see she was moved by her words. "No one ever be thankful for me. I glad you feel better."

"And putting on weight. You are trying to make me fat, aren't you, Mina?" Mina's eyes sparkled as she smiled at the silliness of her friend. Isabella stopped her teasing and gave Mina a serious look. "But I feel like things have changed a little between us since I came back from Jeddah. Have I done something to hurt you, Mina?"

"Isabella, you true friend I ever had. You done nothing wrong. You are Latif's wife; you more mistress than friend. Mina work for you. It a little awkward to be your friend." Mina averted her eyes as she spoke.

"Mina, look at me. Nothing has changed between us. You are my friend, and I don't even think of you as my servant. I am an ordinary woman, just like you. I value your friendship. Without you, I am not sure what I would have done. I believe God has placed you in my life, and I meant it when I said that I am thankful for you." She saw gratefulness in Mina's eyes in response to the words she had spoken.

"Thank you." Mina nodded, then smiled mischievously again. "Now, go! You bother me." Isabella patted her on the back and went in the other room.

Isabella sat on the floor of her bedroom with fabric samples, books, and color swatches all around her. The decorator had arranged several color ideas in front of her. They were talking over ideas for the bedroom, but Isabella could not decide.

Latif had arrived just after breakfast that morning with Gael, the designer. Latif had only stayed for a few minutes during the introductions; then he had left. Gael was a funny, feminine, little French man. Her first thoughts, when she realized her designer was European, were that he might help her contact home. But it did not take long to realize he was superficial and self-centered. He droned on and on about himself and never asked anything about Isabella, except to find out her tastes in decorating. Isabella thought he had too many opinions about everything. Several times throughout the morning he had insulted her about her design tastes. He was an authority on everything, and in a few short hours, this decorating process had lost its appeal.

Isabella looked again at all the ideas that Gael had offered, but none of them seemed to fit her style. They had made some progress on the sitting room, but he was not listening to anything she had suggested about the bedroom. She was getting increasingly frustrated and that surprised her. After nearly all of the morning and part of the afternoon sorting through idea books and color suggestions, Isabella was exhausted. It seemed they had not made any progress in any other rooms. She was even tempted to leave the bedroom just as it was. But when she offered the idea to Gael, he scoffed at her.

"Can't you see this room is unsatisfactory? The tapestries around the windows are faded. The color scheme does not work together, and the furniture is oversized for the room. It's a mess." Gael moved his hands to express every word that he spoke. Sometimes his hands got moving so maniacally he nearly hit her in the face.

Isabella was so frustrated she nearly laughed. Just a few hours earlier, she had looked forward to the distraction of remodeling. Now, she was ready for this man to leave her alone. Isabella took a deep breath before she spoke. "Gael, can we make an appointment for another day to discuss this? I feel a little overwhelmed by all your great suggestions. Maybe I just need a little time to think over the ideas. What is your schedule like later this week?"

"Let me look at my calendar." She watched as he sorted through the catalogs, color swatches, and fabric samples looking for it. "Lets see. Tomorrow is full, but I can come the next day at 10:00 a.m."

"That will be perfect. It will give me some time to sort through all of this. Maybe I will be able to narrow it down by then. Also, I would like to replace the table in the dining area with a table more like one from the United States. When you come, can you bring some additional ideas for that room as well?" Isabella sighed, relieved he was leaving.

"Good. I will leave these things with you to look over. Here is my card in case you have any questions. Decorating is a tedious process if you have not been professionally trained. Of course, everyone thinks he is an expert. It just drives me crazy." He grabbed his calendar and placed it in his bag. Then he got up to leave. "I will see you in a couple days. It is very nice to meet you, Isabella."

"Nice to meet you, Gael. Thank you for your help today." Isabella smiled at him as she opened the door, closing it behind him as he left. She placed her hands over her face and sighed. Then she rubbed her eyes and leaned back against the door. She was exhausted. While she was standing there, someone knocked, and the unexpected sound made her jump away from the door. When she turned around, Latif entered.

"Did I startle you?" Latif looked concerned as he closed the door.

"A little. Gael just left."

Latif smiled at her. "So how did it go?"

"Well, I guess we made some progress." Isabella frowned a little as she thought about the tedious hours they had spent making few decisions.

"You don't seem very happy. What happened?"

Isabella waved off his remark with her hand. "Everything is fine. He is just a bit difficult; that is all." Isabella tried to look at the experience objectively. Then she started giggling.

"What is so funny?" Latif seemed puzzled by the change in her demeanor.

"I don't know. The man makes me crazy, and I just had to laugh." Isabella shook her head as she looked at Latif. "He is not like any man I have ever met. Where did you find him?"

"My mother recommended him. Isabella, if you do not like him, then we can find someone else."

"No, let's give it a few days, and we'll see how it goes. Maybe once I look over all of his suggestions I will not feel so overwhelmed. I have to tell you I have never worked with a designer before. The whole experience was just … different than I expected. I don't know what I envisioned, but I did not anticipate it being so exhausting." Again, Isabella laughed at the absurd man that had just left her house. "What are you doing here?"

"I want to have dinner with you. I told Mina that I would be joining you for dinner. She will be bringing some help over from the main house to serve us. I have had a stressful day, and I wanted to see you to find out how the remodeling was coming. I thought you might enjoy walking around the gardens a little while we wait for them to prepare our dinner. Would you care to join me on a tour around the beautiful grounds of my home?"

"Sure. Can you just give me a minute? I have been with Gael for several hours. I will be right back."

The grounds of his estate were filled with an assortment of trees, plants, and ornamental grasses meticulously maintained by the gardeners Latif employed. They cultivated the land and raised several crops including tomatoes, watermelon, cucumbers, dates, and a variety of citrus fruits. Sustaining these crops with water and care required a full staff of eight gardeners and additional laborers at harvest times. Latif was proud of his paradise in the desert and enjoyed sharing it with Isabella. He guided her around the large grounds, explaining the purpose of each plant. His estate was elaborate and beautiful. He enjoyed impressing her with his wealth, and he was certain she was impressed by this place he called home.

She often stopped and asked him questions about individual plants or flowers. She was fascinated by the lushness of the gardens, and her interest pleased him. The terrain of the kingdom was very different from the world she had grown up in, and he was amused to learn Isabella had never even tasted a date before. This abundant crop was an everyday staple for everyone in his country, and these little reminders magnified the vast differences between them.

He gazed at his young wife. She had her hair pulled back in a ponytail, making her look youthful and carefree. She was relaxed and nearly smiling as he led her through the women's garden near the main house. She had an eye for beauty that he admired. In the shade of a large date palm tree, he pulled her into his arms and gave her a lingering, sweet kiss. Her physical response to him was still reserved and hesitant, but everyday she was getting closer to enjoying his embraces. He buried his face in her soft, fragrant hair, choking back a groan from the enjoyment of their brief intimate hug.

When he released her, she turned and walked a few steps away. Glancing back to him, she asked. "Latif, do you have children?"

"Yes. I have two sons and a daughter."

"I would love to hear about them. What are their names and ages?"

"Youssef is my oldest son. He is twelve. Raja, my second son, is four. My daughter Aisha is nearly two. They are all very special. I love my children and pray that Allah blesses me with many more. I even desire for us to have a son. Maybe he will even look like you. Isabella, the thought of us having a child thrills me."

She had turned back and continued walking down the path as he spoke. He tried to peer around to see her expression at his comment, but he could not see her face. She continued to stroll through the garden just out of his reach. He did not think she was avoiding him, but neither did she turn and acknowledge his remark.

Again he broached the topic to determine the nature of her feelings. "Isabella, would it make you happy to have a child with me?"

She still did not turn and look at him. Instead, she

stopped and looked around at the enclosure of the garden. She was slow to answer his question, and he desperately wanted to know her thoughts. Silently, he stood waiting for her response. Taking a seat on a nearby bench, she looked at a small stone that was near her toe. She kicked it and then spoke just above a whisper. He moved toward her, straining to hear her response. "I am just not ready to talk about this."

Latif exhaled, not even realizing he had been holding his breath. Her answer to such a simple question was more important than he realized. He wanted her desire for a child to mirror his own, and her reaction disappointed him. In his heart, he reminded himself to proceed cautiously. He softly clapped his hands in front of his face, pressing his fingers against his lips and watching her profile. In the soft, filtered sunlight of the garden, she had an angelic glow. He savored the moment, aware of the emotions she invoked deep in his soul. The emotions were consuming and unexpected, and with a brief hesitation, he realized he was falling for his cherished wife. He relished the intoxicating moment in this perfect place for several minutes before pulling himself back to the present.

"I think we should head back for dinner. The servants are probably waiting for us."

She turned, nodding as she stood. As she walked up beside him, he took her small hand into his own. Loosely, he held it as they made their way back through the estate.

Imperceptibly, the days grew into weeks and then months. Frequently Isabella would be reminded of events from home that she missed. When Katherine's birthday came, she spent the entire day in bed. Thanksgiving and Christmas passed in the kingdom without any celebration, and Isabella fought becoming overcome with depression. In Islam, no one celebrated these holidays or birthdays. Some days, Isabella was just a fish out of water. Knowing she would always be a stranger in this place made her sad and despondent.

On tumultuously emotional days, Isabella was over-wrought. Her anger had chilled with time, but she was still frustrated by the uncontrollable nature of her life. In the most desperate times, she still found words of consolation in her Bible and recorded them all in her notebook. It was a comfort to know the Holy Spirit guided her life. She continued to pray daily for her family and her friends, but most of all, she prayed she would not conceive. Her fear of having a child con-sumed many of her sleepless nights. She had already filled an entire notebook encompassing many of her thoughts from the last several months. When she looked back at the near rage of those first few weeks, she was astounded she had survived.

Still, occasionally, she had good days that surprised her. She accepted her life would never be like the one she had known before, but she was determined to make the most of this bizarre situation. Her friendship with Hafa had developed more than she had hoped, and Isabella had been openly accepted into Hafa's group of friends. She was cognizant they considered her a novelty while still relishing the companionship. Hafa continued to come to her home for visits nearly every week, and a couple times a week she would be invited to a party hosted by one of the other ladies. Bahira hosted most of the parties, but sometimes Hafa or one of her friends would offer a party in their home. The parties were always the same and mostly filled with as much gossip as could be crammed into one afternoon.

The other days, when she was alone, continued to be monotonously boring. Even the distraction of the remodel was nearly complete. Within the next few days, everything would be finished as even now the workers were completing the last few details with only a few furniture pieces left to be shipped. Not that she would miss seeing Gael. While he was still pompous and infuriating most of the time, she delighted in the changes to her home. Gael was ecstatic about the remodel, taking credit for many of the suggestions and ideas Isabella had proposed and even argued for. There were certainly times she had desired nothing more than to knock him in the head, but she had refrained.

Throughout the remodel, she had continued to hope Gael would provide a way of escape, but every hint she subtly dropped was always ignored. She had even begun to suspect that Gael had been threatened about helping her.

The kitchen and dining area had been completely remodeled. She had added new cabinets and appliances to the entire space. One of her favorite elements was the dining table. It was a very classic American style in a lovely rich maple stain. The floors were tiled in an ecru-shaded natural marble. The window tapestries were elaborate designs made by local artisans and then fashioned into classical styles. It was familiar and foreign at the same time, an enchanting mix of the two cultures. Upon Gael's insistence, she had agreed to remodel the bedroom using some of the original furnishings. It still reflected the Bedouin style similar to the original design, but the new color scheme of deep purple, brown, and green added to the allure. It was a wonderful retreat, and the place she shared most often with Latif.

How did her mind wrestle with this man so much? The antipodal difference between him and Sam made her head spin. Sometimes, there had even been happy moments with Latif. She tried to deny the intimacy that pulled her ever closer to this man she resisted. In moments of weakness, she used Sam's love as a barrier around her heart from this foreign man. When Latif pierced through the safeguards she had created, she did not know how to handle him. He had become too familiar. She was intimately acquainted with the sound of his voice, the smell of his skin, the touch of his fingertips. She still wrestled with God's opinion of this abomination of her marriage to Sam, often praying for forgiveness when she felt her body weaken to the pleasures of the flesh. How complicated the situation with Latif had become.

She still missed Sam but was too ashamed to hope they would be reunited. She would never be able to explain the circumstances to him, nor did she want to, even though she constantly longed for home. She still had a mother's heart filled with love for her family, and time could never change that. When she was alone, she often cried thinking of all the skinned knees, dandelion bouquets, and squeals of happiness she had missed.

Her relationship with Mina was still strained as she continued to hold Isabella at a distance. When they would visit, Mina was always interested and attentive, but Isabella sensed something had changed. She loved her dear friend and prayed for her often. Mina lived a hard life, and Isabella wanted to offer her hope, kindness, and love to ease all she had endured. However, pain can be a great insulator to love, and Mina was using her pain and fear as protection. Most of all, she knew that her special friends needed the love of a Savior, but most days Hafa and Mina were more resistant to her faith than willing to listen. She sought perseverance, believing time and her comments were cultivating their hearts. When God planted a seed, she prayed it would take root.

Isabella heard an unexpected knock on her door. She shivered, thinking Latif might come for an afternoon visit. With reservation, she walked to the door. When she opened it, she was surprised to find a distraught Hafa before her.

"Hello, Hafa. You look awful. What is wrong?"

Hafa quickly stepped into the door, accepting the embrace of her friend. Isabella could tell she was nearly in tears, but she patiently gave her comfort, waiting as she gathered her composure. Isabella guided her to the sitting room, keeping her arm around Hafa's shoulder for support. When they were seated on the sofa, her friend began to explain.

"My husband, Jabbar, is taking the boys. He is planning to travel to Cairo and London on business. They will be gone for at least three weeks. He has never talked about taking them. He often travels for business, but he has never taken them."

"Hafa, I know you love your boys, and you are a great mother to them. But Jabbar is only taking them for a short trip. They will return to you. Why is this making you so upset?" Isabella questioned.

Panic and fear resonated from her friend. "I am afraid. I am afraid Jabbar will take them and never return. I am afraid they will be in an accident and never come back. I am afraid I will be alone. A widow alone in this country with no sons is at the mercy of men. If they do not return, then…" Hafa silently buried her face in her hands.

Isabella thoughtfully considered Hafa's fears. The qualms about this trip were irrational, but she needed to see the situation from her friend's perspective. She had lived in this country for nearly six months, but she still did not fully comprehend how isolated and dominated Saudi women were. She had not grown up in a country that stifled the thoughts, words, and ideas of women. Hafa was intelligent and charismatic, but her life's purpose had been reduced to caring for her sons and entertaining women. She had little, if any, intellectual stimulation and no individual rights of her own. Accepting this must be difficult, and her lack of control had bred fear.

"Hafa, tell me about your husband. You have never spoken of him. What is he like? Why do you fear him?"

"Jabbar is a decent man. Sometimes I really believe

he loves me. He has never asked to take another wife and that is unusual. I think he knows it would hurt me if he were to marry again. He is a good father, patient, loving, and kind. But there is a distance between us. I do not trust him and that makes him angry."

"Why don't you trust him?"

"I don't know. Maybe it is because trust is the first step toward love, and love is scary. If I let my heart love him, then he can wield that love against me like a weapon. I saw it many times with my own mother and father, and I refuse to let it happen in my own marriage." Anger and fear darkened Hafa's brown eyes as she spoke.

"Is your husband like your father?"

Hafa hesitated thoughtfully. "No, he is very different, but it does not matter. All men are the same."

"You are close to your brother, Latif. Is he the same as your father?" Isabella did not know if her line of thinking would help her friend, but she was willing to try.

"Yes and no."

Isabella patted her friend's hand before she spoke. "Hafa, you are right to believe marriage is complicated, and love can be used as a weapon. But I think the missing ingredient in a good marriage is commitment. If Jabbar does love you, then he deserves a chance to prove his love. It sounds as if the fear in your heart is causing a wedge in your marriage." Isabella paused, searching her friend's face as she considered whether to proceed. "You know my God has given his words as a guide for life. I follow these words because of my trust in him. God's Word says the key to a happy marriage is submission." Isabella sensed a smoldering anger building in her friend, so she proceeded carefully. "I do not believe that means letting a man walk all over you. It means you are willingly giving up your control because of commitment. Submission says I will walk beside you. I can even walk behind and let love be a shield of protection. Maybe submission, and eventually trust, could remove the wedge in your marriage."

Hafa was brooding over Isabella's words as she considered what she had said. "Why would I willingly give up control?"

"Do you have any control right now? Instead you have only fear. Maybe if you concede, then you will begin to really have some control."

Hafa's face registered confusion. "How will a concession give me control?"

Isabella took a deep breath as she prayed for divine wisdom. "It is hard to explain, and there is a risk it might not work. I only know the little about your husband you just told me, but maybe it is worth considering. In marriage, there must be a balance of power, or only chaos will reign. If you acknowledge Jabbar's right to lead your family, then in response, you might find he will repay that with respect and trust. I am not suggesting you use it as a manipulation to get what you want. In the end, that will only drive you further apart. Instead, I am suggesting you try to work together as a team. If the two legs on your body tried to go in different directions, then you would fall down. If your legs work together, then you can walk and even run. That is what marriage should be like. But in order for there to be collaboration, someone has to be willing to concede to allow you to move forward in the same direction. Does that make sense?"

"I suppose. If I give up my right to control, then in response Jabbar may come to trust me. But I still do not understand how that will give me any control." Hafa's puzzled expression suggested she was turning Isabella's words over in her mind.

"When he knows you are his advocate and not his aggressor, then he will come to you seeking advice and direction. I believe God has placed a natural desire within a man to lead. If you willingly follow, then he will trust you. In time, he may even come to see you as a partner and confidant. I make no promises, but maybe it is worth considering." Isabella was unsure if her words had made sense to her friend. She quietly watched as several emotions played across her face.

"How do I do that?"

"Tell him you approve of him taking the boys. It will be educational for them to travel and see more of the world than Riyadh, but be honest with him about your fears. I don't think he will be angry with you for worrying about him and the boys."

Hafa's expression of doubt about Isabella's strange idea was evident, but Isabella could see that the idea had begun to take root in her mind. Now, she would pray that God would do something amazing in their marriage. She could not help the smile of confidence that came over her face.

"Why are you smiling?"

"I don't know. I guess I am just hoping our talk will make something special happen."

"I will consider your advice, but I am not hopeful it

will produce anything good. The whole idea is crazy." Hafa shook her head as she spoke, but Isabella could see a slight smile just beginning to surface. She hoped some of her fears had subsided.

Their conversation returned to more casual things before Hafa excused herself and went home. When Isabella was alone with her own thoughts, she said a quick prayer for her friend and then took out the Bible. She ran her hands over the smooth leather cover. The motion had become a routine. She thought of this strange land and the people that had extended themselves so far from the God of Abraham, Isaac, and Jacob. She knew God was grieving for this lost people; even she began to feel the pain of that loss. They were lonely, desperate people. They had turned from salvation with little or no hope of ever returning. She knew God was jealous and wanted them to return. Revelation dawned in the midst of her prayer. These people might have hope if only they would listen. A growing desire to share truth to this lost people filled her heart. "Please give them ears to hear."

CHAPTERFIFTEEN

Isabella woke the next morning overcome with nausea and barely made it to the bathroom before getting sick. When Mina arrived that morning, she was sitting in the bathroom hoping her stomach would settle. She had counted back through the weeks since her last cycle, refusing to consider that she might be pregnant. Concern was evident in her expression as Mina poked her head into the bathroom to check on her.

"Isabella, you think it a baby?" she asked, her forehead wrinkled in concern.

"Can you get a pregnancy test? Maybe it is just the flu."

"I go to store today." Mina looked sadly at her friend.

"Oh, Mina, what am I going to do?" Isabella was still in denial, bordering on hysteria.

"If you pregnant, you have beautiful baby to love. Is that all bad?"

Tears flowed down Isabella's face. She could not answer. Instead she just looked into her friend's face. She could not bring herself to consider that a baby of Latif's was growing inside her. She felt great sobs of fear and panic rising within her. She lifted the toilet seat she had been seated on and got sick again.

Mina lovingly held her hair from her face and gently rubbed her back. She purred words of kindness into her ear. "It okay, Isabella. It okay. Be calm, and sick feel go away. Breathe through nose. That it, that it."

When the wave of nausea passed, Mina left her to find something to settle her stomach. She quickly returned with some dry toast and a warm herbal tea. Isabella was distraught with restrained emotion.

"Take sip of tea. It settle your stomach." Isabella obeyed. The aroma of the tea was strong and so was the taste, but immediately she felt her stomach begin to relax.

"Better now?"

"I think so, but I don't think I can eat the toast."

Mina kindly encouraged her. "You try to eat it. It make you better like tea."

Reluctantly, Isabella complied with her request.

"That good. Eat it all," Mina encouraged as she got up to leave the room. "I be back. I tell Chen you sick and need stay with you today. You feel sick, take drink of tea." She turned and left, leaving Isabella alone to wrestle with the fears that churned inside her heart.

Hafa climbed in the car that morning excited to make the short ride to see Isabella. The night before, she had reluctantly taken Isabella's advice. After the kids had gone to bed, she had timidly approached her husband to talk about the trip. She had already determined that being open might help. She offered her support for his decision to take the boys on the trip, and then she had explained her fears about losing them. Jabbar had been deeply moved by her honest concern and had talked over all the details of the trip. At the end of the discussion, he had asked her to come with them. She had not even considered the possibility of joining the boys on the trip, but it was a perfect solution.

When they had first gotten married, she had hoped that Jabbar would invite her on business trips. But he had always made the trips alone for one reason or another. Now they were going together as a family, for the first time in a long time, she was excited about being with her husband. She secretly began to hope that this would be a turning point in their marriage. She was even willing to consider that her friend and the crazy ideas of that book might hold some truth, but she was still more than a little skeptical.

She watched out the window at the desert around her with new interest as her driver sped down the highway. A brief windstorm had blown through that morning, leaving a slight brown haze in the sky. The sun was high in a cloudless sky. Winter in the desert was cool, but not cold. Occasionally, snow fell in the mountains, but the weather was mild in the Najd. She had been born here and loved the desert, especially this time of year. Even though she had enjoyed spending a few years in the United States, she had missed her home. She looked around at the beauty that surrounded her.

It was a barren land, but there was amazing life that survived even in this harsh, arid climate. She breathed in the smell of the dry earth, the smell of home.

She admitted to feeling a bit whimsical about the upcoming trip. How many years had it been since she had traveled? As she thought back over the years, she realized she had not traveled from Saudi Arabia since her honeymoon. The years had grown together into a mindless group of memories. The only highlights had been the births of her sons until this new friendship with Isabella.

She pulled out the small diamond-studded bracelet. It had been a coming of age gift from her grandmother. Now she was going to give it as a thank you to Isabella. She was happy for the first time in a long time, and she wanted her friend to know it. When the vehicle pulled in through the gate of her brother's home, she began to anticipate Isabella's reaction to the news about the trip.

When she knocked on Isabella's door, she was surprised that Mina opened the door and greeted her. "Good morning."

"Where is Isabella?"

"She in bed. She not feel well," Mina replied.

Hafa made her way to Isabella's room. She was concerned for her friend and hoped there was nothing seriously wrong. When she entered the room and looked at her friend, her heart sank. Isabella was as pale as a whitewashed wall. She was covered to her neck in the blankets so only her forlorn face peeked out. As she approached, she saw unshed tears pooled in her eyes. She could not believe the change one day had made.

"Isabella, what is wrong?"

"I have just confirmed that I am pregnant. Mina bought a pregnancy test this morning after I awoke feeling nauseated."

"You are not happy about the baby?"

Tears coursed down the sides of Isabella's face. One tear hung suspended from the bridge of her nose before dropping to the sheet near her hand, but her friend seemed unable to give voice to her sorrow.

"I can see by your reaction you are not happy. I am disappointed." She resisted the urge to reprimand Isabella. Instead she carefully considered the emotional turmoil of the few months her friend had been in her country. She thought of Isabella's family in the United States, and then she understood. "But I understand. What can I do to help?"

"I don't know." Isabella's voice was hoarse from emotion.

"Let's get you out of this bed. If you shower and hear my news, maybe you will feel better." Isabella hesitated and then acceded. After Isabella closed the door to the bathroom, Hafa went in search of Mina. She found her in the kitchen making tea.

"Mina, how has she been today?" Hafa questioned.

"She cry a lot. She very sick. Isabella scared, and that make her more sick."

"She is in the shower. Once she is finished, I will see how she is feeling. If she is even a little better, then I will take her over to the women's garden for some fresh air. Hopefully, we can get her feeling better." Hafa gave Mina a modest smile. She realized it was the only serious conversation she had ever had with Isabella's maid.

Isabella looked around at the beauty of the garden. Only a few months before, she had seen this garden with Latif. Instinctually, she placed her hand on her stomach and imagined the life growing within her. The pregnancy scared her, but already she felt a connection to this fragile life. This life was created from the relationship she shared with Latif. When she thought of him, she tried to deny that their time together had softened her. She knew he would be a loving father. Carrying his child bonded her to him in a frightening way, and it forced her to address the feelings toward him that she had previously ignored. Could she ever really love him? A few months ago, the thought would have been inconceivable, but now it was too complicated to really know the answer. She tried to sort through all the emotions, but in the end nothing seemed clear. Hafa had taken a seat on a nearby bench. Wordlessly, she watched Isabella pace around the large garden. After several minutes, Isabella remembered her friend's words and turned to her.

"I just remembered you have something to tell me. I forgot. I have been so preoccupied with my own grief today; I have not even considered your news. What were you going to tell me?" Isabella asked as she took a seat next to Hafa.

Hafa's face beamed with the untold news. "Last night, I talked to Jabbar, just like you told me to. He was very kind and understanding about my fears." Hafa paused, nearly bursting with excitement. "He has asked me to join them on their trip. We will be leaving in three days. You were right. Your advice has changed everything."

Even in the midst of her sadness, Isabella could not help her enthusiasm. This was a true answer to prayer, maybe even a step in the right direction. She lifted her eyes to the heavens with wordless praise for this small glimmer of hope in her dark dysphoria. "I am glad for you, but you know it was not my advice that I offered. I only gave you the words of hope from my God."

"Wherever the advice came from, I appreciate it. As an offering of thanks, I want to give you this." Hafa presented the bangle to her.

Isabella gasped, placing her hand over her mouth. She just looked at the lovely gift, unable to touch the gift resting in her friend's hand. It was a gorgeous, wide, gold bracelet surrounded by what must have been quarter-karat diamonds. She marveled at the wealth required to own something like this.

"Hafa, it is too much. I cannot accept it."

"It is yours. It's a special gift that I received from my grandmother." Hafa's eyes gleamed as she offered it.

Isabella refused to take it. Shaking her head, again she replied, "It is too much. I do not deserve a gift like this. What was the occasion that you received this gift from your grandmother?"

"The day I became a woman, my grandmother, mother, two aunts, and my older sister went with me to purchase my first abaya. Girls are not required to wear the traditional coverings until their first menses. It is a special day celebrating a woman's coming of age. On that day, I received this gift from my grandmother. It has always been special to me. I hope you will treasure it as I have."

Isabella was moved by this special offer. She tentatively reached for her friend's present and slipped it on her wrist with admiration. "I am honored that you would give me something so precious. I will cherish it always, but please do not feel you have to give me a gift for helping. We are friends and helping is what a friend should do. I do not deserve this."

They both sat there together for several minutes, each lost in her own thoughts. Isabella realized that their friendship had risen to a new place. She was content to be consoled by her friend's presence more than conversation. She silently prayed for her sister's marriage and upcoming trip, and she hoped this was the first step toward accepting the truth of God's Word. For those few moments, even her apprehension about the baby did not dampen the moment.

Latif was elated over the news of Isabella's pregnancy. His sister had secretly shared the news earlier that evening. As he made his way across the dark lawn to Isabella's home, he could barely contain his excitement. This was exactly what he had been wanting for months, and now it was going to happen. Hafa had warned him that Isabella was apprehensive about the baby, and he was ready to ease her misgivings. He quietly knocked on her door and entered the foyer. The house was dark with only a dim light in the bedroom. Latif stopped and listened for sounds of his wife but was met with silence. With quick strides, he made his way toward her bedroom. The light from the lamp on the bedside table draped over her sleeping form while curls of hair cascaded across her pillow and framed her face. The angle of the light gave her hair a radiant glow, and her innocent beauty nearly stole his breath. He loved watching her sleep.

Carefully, he moved a chair beside her bed. He resisted the urge to stroke her smooth cheek, afraid he would wake her. It had been an emotional day for his sweet wife. He knew the first trimester of pregnancy was exhausting for a woman, and the rush of emotions only added to it. Effortlessly, he lifted a curl around his finger. She was perfect. He leaned down to inhale the sweet fragrance and felt her stir beneath him. When he glanced back down at her face, he noticed she was watching him.

He offered a tender smile as he whispered, "Isabella, my wife, I have heard the good news."

She responded timidly. "How did you hear?"

"Hafa told me, but I also learned it from Chen. He said that Mina has been with you to care for you during your morning sickness. Are you feeling okay now?"

Isabella closed her eyes and took a deep breath before responding. "I am feeling better now, but I am still trying to grasp the idea. The day has been an emotional roller coaster ride, but the visit from your sister made me feel better."

Latif carefully pulled the covers down to her feet and lifted her nightgown to expose her stomach. He could hardly contain his delight. Gently, he leaned down and kissed her tummy and rested his hand on the place he had kissed. Then he looked back at her face.

He snickered at her astonishment. "I am sorry; did I surprise you?"

For the first time that night, she gave him an affectionate smile that warmed his soul. "I guess you did surprise me. I can see you are happy about the baby."

"I cannot begin to explain the joy I feel about him. I hope it is a boy, but I will be happy to have a girl too. It is more important that we have a healthy child, one with his mother's charm and good looks. If so, he will be a prince befitting the throne. Of course, he will never come to that, you know." Latif could not hide the twinkle in his eye as he spoke.

Isabella had a look of confusion as she spoke. "He will never come to what?"

"The throne. There are so many princes in Saudi Arabia; we do not have to worry about our child becoming crowned prince. You do know that, don't you, Isabella?"

"Yes, Latif." Isabella chuckled at his remark. "Hafa explained it to me when we returned from Jeddah. I was very surprised to learn I had married the prince of Saudi Arabia. She told me the notorious story of Abdul Aziz ibn Saud and his numerous wives. It was a fascinating story explaining how he took a wife in every region he conquered. Isn't it believed that he fathered between eighty and one hundred children in his lifetime?"

Latif openly laughed at the appalling grimace on her face. It was a fantastic story outlining the history of his country and home, but he loved it. It encompassed the conquering spirit of the people in his land.

"Yes, something like that. It is much different from

the history of your country. I am sure you find it barbaric, but I find it intriguing. Who else could have organized and lead such an arduous and aggressive group of people? It is a testament to ingenuity and maybe a little lust…" He gave her a slight smirk before placing a tender kiss on her lips.

He was finished talking. Tonight was a night to savor. He gently lifted her onto his lap and embraced the woman he loved.

CHAPTER SIXTEEN

It had been a wearisome first trimester of pregnancy. She had felt nauseated and unwell most of the time and spent all of her time at home and even turned down several invitations to parties in the main house. But Latif had allowed Mina to remain with her everyday to ease her sickness. She had enjoyed the time with her friend, especially during the three weeks that Hafa had traveled with her family. The weeks with Mina had lifted the tensions that had formed between them after her marriage to Latif. Over the last several weeks, the depth of their friendship had eased some of the pain from the pregnancy, and Mina had protectively nursed her through the worst of the days. Isabella knew that Mina was younger than she, but sometimes Mina treated her like a child. Most days, Isabella loved the pampering, but occasionally it became cumbersome to have someone always doting.

Mina often made dry toast and her infamous tea

to ease the nausea. It did not always work, but most days it held the worst of it at bay. They spent many relaxing days in the remodeled sitting room or out in the small garden during the mild days, sharing everything. Mina told stories about her home and all the things she missed about it, and Isabella shared everything about her family back home. With Mina, she had been able to share all the hopes, dreams, and memories from home, things that were difficult to share with Hafa. Their common subjugation made them sisters in captivity. Isabella understood Mina's desire to return to her family and longed for the same. In just a few months, Isabella had been blessed with a new family and two friends who filled the emptiness with love and companionship.

Isabella realized the importance of this gift, often thanking God for leading these great women into her life. She prayed everyday for an opportunity to share her faith with Mina, knowing she continued to be skeptical about the possibility of any deity greater than self. So Isabella remained patient and prayed, and in those days, her Savior was enough to sustain her through this trial. In her times of prayer, she would mentally climb into the cleft of the rock and rest. She still begged for help and rescue, often aching for the love of Sam and the girls, but she had learned to trust their care and safety to the Father.

Mina was exuberant about the baby, and her excitement was beginning to rub off. Occasionally, Isabella was still indifferent about the pregnancy, but Mina's joy was unexpectedly contagious. Sometimes she was even excited thinking about the child growing inside her body.

Hafa had returned from her trip happy and excited. Something amazing had happened during the few weeks she had been away, and Isabella knew it was a good sign. Hafa began to talk about Jabbar with great affection. She even suspected that love was growing between them. It was amazing to watch the transformation. Hope was blooming all around her, just as this new life was growing inside her.

She gently rubbed the slight swelling of her abdomen, thinking she had felt the flutter of the baby. At fifteen weeks, she guessed it was a little soon, but the movement seemed unmistakable. Her heart was torn with emotions. The life within her was a creation of an unnatural union, but it was still a growing person, flesh of her flesh. Isabella was frightened about how this would change her life in this new land. It was too dangerous to consider this tie that bound her so tightly to Latif and all that it symbolized. Hafa had imperturbably explained the lack of rights for mothers in Saudi Arabia, and it frightened Isabella to think about the laws that awarded children to the husband. As a mother, she would not be granted control of her child once it was weaned. It was preposterous to consider, so most of the time she just pushed it from her mind. Returning home would always be a dream, but never without her child. The logistics of accomplishing such a task were more than she could fathom.

The baby had changed Latif in a way that unnerved her. She had started to predict the timing of his visits most days, but occasionally he surprised her. The affectionate attention he offered weakened her resolve against him, and sometimes she even missed him when he left. In so many ways, their relationship was super-ficial. Living apart and sharing such small aspects of each other's lives made this marriage incomparable to the one she shared with Sam. A love like Sam's was rare and precious. But Latif was growing on her, even when she resisted it. To him, she was simply a lovely trophy for a rich prince, a priceless jewel. He tried desperately to buy her love with words and acts of genuine kindness, but the emotion was aroused by passion and desire, not love. Maybe he loved her, but he was incapable of rich, deep, unconditional love. His actions were inspired more by what he would gain than what he could give of himself, and as the days grew into weeks, Isabella sensed the differences more and more. If only she could keep her heart aware of them. She needed to keep a clear perspective of all that had happened, how she had come to be his wife, and his refusal to give her what she wanted most. In those moments of stark realization, she puzzled over the absurd idea that they would have a child together, and yet that was exactly what was going to happen.

In the last week, Isabella's morning sickness had lessened, and Mina had been required to return to her previous duties. It was time to return to the society of women, and Hafa had reminded her that Bahira was having a party the next day. The tension between Latif's wives had not dissipated, and Isabella hoped the news of her pregnancy would not heighten the apparent tensions that had formed between them. Her retreat was over, and tomorrow she would learn the truth of their feelings about her and the baby. She prayed for guidance and peace that night as she prepared for bed. Tomorrow, she could not fathom what it would hold.

Hafa had knocked on her door late the next morning with a delightful smile. If only Isabella could sincerely have something to smile about.

"What's up?"

Hafa let her smile slip a little when she saw the anxiety in Isabella's face. "Oh, Isabella, it is silly."

"I want to know what's going on. Tell me."

"I am just happy and maybe in love…and I am pregnant. I shared the news with Jabbar this morning. Isabella, I have never been so excited. Of course, with the boys I was happy, but not like this. This baby is different. It was conceived in love. I have not told anyone else about the baby yet. Can it just be our secret for a little while?"

"Yes, your secret is safe with me. Congratulations! I am so happy for you. How did Jabbar respond?" Isabella genuinely shared her friend's joy.

"He was so sweet. I could tell that he was elated over the news of another child. And when I told him, he looked right into my eyes and told me that he loved me. When he said those words, I felt them all the way down to my toes. He spoke right to my heart, and for the first time in my life, I know that I am truly loved by that man." A glow of happiness emanated from deep within her friend as she spoke.

Isabella's eyes filled with tears. She completely understood her friend's words. She had experienced that kind of love with Sam. It was a love that bridged time and space and took her heart right back to the man she loved and to the girls their love had created. When she closed her eyes, the tears spilled down her cheeks. She was happy for her friend, but this happiness she saw in her friend made her yearn for the love she had lost.

"Isabella, what is wrong? I expected you to be happy about my news."

"Hafa, my dear sweet friend, I am so happy for you. I know this is more than you dreamed would happen in your marriage. That makes me delighted, but to see the happiness in your eyes makes me miss the love that was taken from me. True love is a blessed gift, something rare and valuable. Cherish it, Hafa, cherish it, for it is more valuable than all the oil under this rich country." Isabella lightly wiped the tears from her cheeks and embraced her dear friend.

"Don't you ever think you will feel this kind of love for my brother?"

Isabella pulled away from her friend but could not look her in the eye. Instead she looked down at a stray leaf on the entryway tile. After a few moments, she shook her head. When she finally met Hafa's eyes, she knew her friend understood her unspoken emotions. Isabella wanted to explain, but somehow she knew she did not need to.

Hafa changed the subject. "Well, are you ready to return to the world of the living? I am sure the party is already in full swing. It is even possible that Uzma is on her way to a drunken stupor. I am worried about her. Her drinking has escalated over the last several months. If my father finds out, I am not sure what he will do to her. As I am sure you have guessed, he has no patience with indecency in his wives."

Isabella considered the implications of Hafa's words. They lived in a world of conflict, and keeping it all straight was a challenge. Alcohol was forbidden in the kingdom, but it was smuggled into the country by all the royal family. Anyone that could afford the high prices had it and served it. In the secrecy of their homes, alcohol was the norm. While Isabella had lived in this strange place, she had watched many women drown their sadness, loneliness, and emptiness with alcohol. She even suspected that a few, like Uzma, had developed addictions. But Uzma's situation was different. Isabella and Hafa had suspected that Fakhir, her husband, was abusive to her. Many times they had gently questioned her about the unusual bruises that appeared on her body. At first she had been able to hide most of them, but lately they had become less and less inconspicuous. Isabella had questioned Hafa on what they should do to help her. But Hafa had been adamant that interfering would only make the situation worse. The powerlessness of women in this world infuriated her. If only there was a way to help them, but the insignificant voice of one woman would never be heard over the overbearing dominance of men.

Dressing for these parties was something Isabella did not enjoy. Because women must cover themselves in public, an opportunity to display their expensive designer clothes for all to see was almost a competitive game. Isabella just could not get into it. Hafa was always offering to take her shopping to buy new clothes, and one or two times since the wedding party, Isabella had gone. She just did not enjoy spending thousands of dollars on top-of-the-line designer clothes just because Latif could afford to buy them. She already had more clothes then she really needed. But today she was nervous, so that morning she had taken special care in choosing her outfit for the party.

As Hafa and Isabella made their way over to the main house, Isabella tugged gently on her jewel-green cashmere sweater and removed a stray hair on her shoulder. She also checked for lint on her Armani wide-legged, black, pinstriped pants. It was silly to worry over how she looked, but she anticipated that all the women would be appraising her.

Already Isabella was beginning to notice changes in her body. Because this was her third pregnancy, she guessed she would soon be shopping for clothes with a better fit. Today, however, the pants were just a little snug around her waist, even though they did not completely disguise her swelling tummy.

"Hafa, does everyone know about the baby?"

Isabella saw the knowing smile on her friend's face. "Yes, Latif told my mother right away, and she could not help sharing the news with everyone. Why? Are you nervous about it?"

Isabella chuckled under her breath. "Is my anxiety that obvious?"

Hafa's eyes held a mischievous gleam as she spoke. "Silly girl, I have never seen you fuss so much over your appearance. Now, tell me, what are you worried about?"

"I am afraid of Bahira and Dalia's reactions. I still cannot comprehend how wives can live like this. We are together, knowing too many details about the relationships with our common husband. It is unnerving. Besides, you know neither one of them has ever been exactly friendly to me. They cannot be happy about the baby."

"Isabella, they will accept and love your child or receive Latif's wrath. It is no secret to either of them that you are the favored wife. Sooner or later, they will accept it. If anything, having a baby gives you more leverage. Don't assume anything, just relax."

They had reached the main salon. Isabella took a deep breath and followed her friend inside. Immediately, several women approached Isabella. Some offered congratulations and others asked how she was feeling. Everyone seemed very excited about the baby, and very quickly Isabella felt herself relax. Maybe Hafa had been right.

Then she saw Bahira approaching out of the corner of her eye. Isabella offered a small smile as she turned to greet the approaching woman, but her smile was returned by a formidable stare, and her courage began to falter. Bahira approached very closely and whispered in Isabella's ear. "We need to talk. Follow me."

Isabella turned to find Hafa, but she had already moved over to her usual circle of friends. She hoped that Hafa would notice as she was led from the room, but she appeared to be firmly addressing Uzma and did not notice what was happening.

Isabella had never had a private conversation with Bahira, and her mind scrambled to understand why she wanted to talk to her now. Quickly and silently, she asked for divine guidance in the exchange that was about to transpire. Within moments, they were in a small corridor outside the main room. Bahira pushed her aside and closed the door to give them privacy, then turned to address Isabella. Isabella tried desperately to comprehend the true motive for this meeting from the expression on Bahira's face. It was clear that she was angry, but there was something more. Something that Isabella could not read, and then Isabella saw the truth. For just a moment, it was visible and clear—disappointment. In response, Isabella's heart understood.

Bahira spoke just above a whisper, but her anger was evident. "I am expected to receive you in my home with hospitality, so you are always welcome. But do not think that I am deceived by you. You put on a kind and loving front, but I know you are not what you seem. Your beauty has drawn Latif's favor and attention, but remember I am the first wife and the mother of his oldest son. Things do not work the same here as in your own country. You must remember your position in this family."

Isabella hesitated before she spoke, and in that moment, she thought of the age-old story of Hagar and Sarah, the wives of Abraham. This was not God's ideal for marriage because it would always cause division and rivalry.

"Bahira, I do recognize and honor your position as Latif's first wife. I do not desire or seek his favor." Isabella paused to offer her an honest smile. "I do not despise you or try to acquire your position. Do not hate me for something I cannot control. If I could give you Latif's attentions toward me, I would gladly hand them over to you."

Isabella watched the changing emotions on her face in response to her words. Then her anger returned as she spoke. "You do not fool me. You have bewitched him. Since you have become his wife, he almost never comes to me. It is my duty to bear him sons." Bahira nearly choked on the emotion from the words she had spoken.

For a brief moment, it was evident to Isabella that Bahira truly loved Latif, and she sensed she was trying desperately to hide the searing pain in her heart. How ironic it was that Isabella had unknowingly and unwillingly hurt this woman. Out of the blue, Isabella dropped to her knees and took Bahira's hand.

"I am sorry. I have never intended to cause you pain. I do not love Latif or wish to gain all of his attentions. Please forgive me. I have no desire to hurt or anger you."

Isabella recognized the shock on Bahira's face in reaction to this spontaneous response from her rival. Isabella leaned against the wall. When she looked again at Bahira, she saw tears brimming in her eyes. Instinctually, Isabella embraced her. She was stiff and unresponsive to Isabella's hug, so she quickly released her. Bahira quickly turned and left her standing in the hall alone. For several minutes, Isabella just stood there. She was mystified by all that had just happened and shocked by her own impulsive response. Desperately, she wanted to leave the party, but instead she quietly returned to her friends.

For the next few weeks, she became more cognizant of how much time Latif was spending with her in comparison to his other wives. She wondered if it was appropriate to talk to him about it. In the end, she decided to mention something about it, but each visit just never seemed to be the right time.

Tomorrow, Hafa planned to take her on a shopping trip. She knew it was time to get some maternity clothes, and as usual, Latif had been agreeable to her spending money, giving her a personal credit card to use. She still hated wearing the abaya, but she had accepted that there was no other way to consider moving about in public. Often when she was out, she would wonder if there were other American women concealed under the black clothing. If there were, how would she ever know?

Today, with nothing better to do, she was spending a quiet day alone. She still had not learned how to deal with the tediousness of being completely alone. Isabella had read nearly all of the books that Mina had brought to her, and there was nothing new to draw her interest. She missed watching television and movies, talking on the phone, dinner at restaurants with her family or friends. There was no radio, no talk shows or music, just silence. Again, she walked through all the rooms of her home looking for something to amuse her. Finally, she flopped down on the sofa in an ungraceful manner. She was bored.

Pausing to listen, she thought she heard a quiet knock on the front door. As she made her way to answer it, she wondered whom it could be. If it were Latif, he would have already let himself in and come looking for her. She did not expect Hafa. She knew that she was spending some time with her children this afternoon.

Mina had already been over, made lunch, gathered her laundry, and dusted the furniture. She wondered if maybe she had forgotten something, but Mina usually did not knock unless Latif was visiting her. When she opened the door, she was shocked to see Bahira. For several minutes, she just stood there staring at her.

Registering the woman's uneasiness amidst the shock of her visitor, Isabella offered, "Bahira, I am sorry. You surprised me. Please, come in." Isabella stepped aside for her guest to enter.

Bahira stepped over the threshold and shrugged as she spoke. "Maybe I should not have come."

Isabella offered her a kind smile. "I have been very bored today. I am glad you came by. But I must admit your visit is very unexpected."

Bahira's eyes were large and sad. Her expression was like a guilty child's. "Isabella, I have treated you badly, and I would like for us to make peace."

Isabella was stunned into complete silence. After a few seconds, she simply nodded her agreement. "Would you like to come in and visit?"

For the first time, in all the time Isabella had known her, Bahira presented her with a simple, sincere smile. "I really cannot stay long."

Awkwardly, they tried to make conversation as Isabella struggled with what was appropriate to say, but in a short time, they both began to relax a little. Bahira shared a little about the unusual relationship her parents had shared. They had sincerely loved each other, and her father had never chosen another wife, even after only having one daughter. This was uncommon among the men in Saudi Arabia and a testament to the love they shared.

Isabella also shared a little about her own parents, and the small family by Saudi standards that she had grown up in. Like few parents in the United States, her parents had been happily married for forty years. She told a little about her bossy older brother, John, who was always attempting to get her into trouble when they were kids. And about her pesky twin sisters that were always tagging along with her and her friends. It was crazy to think of all the squabbles and power plays they had made as kids. Now that they had grown out of the typical sibling rivalry, they had remained close. John had moved from Indiana to Georgia after college, but he returned with his family for visits during the holidays.

Discussing her family made her wonder about them, like Sam and the girls. Her disappearance must be very painful for all of them, but she shared none of these feelings with Bahira. In time, maybe she would feel comfortable sharing the truth of her abduction, but for now she kept those details to herself.

By the time Bahira was ready to leave, a little of the tension had lessened between the two women. She did not feel the instant friendship she had experienced upon meeting Hafa or the trust she felt with Mina, but somehow she sensed maybe the seeds of friendship had been planted between them.

As she walked Bahira to the door, she asked, "I would like it if you could come and visit with me again another day."

"I would like that. Like you, I am often bored with

nothing to do. I hope we can put away the hostilities and become friends."

Isabella reached out and took Bahira's hand. "I believe we already have. I look forward to visiting with you again."

Isabella closed the door and walked back to the sitting room, astonished by what had just occurred. She could not wait to share the details with Hafa the next day.

CHAPTER SEVENTEEN

Hafa had spent the entire afternoon at the mall with her friend. Both of them were shopping for maternity clothes. Because Hafa was only about seven weeks pregnant, she had not even started to show. But Hafa was so excited about the pregnancy she made several purchases, anticipating the coming months. Isabella was just beginning to show, and pregnancy only added to her beauty. Hafa never imagined she would form such a close, comfortable bond with one of Latif's wives, especially the reluctant bride from the United States. Yet, effortlessly, they had nearly become instant friends.

Over the last several weeks, Isabella had continued to talk about her strange and foreign God. In all her life, she had never heard about this God that loved and sent his Son to rescue men. The few years she had spent in the United States had exposed her to girls with religious ideas that had differed from her own, but none of them were like Isabella.

Sometimes Isabella's words angered Hafa, and even a couple of times she had told her to stop. But no matter how much her words of hope angered her, there was something moving about this God and the relationship that Isabella talked about.

All her life, she had been certain of Allah. She was afraid to face the judgment that would come to those who did not claim allegiance to him, but never had she hoped to receive mercy, hope, or love from her god. When Isabella had shared the words from her God about marriage, Hafa had only doubted the sanity of following him. But when the simple ideas had transformed her marriage, it made her pause and consider the validity of all she had believed.

They had just arrived back to Isabella's home to deliver the purchases she had made. When Isabella offered for her to stay for dinner, Hafa had agreed. Tonight, Jabbar was taking the boys with him to stay overnight for business, so she had no reason to hurry home. Just for curiosity's sake, Hafa wanted to really know about Isabella's God. She wanted to understand what made him different from Allah and the teachings she had learned from her parents.

Mina had just finished serving the meal and returned to the kitchen. Hafa noticed that Isabella said a quiet prayer before she started to eat the traditional dish of kapsa served with fatir. Instead of using the bread to scoop up her food as traditional Saudis do, Isabella used a fork. When Isabella saw her watching, she stopped.

"Hafa, did I do something wrong?"

Hafa smiled at her friend. "No, I just did not realize

you used a fork when you were eating. I guess we have only eaten at parties together and not alone in your home. You seem to have adjusted so quickly to our way of life, your American utensil just surprised me."

"I guess I will always be partial to flatware. I am beginning to adjust to the changes here when I am forced to, but eating with my hands is not one that has been easy. It still feels very cumbersome trying to respect these strange customs, especially when the hot food burns my fingers." Isabella grinned shyly at the awkwardness of her words. "When I remodeled and added this new dining table, I ordered flatware. Does it bother you?"

Hafa smiled again and shook her head. "No, we are in your home, and I want you to enjoy your meal. Using a fork does not offend me, silly girl."

Isabella offered a smile of thanks and returned to eating. Hafa noticed Isabella's appetite had returned after the prolonged morning sickness had passed. Hafa had not suffered from morning sickness with either of the boys and hoped she would not with this baby as well. However, today, she just did not have much of an appetite. She took a few bites of the food but moved most of it around her plate.

"Hafa, is something wrong with the chicken and rice?"

"No, it is delicious. I am just not hungry today. I am not sure what it is."

"Would you like for me to ask Mina to bring something else for you? Maybe a glass of laban would taste better?"

"No, thank you. I am fine. But I do want to talk,

and the topic might surprise you." Hafa hesitated. She suddenly felt shy and a little guilty bringing it up to her friend, but she was curious. Would there ever be a better time? "I have some questions about your God."

The smile that Isabella offered in response to her comment made light shine in her eyes. "I would be glad to answer any questions you have."

"I want you to start from the beginning. I just can't get my mind around why your God would make a sacrifice for anyone. If he is God, then he shouldn't ever be subject to men."

"You are right, my friend. Let us start from the beginning. If I say anything that confuses you, stop me and I will try to explain. Okay?" When Hafa nodded in agreement, Isabella began the story. "God created everything on the earth, the sun, moon, stars, the plants and animals, and then man. The first man was Adam, and then he created Eve, his wife. They lived together in a beautiful garden where everyday God came to spend time with them. There in the garden, everything was good." Isabella paused and looked intently into her eyes. Hafa was surprised at how quickly Isabella had drawn her into the story. She was very animated as she told it, reminding her of her grandmother and the oral style of narration. "Then Adam and Eve were deceived by a serpent encouraging them to eat of the forbidden fruit in the garden. When they did, sin was introduced into the world. Because God is holy, he cast them from the garden forever and did not let them return. In that moment, everything that was good was ruined, but worst of all, Adam and Eve and all their descendents were separated from God. The closeness they shared with their God and creator in the garden had been broken, and there was no way for them to repair it."

Hafa imagined the beauty of a garden made by God where he came to fellowship with Adam and Eve. She could not fathom the pain that followed after their sin had destroyed this marvelous thing. Hafa contemplated the loss, and it revealed an empty void in her soul. When Isabella resumed her story telling, Hafa was relieved.

"It is a sad story for man, and without God intervening, there would still be no hope of restoring what was lost. But do not be sad, my friend. This is the best part of the story." She hesitated for a moment, giving Hafa a knowing smile before continuing. "In the Bible, the book of John states that God loved us so much he wanted to make a way for us to have a relationship with him again. He knew that we could not repair what had been broken, but he could. It had been his plan from the beginning. He sent his only Son to earth to live among men. This man was Jesus. I believe you have already told me that Muslims believe Jesus was a prophet like Muhammad, but the Bible states that he was God's Son, God come to earth. The Bible records his life. He was without sin, and many on this earth were drawn to him and flocked to hear his teachings. But some of the people hated him and wanted him dead, so they plotted to have him killed."

Again, Hafa was puzzled by the emptiness she felt in her heart as she listened to the story. There was a familiarity to it that drew her, even as she reminded herself that it was just a story.

"And they did kill him. They hung him on a wooden cross, the perfect man that was God's Son. The evil men that killed him believed that they had won, but they did not win. You see, Hafa, God sent Jesus to die. It was part of his plan. It was the way for him to make atonement for the sins of men. God could have let us die to pay for the sins that we have committed. The Bible says that the punishment for sin is death. When Jesus died, he paid that punishment. If you believe in Jesus, he will restore the relationship that was lost. Really, he is longing for it. His death made a way for us to again have communion with God. It is a beautiful and sad story, but the ending promises only hope. Hafa, what does Allah promise you?"

Hafa sighed and then responded, "Isabella, you are right; it is a great story, and you are a wonderful storyteller. But how do I know that it is true? In some ways, it is not so different from the stories I have heard all my life. How do I know what to believe?"

Hafa saw the light dim in her friend's eyes. "Do not decide tonight, my friend. Consider the story I have told you. I know it is the truth, and someday I pray that you will believe it too. Until then, I am happy to answer your questions."

That was fair enough, and Hafa resolved to consider her friend's story, even if it sounded too good to be true. It was time for her to return home. She stood and turned to her friend.

"Isabella, I have had a wonderful day, and I did enjoy your story. Now, I really should be going. Thank you for dinner."

They both walked to the door in silence. She hoped her disbelief had not affected their friendship.

"Good-bye, Isabella."

"Good-bye. I hope to see you again soon." When Hafa looked into Isabella's eyes, she saw the kindest, sweetest smile. It was a look that warmed her heart.

She looked up at the stars as she made her way to the main house to have her driver bring around the car. The exquisiteness of the night sky spread before her, appealing to something deep within her heart, something she could not begin to grasp.

Isabella was disappointed. Part of her had truly believed that Hafa was ready, but in the end, she had left still not believing. And for the first time, Isabella really wondered if her friends would ever believe. All her life, Hafa had been taught a lie, and sometimes that was easier than the truth. Haven't men created their own religion for all of ages passed? They had even fashioned them out of clay and worshiped them for centuries. But all the other religions expected man to earn salvation. Only Jesus offered the payment that we can never earn. It was simple and complex. It was perfect.

Isabella knelt beside her bed. She was so thankful that the truth had been revealed to her so many years ago when she was a child. She did not deserve what she had been given, but she was grateful for it. Then she pleaded for Hafa, Mina, Bahira, Dalia, Uzma, and even Latif. She did not know if their ears would ever be open to the truth, but she prayed anyway. When she doubted whether God would ever use her in this land, she reminded herself that with God all things are possible. When she was exhausted and her knees ached from the loss of blood, she silently prepared for bed.

CHAPTER EIGHTEEN

Isabella was not having a good day. She had woken that morning from a vivid, lifelike dream of home, and she had been unable to shake the familiarity of it. As the months had passed, she had resigned herself to this place, and again she was reminded of the foreignness of it all. In her dream, she had seen the faces of Sam, Rebecca, and Katherine, and she had heard their voices calling to her. She could not shake the feeling that they were close by.

She was expecting Latif to come that afternoon after lunch, and the idea made her restless. It was the first time in months that she felt like a caged animal looking for a way to escape. She prowled around the house and out through the garden. At any moment, she expected something to happen. She needed help to be on the way; she longed for it.

For the first time since her wedding day, she again considered escaping into the desert. She had even walked to the front door and held the handle ready to bolt, but every time, something stopped her. It was an emotional and irrational day. Yet she could not shake the idea that her family was near, even though the idea was preposterous.

When several hours passed and silence still followed her around like a ball and chain, she decided to take a nap. But when she lay down on the bed, she just stared at the ceiling. She was afraid to close her eyes. The dream had been so real it had pierced her heart. Sometimes remembering was excruciating, and the lack of control over her situation was pushing her too close to the edge.

Most days when she felt she was losing control, she would pray or write in her journal. Today, she couldn't. Instead she just lay on her bed and looked at the ceiling. She even surrendered to short bursts of tears, but nothing eased her discontent. How would she ever survive a lifetime of this?

For hours, she succumbed to the memories, recalling some of the oddest things, like when Katherine lost her first tooth. She had refused to let Sam or Isabella pull it, even when it was hanging by a thread. Then, one night when they had thought she was asleep in bed, she had come to them carrying it in her hand. Proudly, she had showed them her toothless smile.

Later, she remembered when Rebecca had received a merit award at school. The principal had explained that she would shake her hand and give her the award while the photographer took her picture. Rebecca, nervous about getting it wrong, had snuck back to their seats and confirmed which hand to offer to shake before returning to her own seat. She remembered the amusement and pride on Sam's face from this simple action.

They were all so precious to her, every memory. For just a little while, she let those memories keep her breathing like oxygen to a drowning man. Even if she could never return to them, she vowed to never forget all she had experienced.

She heard a knock at the door, the one she dreaded. She looked around the room, wishing for a place to hide, but there was nowhere to escape. When Latif made his way to her bed, she could not even look at him. When he tried to touch her, she recoiled away.

"Isabella?"

She could hear the ache of sadness in his voice, but it made her only want to withdraw further from him. Today, facing him seemed harder than the first time.

"Isabella, look at me." She felt him gently reach for her face. When she looked at him, his pain was evident. She tried to resist the sympathy that welled up in her heart. She just wanted to be alone, and she was torn between rebellion and concession.

Latif held her face and attempted to give her a kiss. "Latif, please don't," she gently pleaded, and his face registered confusion.

"Isabella, don't pull away from me. I can see you are hurting, but I won't let you go. Don't you know that I love you?"

Isabella just looked into his eyes. If only his love could be enough, but it wasn't. She belonged to Sam. If only she could tear herself away from this man, then would he let her go? As she continued to look into his soft brown eyes, she knew. Hurting him would not help her. Hurting him was not even something she wanted to do anymore, but just now her memories of her family haunted her. She had started to need him, and his tenderness was softening her resolve.

"Today, just today, can I say no?"

"Why?" He withdrew a little as the pain in his eyes turned to frustration.

"I don't know. I just feel very melancholy. I suppose the baby is making me emotional. I am not trying to hurt you. Please, don't be angry."

But it was too late; she watched his eyes harden in anger. In response, Isabella began to cry. It was an impossible situation in an impossible world. She expected him to leave, but he didn't.

"Today, I will let you say no, but only today. I will return tomorrow." The anger had changed to firm resolve, and his message was clear.

Sunlight streamed in through the window. It was a luminous, pleasant morning. She listened to the birds singing outside her window, rejoicing a new day. She had slept well with fewer dreams from home. While she still felt gloomy, she could also feel hope dawning in her heart. The baby was very active, and it was unmistakable that there was life fluttering inside her. She picked up her Bible and flipped to a passage. She ran her hands over the smooth, cool, translucent parchment page. No matter how many times she looked within these pages, she was always awed by the power of this written word. Even when she could not comprehend its meaning, it spoke peace to her heart. As she had done so many times before, she prayed. Like the sun flooding in through the window, encouragement fed her soul.

It was a battle in her heart to remember the promises of God. In every situation, she must learn to rely on him for hope, strength, and purpose. She did not like this life that had replaced her safe and loving one, but she was again resolved to be beneficial to God's plan for her life. As long as she was alive, she knew he had a function for her to fulfill.

She took a deep breath and slowly exhaled it. She again looked out the window at the world that had become her home. Winter had passed here, and the days were again becoming longer and hotter. She flipped through the pages of her most recent journal, realizing she had been gone from the United States for nearly eight months. She was amazed at how much time had passed, and in a little less than six months, her baby would be born.

Would it be a boy, like Latif had concluded, or a beautiful little girl? Would it have dark hair and dark eyes like its father? Was there even a genetic chance that red hair and green eyes could prevail? She doubted it. Regardless, she would love it. When she rubbed the growing mound where the baby was moving, she felt a connection deep in her heart. Soon she would be a mother again. As the idea penetrated her thoughts, she smiled.

Her life was like a river flowing through a fallow land. Time continued to pass by her, bringing more distance from the life she loved. Many times over the passing weeks her heart continued to be pierced by thoughts from home, but she was learning to trust in the midst of this suffering. The circle of her existence revolved around a few people, a few activities, and plenty of solitude. The quiet moments were becoming more familiar. They were times of reflection and conversation with her guide and protector. In her old life, the busyness often overshadowed the dialogue in her soul. It was easy to forget or simply ignore this discipline. For the first time since coming here, she could embrace joy in suffering. It did not diminish the desire to see her family or return home, but somehow trusting brought a steady, simple joy.

She had been to several parties hosted by Bahira since her unexpected visit so many weeks ago. Their friendship was still distant and a little strained, but the anger and jealousy had diminished. Isabella celebrated this small victory. On one other occasion, Bahira had even come for another short visit to her home. From these brief encounters, Isabella was beginning to understand her. Bahira had grown up in a loving, doting home with unusual parents by Saudi standards. She had received more attention, admiration, and encouragement than most women in this society. Then she had married Latif. When her high expectations of the marriage had been dashed by reality, she became bitter. Bahira still wore her pride like a chip on her shoulder, but Isabella did not mind. She knew that love and friendship could surprisingly cure many ills, and she resolved to set aside pettiness in favor of this. She also learned that Bahira had nagging doubts about Islam. Her parents had only been nominal followers, and Bahira lacked faith in the government-imposed religion. More than anything that she had seen and heard in her new home, this encouraged her, and she prayed diligently for God's work.

Hafa had become like a sister. She had even been invited to Hafa's house to meet her boys and her husband for dinner. Isabella had relished the time spent with Hafa's family. Meeting Ali and Jalil had wrenched her heart, reminding her of her daughters. They had both animatedly talked about their desire to have a puppy. It was an idea that had been hinted at by their parents but not fulfilled. The excitement glowing on their faces was contagious, even making her giggle.

Watching the budding love between Jabbar and Hafa had been bittersweet. She was so happy for her friend, but watching it play out in front of her eyes was still painful. They all openly welcomed her into their family, and Isabella was instantly drawn in by their kindness and hospitality. On that night, she had even discussed at length with Jabbar and Hafa about her God. They had both been interested, asking many questions. But in the end, Hafa still resisted acceptance. In the hours that had followed their visit, Isabella had been plagued with doubts. She desperately longed for her dear friend to believe, but in the end, she knew that she was only a vessel. She prayed that God would find her usable to bring her friends to him.

Isabella looked in the mirror at her reflection. And what she saw made her shiver. She was wearing the shroud of black chiffon required to enter the public streets of Saudi Arabia. Wearing them was still strange and unsettling, but looking at her reflection was repulsive. She was waiting for Latif. They had an appointment with the doctor that would be delivering the baby at the King Fahd Medical City in a few months.

In the other room, she heard him knock and then enter the foyer. Her belly was growing more every day. She estimated she was near twenty weeks, about halfway through the pregnancy. In this country, it was common for the father to name the child, but she was insistent on being involved in the process. The Arabic names were all unfamiliar to her, but an American name seemed out of place for their child. She liked the name Ibrahim for a boy and Hana for a girl, but Latif wanted Nadir and Malaika. At this point, they had not made a decision.

Isabella tried to convince herself that her relationship with Latif had not changed. In quiet moments alone she often wondered where he was or what he was doing. Most of the time, he was a tender and loving husband. She still carried her precious love for Sam protected from these conflicting emotions, but life had continued on, and her hope of ever returning home had dimmed. In her heart, she wanted to deny the depth of her love for Latif. Admitting it would be a betrayal. Her feelings were confusing, and she found herself pushing away the parts that were too complicated to contemplate.

When she met him in the foyer, he was wearing his

traditional Arab dress. The stranger in foreign clothes that greeted her when they were going out in public always unnerved her. When he was dressed like this, he seemed more like a terrorist than a husband. It was an incorrect stereotype, but something she could not resist feeling. She followed him out to the waiting car in silence, unsure of what to expect.

When they arrived at the medical office, she was surprised to see that the facility was modern and well equipped. Some of her friends had asked if she would be leaving the country for the birth, but Latif did not like the idea. Because most women in the royal family delivered in other facilities outside Saudi Arabia, Isabella was not sure what to expect from the local hospital. She just hoped the delivery would not have any complications. Her past two pregnancies had been normal, so she hoped this one would be as well.

When Isabella and Latif were in public together, he never touched her and often did not even acknowledge her company. But when he heard the baby's heartbeat in the doctor's office, he instinctively rubbed her tummy. He was so excited about this baby. The love and pride in his eyes was engaging, making her heart swell for the child they both loved. It was an undeniable bond, one that was hard to ignore.

Isabella had been surprised again by another visit from Bahira. She had arrived late in the morning with something clearly on her mind. They had been casually visiting for about a half an hour, but somehow Isabella knew Bahira had something specific she wanted to talk about. Isabella wondered if she should be patient and wait for her to bring it up or broach the subject first. She was still considering what to do when Bahira came straight to the point.

"Isabella, I want to talk to you about Latif."

"Okay. What do you want to talk about?"

"I just cannot understand what your secret is." Bahira spoke candidly without anger.

Isabella was confused, but she admired her friend's tenacity. "Bahira, if I have a secret, I would be happy to share it with you. What secret do you think that I am keeping?"

"How have you charmed Latif into loving you? I know you are beautiful, but so is Dalia, and she has never influenced him. I just cannot figure it out. So what is it?"

"I wish that I knew. To be honest, I am not sure. If you could persuade him to love you instead, I think I would be happy. Sometimes I think he loves me because I am American. Other times, I think he is drawn to the real me. But if I had to guess, I wonder if he is intrigued by my openness." Isabella gave her friend a smile.

"When I am with Latif, I do not know what to do. I want to please him, but I don't know how to make him love me." For the first time, Bahira seemed vulnerable.

"Tell me, Bahira, do you love him?" Isabella asked tenderly.

Bahira did not answer right away. The truth was written on her face, but she was slow to give words to the truth. "Hmm... I have never had anyone ask me such a pointed question. But the truth is I do love him, but I don't know why."

"Love is a mysterious and beautiful thing, but it can also be cruel and painful. Love has the power to enhance or destroy. But I don't think any secret I might or might not have will help you. Instead, we must find your secret to making him love you. Tell me, how do you feel when you are around him?"

"Nervous and intimidated. Sometimes I enjoy being his wife, but I cannot relax when I am near him." Bahira seemed anxious just talking about being around him.

"First, you must remember he is only a man, nothing more and nothing less."

Bahira sighed. "But I have not been around many men."

"True, but you were close to your father. Latif is not so different from your father. You need to learn to relax around him."

"How?"

"Well, let's see. What do you talk to Latif about when he is with you?" Isabella asked, searching for a way to help her friend.

"We don't really talk."

"What? You don't talk?" Isabella was surprised by this admission.

"Well, sometimes we talk about Youssef, but usually he comes to me because he is required to." Shame registered on Bahira's face.

"So, you are really still strangers after all these years?"

"Yes," Bahira answered with a whisper.

"Do not feel ashamed, Bahira. Marriage should be a relationship, not just a means for procreation. But you cannot know or understand that if you have never had a chance to experience it." Isabella felt sympathy for this woman and wanted to help her.

"My mother told me marriage would be rewarding and beautiful, but she was wrong." Bahira's insolent nature began to resurface.

"No, she was not wrong. We just need to help you find out that marriage can be those things and many more, but it is not easy."

Isabella agreed that Bahira needed some solutions that would help her marriage. Over the next hour, they worked through ways she could relax when she was with Latif. Isabella talked to her about flattery, not vain flattery, but giving him sincere compliments. It was a perplexing conversation, coaching one of Latif's wives, but she enjoyed helping her friend. Isabella reminded her she must be willing to share from her own life and experiences in order to draw him into conversation. She shared a few things that Latif had told her to help Bahira feel more comfortable. It was a strange kind of matchmaking, but she enjoyed helping her. If Latif's attentions and affection shifted to Bahira, it could be good and bad for Isabella. But instead of thinking about it, she focused on helping Bahira. When they had finished talking, Bahira got up from the sofa to leave.

"Now, if only Latif will leave your bed to come to me. Do you have any suggestions on how to do that?" Bahira was not angry, but her voice was clearly laced with sarcasm.

"No, I am not sure exactly how to accomplish that part, but in time he will come to you again. When he does, you must be ready. Do not become bitter while you wait. It will not help your relationship with him.

Just remember it is not my intention to keep him from you. Do you think you will be ready?" Isabella wondered if this whole thing was possibly a long shot.

"I am ready, and you are right." Bahira did not apologize, but there was concession in her tone.

"I will be praying for you, Bahira. I really do hope you can make him love you." Isabella reached out and squeezed her arm for comfort.

"Isabella, you are not like anyone I have ever met. I am surprised by your willingness to help, but yet somehow I suspected that you would."

"I am so glad to help. Once he comes to you, tell me how it goes."

Isabella opened the door and watched Bahira make her way to the main house. It had been a strange morning. She had sincerely enjoyed helping her new friend, but she was also a little apprehensive about what changes it might cause. She shook her head and closed the door. It was a complicated place and a strange situation, so she resolved to leave the details to God.

CHAPTER NINETEEN

Latif puzzled over the events of the previous night. He had traveled part of the past week for business. Upon his return, he had visited Bahira as usual. This was part of his typical routine after traveling, something he did out of formality, not desire, and until last night there had always been a cold distance between them when he visited her. In the past, whenever he had tried to make conversation, she had withdrawn from him, but last night had been different. She had asked about his trip and volunteered an update on Youssef. She had encouraged the visit, even sharing details of her week. For the first time, Bahira was open and engaging, and he had enjoyed spending time with her. Was it possible he had imagined it? He shook his head. It was a real mystery, but maybe he would have to consider visiting her again soon. The thought nearly made him smile.

He thought back over the past week. Things were

good in his life. Isabella was pregnant, and being with her made him feel intoxicated. He had completed a lucrative business deal with a London firm that promised to make him millions, and then as icing on the cake, overnight things had improved in his marriage with Bahira. It was too soon to hope for any lasting changes, but the possibility was appealing. To have two beautiful, loving, and responsive wives would be a dream beyond imagining. It was something to savor and keep him company throughout the coming day until tonight when he would see Isabella.

Isabella was dressed for another party and waiting for Hafa to join her. It had been a rather boring couple of weeks since Bahira's last visit. Both Hafa and Latif had traveled out of the country. Latif had traveled to London on business while Hafa had gone to Egypt again with her husband and sons. She had attended a party hosted by Bahira while they were gone, but it had not been the same without Hafa. Isabella was a social person, but the language barrier and the cultural differences made most of the relationships feel strained. In wealthy Saudi Arabian families, it was not uncommon to learn English, but some of the women had not received much education, so their English was lacking. Isabella had picked up a bit of Arabic. But because Hafa, Latif, Bahira, and Mina all spoke English, she had not been fully immersed in the language.

Hafa had returned a few days ago from her trip but had not been able to visit until today. Latif had returned yesterday, but she had not seen him either. She wondered if he had visited Bahira. If things had gone well, would Bahira tell her? She was unsure. Bahira was a proud woman, and she would not want to admit Isabella's advice had worked. She prayed that changes would not add to the rivalry between them. Isabella believed Bahira loved Latif, and she wanted them to be happy. She tried not to imagine them together. Strangely, the idea was more unnerving to her than she had expected, so she did not think about it. She refused to resort to pettiness, and in her heart, she did want things to be right between them.

Her wandering thoughts were interrupted by a knock on the door. When Isabella answered it, she was surprised by the look on Hafa's face. She could not tell if something good or bad had happened, but the shock on Hafa's face was obvious.

"Hafa, are you okay?"

She continued to stand at the doorway without saying anything for what seemed like forever. When she spoke, Isabella did not know what to expect.

"The most bizarre thing happened. I am almost afraid to say anything. I think it might be scary. I just don't know." Hafa's wide eyes glistened from unshed tears.

"Come in and tell me. I am sure we can sort it out. What happened?"

Isabella guided her friend into the salon. When they sat down, Isabella faced her.

"I had a dream..." Hafa shuddered from the memory.

"Tell me about the dream." Isabella could not understand what was going on with her friend. She had never seen her act like this.

"Well, I was dreaming I was in the desert at an oasis. It was beautiful, like just after it rains. The sky was clear and blue. I was all alone enjoying the beauty of the flowers and the crystal pool of water ..." Hafa hesitated. "Then a man came walking toward me from the desert. He seemed familiar. But when I looked closely at him, I knew he was a stranger. Then he spoke my name."

"Okay, Hafa, but it was just a dream." Isabella was shocked by her friend's reaction to a mere dream.

"He said, 'Hafa, I love you. Come to me and have life.' When he reached out his hands, there were scars. I don't know what this means. I have never had a dream so real and powerful. Since I woke from the dream, I have not been able to forget it. Isabella, tell me what this means. I am very afraid."

Isabella was shocked and did not exactly know what to think about Hafa's dream. It sounded like Christ, but it seemed supernatural and beyond anything that Isabella could comprehend. God revealed himself in dreams in the Bible, but would he still reveal himself that way today? Isabella did not know the answer to her questions, but she did not want to share that with Hafa. Instead, she just asked her, "Hafa, that was truly an extraordinary dream. Who do you think the stranger was?"

Hafa just stared at her and shook her head. Her face registered the fervor of all the emotions battling in her soul. Realization dawned, and after several moments, she spoke. "I know who he was, but I cannot say his name."

Isabella hugged her friend and whispered in her ear. "I am here with you. Tell me his name."

"It was Jesus. I know it was Jesus. He came to me in a dream. He wants to give me life. Is that possible?" Hafa pulled away and looked into Isabella's eyes.

"I know that Jesus is real. I know that he does offer you life. So yes, I think it is possible. And my question to you is, what do you say in response?"

The shock never left her face. "I don't know … but if he is real … then I do want to believe. But I don't know how. Isabella, how do I believe?"

"You should pray to him and tell him that you believe. Ask him to take away your sins and give you life. Let's pray together right now and ask him. What do you think?" Isabella was shocked and excited by this strange turn of events.

"I don't know how. Will you help me?"

"Yes, my friend, I will help you." Isabella did not know what to think of this miracle that had occurred, but she was ready to help her friend take this step of faith.

They prayed together. And when they finished, Hafa drilled her with questions. Isabella patiently tried to answer them all. Sometimes she did not know what to say, so she just told her she did not know. She was looking forward to exploring all the answers with her together.

They both decided to skip the party. They had missed so much of it, and neither one of them had a desire to go. So they just talked. In an instant, their friendship had risen to a new level. This common belief made them even closer. Today, God had answered Isabella's prayer, and she would never forget it.

When Hafa finally got up to leave, Isabella told her to wait in the foyer. She ran to her room and opened the drawer to her bedside table. Inside was the precious leather Bible she had mysteriously received from Mina so many months ago. She did not want to part with it, but she knew she had received it for this very moment. She paused and ran her hands over the cover as tears came to her eyes. This book contained the words from her God, and they were faithful and true. Now she would be passing them on to her sister and friend. God was still in the miracle business, and no one would ever convince her otherwise. Thankfully, she had already written down in her notebooks each passage she had received during her times of meditation.

She made her way back to Hafa and offered her the Book of Life. "Start in the book of John. It tells about Jesus' life. It is a great place to start. Whenever you can, come by and we can talk about what you have read." Isabella prayed that Hafa would find the right place because she could not read the Arabic words to show her. Then she hugged her friend before she left. Hafa's eyes were shining.

Isabella's heart overflowed with happiness as she watched her friend leave. It had truly been an extraordinary day.

CHAPTER TWENTY

Isabella was peaceful. Several times over the last two weeks, Hafa had come by to discuss the passages she was reading. For the first time in months, God had given Isabella meaningful purpose. Hafa's hunger for God's Word was refreshing, and talking about it with her friend was exhilarating. Watching Hafa pore over the words of her Bible also made Isabella long for one in her own language. There was a beauty in the love and fervor of Hafa's love for God that was contagious to Isabella. Watching her fortified the love in her own heart.

Unexpectedly, Jabbar, Hafa's husband, had also been very interested in this new faith that Hafa and Isabella shared. Isabella had feared Hafa's faith in Christ would interfere with the growing love in her marriage. Instead, it appeared to only improve their relationship. Isabella sensed God was beginning a mighty work in this dark and defunct place. It was a miracle that she embraced without completely understanding it.

But even within the momentous peace and promise of the past weeks, Isabella had also become worried. She suspected that her body might be going into preterm labor. For a while now, she had begun to feel contractions. At twenty-four weeks, she guessed that it could possibly be Braxton Hicks contractions, but she was not sure. Hafa had gone with her to the doctor. He had not been concerned. To him, the pregnancy was progressing on schedule with no notable changes to her body. She tried to let his confident words be a reassurance.

When she was afraid, she would pray for strength, wisdom, and guidance. She knew that her God was in control, and she resolved to rest in that knowledge. It was out of her hands.

Bahira had come by just a few days ago for another visit. Isabella had been astonished by the change in the woman's demeanor. For a brief moment, Bahira's happiness had torn Isabella's heart. Since Latif had returned from his London business trip, Isabella had noticed a slight change in the frequency of his visits. She had suspected that he was choosing to spend more time with his other wives. Until a few weeks ago, Isabella had been the favored wife, something she had enjoyed more than she realized. Now her position was becoming threatened. Jealousy was a dangerous weapon that could undo everything good God had begun. She resolved to take the high road and let it go.

Bahira had been kind enough to relate only vague details of the time she had spent with Latif, but it was evident something good was flourishing between them. She reminded her heart that what was happening was wonderful. Bahira's visit had been brief, and at no time had Bahira appeared to gloat over the changes in her relationship with Latif. She had really only been grateful at Isabella's willingness to set aside her own feelings to help her. Hope and love were growing in Bahira's heart. The whole thing was a strange dichotomy to Isabella. Isabella fought to deny her love for Latif, even as Bahira's love for him continued to grow. She wanted them to be happy, but she could not explain the sadness that resonated with this truth. If only life were simple.

When Isabella opened the door and greeted Hafa that morning, she was surprised to see she was offering her another gift. Their visits had become routine and frequent. Isabella followed her friend to the sofa where they always sat during their conversations. Once they were seated, Hafa offered her the wrapped box. Isabella was filled with anticipation. She guessed it was something for the baby.

Hafa had even suggested at their last visit that in the next few weeks they should begin shopping. Isabella had already made plans for the small second bedroom in her house but had not made any changes or purchased any furniture. She planned to keep the baby with her in her own room for several months before moving it to the nursery. She could not resist the excitement over this small one that was already welcome in her heart. When she imagined the child growing within her, her heart was overflowing with joy and love.

She reached for the gift from her friend as she set aside her thoughtful hopes for the future. She carefully opened the box to reveal a Bible. It was an English translated Bible. She removed the brown leather book from the box. She could smell the new leather and feel the smooth unopened cover to this beautiful timeless book. She held it to her heart and looked through tear-filled eyes at her special friend.

When she could finally control her emotions, she whispered, "How did you ever get a book like this into this country?"

"Jabbar brought it from England. You know that he had a short business trip there earlier this week. I asked him to consider buying one for you as a gift. He was initially resistant to the idea. But when he returned from his trip, he gave it to me. He had traveled with Latif in his private jet, so no one checked his bags in customs. After I asked him to get it for you, I became very afraid he would get caught, maybe even imprisoned or worse. So I prayed and prayed for him. When he presented it to me, I nearly fainted. It was like an answered prayer."

"Thank you, Hafa. And please tell Jabbar I am forever in his debt. He made a huge sacrifice getting such a valuable and dangerous gift for me."

"Isabella, I have been praying for him and the boys to believe in Jesus. I do believe he is beginning to. If only there was someone else to help us." Hafa seemed a little overwhelmed by this burden.

"Hafa, my friend, remember that we are never alone. God is with us. It may seem at times we are inadequate for the task of sharing about him, but we are never alone. God is working in and through us to accomplish his good works. Trust in that because he is sufficient."

Isabella offered an encouraging smile to reinforce her words.

"You are right. I need more faith like yours." Hafa shrugged her shoulders after she spoke.

"I am not perfect, and I have plenty of doubts. When I was sharing with you about God, there were times I doubted that you would ever believe. We must trust in God's timing and plan. He will accomplish all things at the appropriate time, that I am sure of." Isabella gave her a hug. "Don't lose heart, my friend."

While Isabella and Hafa visited, she could see the courage and hope return in her friend's heart. She was so thankful for this remarkable woman and all that she represented. Even as she taught and encouraged Hafa, she received hope and encouragement in return. The exchange was a wonderful mystery.

Eventually Hafa had to leave to return to her family. When they said good-bye, they were both aware of the comfort they had received from the time spent together. Isabella reminded Hafa of God's promise that where two or more are together, there God will be also. Hafa promised to return soon and to be diligent in her study of the Word. For just a little while, Isabella's life was a celebration.

Later that afternoon, Isabella prepared to read her new Bible. She had opened the curtains so she could see the beauty of the world outside her window and seated herself in the comfy overstuffed brown leather chair in her bedroom. This chair had been one of the many additions with the remodel. She used it whenever she was studying or writing in her journals, but here she would have her first real chance to study in months. She tucked her feet up on the chair and snuggled in, then sat for several moments looking at the special book in her lap. She did not know where to start. In her heart, she thirsted for the words that offered life and hope, but strangely she could not begin.

For several moments, she just meditated, taking in the complete solitude. She was hoping for a revelation, but nothing came. She prayed for guidance. Where should she begin? Again, several minutes passed. Finally, she decided to just open it. There before her were the words of King David in Psalm 150. How befitting. She read aloud the words before her eyes.

"Praise the Lord. Praise God in his sanctuary; praise him in his mighty heavens. Praise him for his acts of power; praise him for his surpassing greatness. Praise him with the sounding of the trumpet, praise him with the harp and lyre, praise him with the tambourine and dancing, praise him with the strings and flute, praise him with the clash of cymbals. Let everything that has breath praise the Lord. Praise the Lord."

She was enveloped in a moment of perfect peace. When she finished reading, tears were running down her cheeks. Her heart was veraciously worshiping God, and for a brief moment, it even seemed she was worshiping with the angels and all the saints of heaven. She closed her eyes and imagined the church everywhere on this earth. She was worshiping with them as well. Time stood still in the wake of these words, and everything in her life made perfect sense.

"Isabella, are you okay?" Mina's voice shattered

the solitude, the beauty, and the peacefulness of the moment. Her heart ached to return to this perfect place even as she remembered the resonating words that Jesus spoke to his followers: "How can they call on whom they have not heard?"

She opened her eyes and lovingly spoke to her dear friend. "I am very well, my friend. Can you come and visit with me?"

"Yes, I will like that. I been very busy with many project from Chen. I not been able to visit you lately. What are you reading?" Mina took a seat in the adjoining chair.

"I have a new Bible, one that is translated into my native language. For the first time in months, I can read God's Word."

"There is light reflecting from you face. Is magic in your book?" Mina looked awed and a little frightened by this idea.

"Not exactly magic, but there is power in the words of this book. The creator of the universe speaks in this book. It is the most powerful, life-changing book ever written."

"I not believe you. You making fun of me." Mina looked a little hurt by Isabella's words.

Isabella coaxingly invited Mina to listen to the words she had just read. As Isabella read them aloud again, she let her heart return to the place of worship she had been before. When she finished, Mina's face looked stricken. "Mina?"

"It time to make your dinner. I not time to listen to nonsense with much to do. I call you when I finish." Mina jumped from her seat and hurried out of Isabella's bedroom.

Isabella called after her. "Do you need any help?"

Mina stopped and turned back. She did not answer but adamantly shook her head.

Isabella quietly whispered to the air under her breath. "Well, Lord, what are you going to do about sweet, loving Mina? Certainly you have a special plan for her."

It was a question without an answer. She was reminded of the declaration she had made earlier in the day to Hafa. "In your own time, Lord, in your own time." Then she smiled and rested in the cleft of the rock, her Savior.

CHAPTER TWENTY-ONE

Isabella awoke that morning with a feeling of dread. Something was not right, and over the last hour, her contractions had increasingly intensified. When Mina came that morning, Isabella met her at the door.

"Please go immediately and tell Latif that something is wrong. I need to go to the hospital." Isabella almost could not recognize the fearful hollow voice that echoed from her mouth.

Mina looked stricken by this proclamation. "The baby?"

"Yes, the baby. Now, please go and hurry."

Isabella slowly and carefully made her way back to the bedroom and sat on the bed. She needed to get dressed, but another strong contraction had come over her. She breathed and prayed. When the pain began to lessen, she gingerly made her way to the dresser to get some clothes to change into. It was a painful and slow process, but she managed to be ready when Latif came barging into her room.

"Isabella, what is wrong?" The fear in his eyes made Isabella's heart ache.

"I need to get to the hospital. My contractions are too strong. If we do not get there right away, I am afraid . . ." Isabella choked on the unspoken words.

"I have already called to the driver. I will help you into your abaya."

"Thank you, Latif."

Within a few minutes, they were speeding down the highway to the King Fahd Medical City. She knew it would be nearly a half an hour before they arrived. Latif lovingly held her against him as she struggled to breathe through the contractions. When the pain was most severe, he would calmly and sweetly whisper words of encouragement in her ear. The driver was racing down the highway, but the drive still seemed to take forever. She began to wonder if she would give birth in the car as they made their way to the hospital. While looking at the time on his watch, she even heard Latif curse under his breath.

So many things were racing through Isabella's mind, but more than anything, she pleaded, "Lord, please. No."

When they finally arrived at the hospital, Latif raced into the emergency door. He returned with an orderly pushing a wheelchair. They were quickly rushed into a room with a nurse and doctor ready to move her to the gurney. A monitor was placed on her stomach. She heard the nurse say that the baby's heartbeat was stable while another nurse tried to start an IV. It was rushing, roaring chaos. Isabella closed her eyes and tried to calm her racing heart. The stress of the moment could not be good for the baby. By this time, she guessed that the contractions were only a few minutes apart.

One of the nurses asked Latif to leave the room. His pacing was getting in the way of their work. Instinctually, Isabella reached for his hand. When he came to her side, she could see the apparent distress on his face.

"Latif, I am afraid."

She sensed that the weight of those words had crushed something inside him. Tears filled his eyes as he spoke to her.

"Isabella, it will be okay."

She felt the tears coursing down her face. In that moment, she knew it would not be okay. She was twenty-five weeks pregnant. The chances of survival were not good for a preemie that young. Her contractions were not letting up, even as they poked and prodded, using all their medical expertise to stop her labor. Latif was there beside her holding her hand, but he could not make it stop. When panic gave way to sobs, the doctor gave her a sedative. She noticed that everything was fading into darkness.

When she awoke, she had been moved to a birthing room. The nurse was beside her looking over the chart and had not noticed she had awakened. She felt her stomach to make sure the baby was still alive within her. She felt another contraction building. The baby had not been born, but the contractions had not stopped.

The nurse's eyes met hers. Without a word, her eyes confirmed the danger had not passed.

"Are you feeling another contraction?" the nurse questioned her.

"Yes."

"It appears from the monitors that they are still coming about ten minutes apart. While you were out, your water broke. The doctor has been in several times to check on you. He is hoping we can slow down the contractions with medication." The nurse spoke directly, but there was kindness in her voice.

"Now that my water has broken, can you keep the baby from being born?"

"It is hard to say. We will just hope for the best." The nurse smiled and patted her shoulder for reassurance.

"Where is Latif?" Isabella looked around the sterile hospital room, trying to find him.

"I am not sure. He has been in and out. I am guessing he will be back in a few minutes." The nurse finished with her chart and laid it aside, turned down the lights, and then left the room.

Isabella closed her eyes and tried to pray, but she just could not foresee how this would turn out. She wondered where Latif had gone, but had no idea where he might be or what he might be doing. And then she realized that she really wanted Sam. She wanted her safe, comforting, loving husband to help her through what might become the greatest trial she had ever faced. When she thought of losing this baby, her heart broke. She imagined Sam holding Latif's child. And somehow she knew that if he were here, he would love this child as his own. She was crying, but it did not lessen the pain. She was afraid, but it did not change the inevitable. When there were no other emotions to express, she realized her only hope lay in trusting, but it was a restless trust. Her body was exhausted from the emotional turmoil, so she drifted back to sleep.

When she had given birth to a beautiful baby girl, they placed her in Isabella's arms. She was bundled up in a stiff, blue and white receiving blanket from the hospital. She was beautiful. Her downy hair was dark brown. Her little face was perfect and nearly peaceful sleeping in her arms. She was a little blue around her mouth from the lack of oxygen. Silent tears poured from her eyes, and she blinked them back.

She was too little. The doctor had said that she would not survive long. Her lungs were underdeveloped and not supplying her body with enough oxygen. Isabella was confused that measures were not being taken to keep her alive, but the doctors said it would not help. She was angry and hurting, but she would cherish every moment with her baby girl. She opened the blanket and looked at her perfect little hands and fingers. She was so tiny. She weighed only one and a half pounds. She was twelve inches long, but she was perfectly formed. Each breath was shallow and forced, and Isabella agonized through every one with her. She prayed for a miracle and hoped the doctors were wrong. It was a foolish hope, but she could not let it go.

Latif had left earlier after Hafa had arrived. Isabella was amazed that he would not stay with his baby daughter. She had seen the hurt and anger in his eyes as he told her good-bye, but she could not understand why he would leave. It seemed he had already accepted the inevitable while she still held out hope.

She wrapped her back in the blanket to keep her warm and rubbed her finger against the smooth skin of the baby's small cheek. Her baby responded with the slightest little smile.

"Hana. Your name is Hana, my sweet little girl." Isabella choked on the sobs that threatened to overtake her. She felt Hafa rub her shoulder. Her friend had not left her side for nearly an hour.

Instinctually, Isabella knew that Hana would not live much longer. Her color was worsening, and her breathing had become more and more shallow. When she finally took her last breath, Isabella thought she would stop breathing as well. But she could not, just like Hana could not continue. She wanted to die, but she lived. She wanted her baby to live, but she died. It was more than she could handle. In just a short time, she had completely loved this little bundle and had wished she could die in her place. Gut-wrenching sobs filled her soul. She wanted to understand, but she could not. Grief poured from within her until she thought she would die from it, and still she lived. Her heart was raw and aching.

When the nurse came to take her baby, she refused. She needed just a little more time.

Hafa leaned down in front of her chair. "Isabella, my dear sweet friend, it is time. She has gone to heaven."

Hafa was right, but she was just not ready to let her baby go. "Please, just give me five more minutes."

Isabella could feel that life had relinquished her

baby, but she could not reign in her grief to release her. When they finally took her away, Hafa immediately grabbed her and hugged her. They cried together for a long time with an acute certainty that a part of Isabella had died as well.

The next morning, Isabella stood next to Hafa and Mina, looking out over the barren desert. Latif and his father were carrying Hana's body to the empty area where they buried the dead. It was not a grave-yard because there were no headstones. Only empti-ness marked the place where she would be placed into the ground. Earlier that morning, Hafa and Isabella had carefully wrapped the tiny body in a white shroud. After a short family prayer time, they had made their way to this desolate place. According to Islamic cus-tom, there was no embalming. It was important for the burial to happen in the morning after she had died. Isabella had received an early release from the hospital to accommodate the arrangements.

The men had gone alone for the burial, according to custom. Grief and keening were expressions of emo-tion that were not accepted at the grave. She would have three days to quietly grieve, and then she must put the pain and heartache behind her. Isabella was con-fused by such rigidity and insensitivity. Grieving was not a lack of acceptance of God's will; it was a natural emotional reaction to the pain of loss. Hafa had care-fully and somberly explained the strange rituals to her, but she still had trouble understanding such limitations to grief.

She had already cried so many tears. She was certain she had no more in reserve, but as she saw them lower her child into the ground, she felt her knees begin to buckle. Her friends responded by giving her the support she lacked to endure this horrific thing. They both reached their arms around Isabella and held her on her feet. It was a beautiful symbol to Isabella of the blessing of friendship. Even in her deepest despair, she thanked God for giving her this simple assistance. Just as Job had despaired over the pain and suffering of his tormenting loss, she grieved. But she remembered that even in the midst of suffering, God was with her. Blessed be his name.

CHAPTER TWENTY-TWO

L atif stretched out in his leather seat on the plane. He was just returning from another long business trip to London. He looked forward to the return. He thought about Bahira. She would be awaiting his arrival tonight, and he looked forward to seeing her. Before the trip, she had enthusiastically shared with him the news of her pregnancy. Only a few months ago, their relationship had been mere formality. Now he carried a very special love and appreciation for his first wife. There was a complexity to Bahira he had only begun to explore. It was a transformation he enjoyed pondering.

He puzzled over the changes in his life over the last several months. Was it all really because of Isabella? She had come into his life and changed everything. First, she had taught him how to love. Possessing her had been an obsession that had haunted him. But then she had brought a new joy into his life he had not expected. When she had lost the baby, Latif had worried that her loss would change something between them, and it had. Latif had watched his beautiful wife grieve for little Hana with empty arms. Seeing her suffering had been difficult. Death was an accepted part of life. As a Muslim, excessive grief was forbidden. One must always be willing to accept Allah's will. But Isabella was not Muslim, and he had expected her to be overcome with grief. Her suffering had been painful to watch, but not the way he had presumed. Isabella had lived a faith in the midst of her pain unlike anything he had ever seen. He had seen many followers of Allah bury their grief in obedience to the Koran. But Isabella's grief over these last six months had been different. She had hidden nothing, even the loss and aching pain in her heart. It had filled her with sadness but never despair. Somehow through the midst of it, he had even wondered if he was seeing her faith grow. So many women in his country were bitter and disillusioned with their lives but not Isabella. She found hope in the mundane and the insufferable parts of her life. His new wife still excited him and made him want to be a better man. She was uncommon; no, she was exceptional. And even as his love for Bahira was ripening, he continued to find a deeper love with Isabella.

He stretched out his arms and locked his hands together behind his head. He sighed as he closed his eyes. He was content and satisfied with the way things were working out.

There was peace in her private garden. She inhaled the familiar scents and tried to quiet her tormented emotions. Winter had returned and with it, cooler weather. She lifted her face to the morning sun and prayed for peace in her heart. She zipped up her sweater to ward off the morning chill. Her journey of grief had been arduous. Her empty arms had made her yearn even more determinedly for Rebecca and Katherine. Her hope that they were safely at home with Sam encouraged her but made the distance more pronounced.

A couple times during her stay at the hospital, Isabella had tried to offer a plea to a friendly British nurse for help in contacting her home. Each time she had begun explaining her plight, Latif had come in to check on her. She had slipped the nurse little bits of information but had never been able to give her the entire story. The day that Isabella had been released, she had not been on duty.

Not a day had gone by that she did not think of Hana. As time had passed, the pain had lessened but was still ever present, especially now that she was facing this new challenge. Hafa was coming today with the baby. She had given birth to a healthy baby boy. Nearly a month ago, Jabbar had flown Hafa and the boys to London for the birth. Since their return only a few days ago, Hafa had been making the rounds to family. She was excited for her friend and the new life she was welcoming, but it was a bittersweet reunion. The thought of seeing Hafa's baby and holding him in her arms scraped the scab off the healing wound in her heart. She had been wrestling to control her tumultuous emotions all morning. Hafa, her dear friend, had experienced all the emotions beside her during Hana's death. They had journeyed through her pain and loss together, learning from the Bible study they completed each week, and had both grown through the process.

Isabella heard a car pull in through the gate. She stepped back through the door; all the while she prayed for courage, peace, and endurance. Hafa deserved a sincere welcome from Isabella, and she determined to give it to her in spite of the pain.

She went into the bathroom to splash cool water on her face. As she wiped it with the towel, she could not help but notice the evidence of the months. She was still youthful, but there was a solemnity in her expression that never seemed to leave. Her hope for returning home had solidified into a desire to be used by God even in the midst of her greatest pain, and right now she needed help.

When the knock came, she heaved a deep breath and welcomed her friend. She could not suppress the tears that sprang to her eyes at the sight of that little bundle in Hafa's arms. She gently stroked his soft little cheek as the emotions surged inside her.

"Would you like to hold him, Isabella?" Hafa's emotions were evident in her tone and expression. She understood the conflicting emotions going on within Isabella.

Isabella quickly brushed away an errant tear as she answered, "Yes, I would love to hold him."

When she took him in her arms, he meowed like a kitten. He smelled fresh, clean, and new. It was exactly the smell she had remembered with all her children. She could not control the emotion. She saw the concerned look on Hafa's face, and felt compelled to explain this rush of emotion to her friend.

"Hafa, I am so happy for you. He is beautiful and perfect. He just reminds me of all my babies. Please do not mistake my sadness for lack of love."

"Isabella, you have suffered a great loss. I knew that on this visit you would battle with the emotions of all that has happened. I have prayed my joy would not bring you pain and sadness. If seeing him is too much for you, my friend, I can come back on another day."

"No. I have missed you and have prayed for your health and the baby's. I do not want my pain to make you uncomfortable. I love him; he is so precious. It is hard, but the pain is not beyond bearing. I really am rejoicing in all God has accomplished in your life. Your son is a symbol of the miracle that God has accomplished."

"I have missed you, Isabella. I even have news that will bring you joy. While we were in London, after the birth of Kamil, Jabbar believed."

"Do you mean he believes in Christ?" Isabella was shocked by this news.

"Yes." The light that was shining in Hafa's eyes filled the room and gave Isabella a new and growing hope in all that God was going to accomplish. "Please come and tell me all about it."

Hope dawned again in this strange and mysterious place. It did not erase the pain in Isabella's heart. She knew her loss would take time to heal, but this hope made it all worthwhile. God was moving and working, and no one could deny it.

A new guest had arrived in their weekly study. Only a week ago, Bahira had arrived at her door asking probing questions, looking for answers. Bahira was seeking. Isabella did not understand how it had come about, but something had sparked a desire in Bahira to know and understand about Christ. During that visit, Isabella had shared openly with her about the hope within, and Bahira had been intrigued. In a way, it seemed sudden, unexpected. But she had been praying for her friend, and God had delivered her to Isabella's door with more questions than she had answers to give. In the process, Isabella had learned so much more about the emptiness of the Islamic faith from Bahira. It had renewed her desire to offer hope and love to these people that she had come to love.

After Bahira's visit, Isabella had asked Hafa if they could include her in their weekly Bible study. Hafa's excitement had surprised Isabella. Immediately, Hafa had welcomed the idea and suggested they begin fervently praying. Isabella ceased to be amazed at the love and passion growing daily in her friend. God had definitely poured the gift of evangelism into Hafa's heart. She had an unspeakable ardor for sharing God's Word. Watching it was exciting and humbling. Hafa was bold and fearless, and it scared Isabella. She often reminded Hafa of the warnings she had given her so many months ago, but they did not dampen Hafa's eagerness to find others who were seeking. When consternation over Hafa's safety overwhelmed her, Isabella prayed. She thought of all the martyrs in the Bible. Would she be so willing to die to proclaim the gospel? It was a scary question to pose, a question without an answer. But even more, she was afraid for her friend. To consider watching her be sacrificed for the gospel made Isabella's heart jump into her throat. It was a formidable thought that brought tears to her eyes.

She looked at the two women in her sitting room. Their expectant smiles were petitioning her for answers, and so she began by praying.

"Dear loving Father, guide us, help us, and give us strength. Thank you for my two special friends and the love you have placed in their hearts. Guide them; guide us that we may grow more like you in everything. Lord, help our doubt and unbelief. When we are weak, make us strong. Prepare us for what is to come and give us hope in you. Amen."

Isabella opened her eyes, and Hafa gave a little wink of encouragement. They opened to the first chapter of the book of Matthew. Isabella began to read. Like a fresh spring breeze blowing through the room, she felt the spirit of God moving. The feeling was so strong that tears of joy sprang to her eyes as she kept reading. Her fear had dissolved, and joy had replaced it. She regarded the women in the room and saw the light radiating on their faces. There was a fire in this room unlike anything she had ever experienced. If ever she had doubted, it was washed away.

CHAPTER TWENTY-THREE

Bahira was sleeping peacefully in his arms. Latif gently rubbed her swelling abdomen, ruminating the events of his life. Was it possible the hard, loveless woman he had married was the same woman that lay beside him? Isabella had befriended her, and it had changed everything. Bahira had transformed over the past months. Astonished by the initial changes, Latif had supposed it would not last. Women are fickle and cold; he supposed it was a matter of time before the bitter woman returned. Even when he felt a stirring, unfamiliar ardor burning within him, he had doubted it. But this growing affection had intrigued him, and he had cautiously explored Bahira's heart. He had sensed her initial fear and trepidation as they had explored their growing affection. Bahira's earliest expressions of love were like exposing a festering sore. Her vulnerability had scared and captivated him. When he got too close, she protected her heart like a fierce lioness protecting her cub. At times, he had only been able to watch her lick her wounds and wait. But other times, she had been open and passionate, and slowly they had found a common language. It had been tumultuous but stimulating. She was a fascinating woman, and he reveled in watching love bloom in her heart.

But in the last few months, something else had changed in Bahira, and it had drawn them even closer. He could not explain it. The thought was bewildering. Often he had shaken off the strange notion, but it continued to reoccur each time they were together. As much as he wanted to deny the truth, it was indubitable. Her heart had become in a faint way like Isabella's. There was still a capricious nature to Bahira, and exploring it intrigued him. But he could no longer deny that something deep within her had changed, and it had nothing to do with their growing relationship.

His mind traveled to Isabella. She had captivated him from that very first moment, and it seemed she possessed something that had captivated many of the people that had come in contact with her. As he held Bahira, he could smell the freshness of her skin and hair. She was pleasing to him. While he shared her bed, he tried to shake free his thoughts of Isabella, but the deep mystery of her heart enthralled him. In a dark and hidden part of his own heart, he suspected that it was supernatural, but he refused to give credence to the God she professed. Her belief was a heresy to Allah. He would not listen to the ramblings of a woman and be persuaded by it. For a moment, the thought caused his anger to flare, but then it settled into a firm resolve.

The foolish thoughts of these weak-minded women would not trap him in the folly of their beliefs. Then a slow, gratifying smile came across his face. Of course, he did not mind enjoying the fruits that resulted. He was content; he would not let foolishness ruin the good he had received as a result.

How would they ever accomplish anything? Isabella smiled as she looked around the room. The little group had grown, and the noise level had increased because of it. Kamil, Hafa's son, whined as she patted his back. She could hardly believe he was nearly six months old. In that time, the group had added new members, and she still could not believe it. She looked around at the precious faces that were chatting and laughing around her. Bahira's growing belly reminded everyone that another new addition would be joining the family. Occasionally, that thought still saddened her, but looking at the joy and peace on Bahira's smiling face erased any of Isabella's misgivings. Bahira had been the second member among them to become a Christian. She and Hafa had rejoiced in having another woman come to accept Christ. Then, tentatively, Uzma had joined them as well. They had each encouraged her, helped her, and struggled with her as she battled her need for alcohol. She had been with them for nearly two months, and her addiction seemed to be a thing of the past. The broken woman of just a few months before was transformed. Her life was still formidable, and the fear was something she daily struggled against, but there was a new serenity emanating from her. She was fragile, but God had given her the strength to make it through each day. Isabella still prayed for her daily, and she was glad she was here and had no new visible signs of abuse.

Within a few days of Uzma joining, Mina had finally conceded. In the background of each conclave, she had silently served Isabella and her friends. For months, she had listened and resisted with all her might. Each woman in the group had been burdened to pray for sweet, loving Mina, but nothing seemed to break through her shield. Nightly conversations with Mina continued to reveal her impenetrable resistance to a God that had ignored her pain. In the end, they had resigned to leave her in peace. They had come to the end of ideas and realized she could not be coerced into believing.

To Isabella's astonishment, within a few short weeks of that day, Mina had come and whispered her desire to join the group. So many months of resistance had so quickly provided a soft and pliable heart open to God's Word. All the women had marveled at the miraculous change that seemed to come about overnight. But Isabella knew that God had been working all along, even when it appeared nothing would change Mina's heart. Isabella had cried tears of joy for Mina's simple, humble faith. Now she looked at that sweet face. She had been her first friend in this dark, foreboding place, the one that had helped her through those first lurid and oppressive days. Of all the changed lives in this special group, Mina's had touched her deepest. She wiped a stray tear as she celebrated the hope growing in her friend's life, and she formulated a plan.

They were studying the book of Romans, and sometimes her friends offered difficult questions. She longed to have the correct answers, but in the end, sometimes there were no answers to give. In those times, she reminded them that God's Word was true and living. She refused to make her own ideas reshape the written Word. Instead they prayed and searched through Scriptures to try to understand the mysteries that had been revealed. She also taught them of the joy of searching. Thankfully, God had provided a Word that did not give a list of laws to follow. Instead it was a guide to a living, breathing relationship with Christ. Eager faces with absorbent hearts always greeted her words, and the gravity of teaching these women such profound truths weighed on her heart. It was a monumental task she would never have chosen for herself. Yet God had placed her here with his divine task. When she became overwhelmed, the Word was a reminder that she was not alone.

At the end of the meeting, Isabella asked if Hafa would stay behind and help her with something. She hugged and offered a farewell to each of them. When even Mina had left to return to her daily chores, Isabella turned to Hafa for help.

"Hafa, thanks for staying behind. I have a burden on my heart that I would like to share with you."

Hafa smiled her reassurance as she spoke. "I would love to hear what you have on your mind. I hope I can help with whatever it is."

Isabella sighed, contemplating how to begin. "I want to do something for Mina, but because of my current situation, I am not sure I know how." Isabella paused as she formulated her thoughts into words. "Mina was brought to Saudi Arabia as a slave from her home in Indonesia. You know a little of the story that she has shared with the group. But she has also told me of her desire to return. She feels the need to learn a usable trade that would bring her family out of the pit of poverty that binds them. You know the customs and laws of this country. Is there any way to make something like that possible, or is it merely a pipe dream?"

"Isabella, you are a special woman. I know in your heart you share the same dream as Mina. If only I had the means to send you home too. But even knowing how much you wish to break free, you have overlooked that desire to offer hope to your friend. Fortunately, her situation is much easier to remedy than your own. Let me talk the details over with Jabbar. If Latif is willing to let her purchase her freedom, then I believe we can send her home. Jabbar may even have an idea of how she can obtain a job that would support her family and give her training for the future. I know he will be willing to help and even offer her monetary support to get her started. I am glad you have brought this to my attention. There has to be a solution that will work. I will let you know of any ideas that I can learn from Jabbar. In the meantime, let's be praying that God will guide us." Hafa squeezed Isabella's shoulder in reassurance.

Isabella could not resist giving her a hug. "Thank you. I knew you would know what to do, and I will pray. I cannot believe the incredible things that God has accomplished in your life and the lives of the other women, but I am honored to be here to witness it. More than anything in the world, I want to return to Sam and the girls. I know that you understand even more than anyone else. But today, I am privileged to be here with this awesome task that God has provided. You all are my family now, and I will choose to be content in knowing that."

Hafa offered a reassuring but sad smile. "I believe one day, just maybe, God will provide a way for you to return to your home as well. I don't know when or how, but in my heart, I do believe it will happen. Until that day, I am honored to be counted among your group of friends. I will come by in a few days with some ideas about Mina. Take care, my friend."

Within a few short weeks, the arrangements had been made. Everything had moved along seamlessly. The days had flown by, racing headlong to this day when Mina would be leaving her. The day before, they had met together as a group. Each of the women had provided her with gifts and notes of encouragement. They had celebrated and talked of the work God was going to do in Mina's future. But now, even though Isabella wanted this with all her heart, she could not let her go. Mina's bags had been loaded in the car. It was time to say good-bye, but the pain of letting her go was breaking Isabella's heart.

Mina was crying; she could see the pain etched on her face. When she spoke to Isabella, her voice was hoarse with emotion. "I never forget what you done for me. You give me more than I ever believe. I go to my family; I tell them about you and God that give hope. Pray for me. I happy and afraid, but I not forget

I have Jesus. I miss you. I think leaving so hard because I never see you again."

Isabella took a deep breath and wiped the tears from her face. She knew it was time to summon the strength to send Mina away with hope. "Mina, my sweet friend, we will see each other again someday. If it is not in this life, then we will see each other in heaven. I am so sad to see you go, but I am rejoicing in the knowledge that you are giving new hope to your family. Even though I am sad, I will not let go of the joy I have in witnessing all that God has accomplished in your life. Go, my friend, and know you have my blessing. I will be praying for you always, and I will never, never forget you. May the peace of God always be upon you."

Stubborn tears continued to slip down her cheeks. She looked into the loving, deep brown eyes of her friend for the last time. "Good-bye, Mina."

"Good-bye."

Isabella watched as Mina made her way down the drive to the awaiting car. Jabbar was waiting next to the open car door. He was taking her home. Isabella smiled in the midst of her torrent of tears. It was such a bittersweet day.

After the black car exited the gate, Isabella reentered her home and closed the doors. She thought briefly of the new maid that would replace Mina. Latif had introduced her the week before. She was so different from Mina, and even now, Isabella could not even recall her name. All she could remember were the harsh and criticizing eyes that had appraised her. The maid had attempted to act humble by lowering her eyes whenever Latif or Isabella addressed her, but Isabella had seen the truth nonetheless. Isabella wondered if anyone would be able to replace Mina. And because of the memory of her friend, she vowed to give this new woman a chance.

CHAPTER TWENTY-FOUR

Fear clung to Isabella's heart like icy drops of rain. Her friends had come today as usual for their weekly Bible study, but Hafa had burst into her door that morning with distressing news. Jabbar had issued a warning to Hafa suggesting that Latif had learned of their secret meetings. Not once had Isabella ever lied to Latif about the nature of her parties, and until today he had never guessed. Now, standing imposing in the middle of her sitting room, he was livid. He glared down at Isabella. His eyes, nearly black with fury, were hard and menacing. Upon arrival, he had howled at Bahira to return home, promising to deal with her later. Fakhir had arrived with Latif, Jabbar, and Chen, but had left immediately, dragging Uzma away in tears. Isabella glanced at Jabbar. He was quietly waiting by the door with Hafa. Concern and anger were evident in his rigid shoulders and stiff demeanor.

Months before, Jabbar had brought a trunk with a

hidden storage area for Isabella to hide all of her illegal religious items. It looked antique made out of rich teak with bronze hinges and clasps. At the time, Isabella had questioned her need for it, but Jabbar had insisted on the necessity to be cautious. Now she was thankful that all the evidence had been carefully hidden before these men had arrived.

She looked down at the large dark hand that easily possessed her small wrist. Latif was strong enough to snap the bone in her arm in a swift, easy motion, and he was angry enough to attempt it. Isabella silently prayed. She knew it was impossible for anyone to know where her Bible was hidden, but the panic in her heart refused to relent. When Latif had barged in unannounced that afternoon to what appeared to be a casual party, he had immediately seen through the façade. No one had spoken, but the guilt and fear had been written on all their faces.

At Latif's command, Chen had started searching her home for evidence. She was certain Latif knew the truth. Someone had betrayed her. Latif had not offered casual questioning or small talk. From the moment the men had burst into her home, Latif had been ready for combat, and no pleading from Isabella had changed the anger boiling inside him.

Isabella was afraid. She tried to control it, but it oozed from every pore, and Latif could smell it. For the first time in nearly two years, she feared for her life. Something primal had snapped inside the husband she had come to trust. She had nearly forgotten this aggressive side of Latif that could resort to violence in order to accomplish his own desires. She reminded herself that this man before her was unpredictable and dangerous.

The air was charged with abhorrence. They had been waiting for what seemed to be hours for the exhaustive search to be completed. When Chen returned empty handed, Latif roared at her for an answer.

"Isabella, I know what is going on. It is time to confess."

In shock, tears sprang to her eyes. His tone made her fighting mad; it was the only way to keep the fear at bay. She leveled her hardened gaze at Latif, swallowed down all traces of fear, and spoke through gritted teeth.

"What are you accusing me of? You have stormed into my house, frightened my guests, and torn apart my home, but you have not made any accusations. So tell me, what is this crime you think I have committed?"

For a brief moment, surprise flashed through his anger. She was certain it had been there, even when the curtain of acrimony returned to mask it. The icy stare nearly unleashed her tightly restrained fear. Her situation was perilous, but the blood pounding in her ears urged her to fight, not just for herself, but also for all the women who were counting on her.

When he met her indignation with a glacial stare, she waited in silence. To speak and give too much information could bring calamity. She would bide her time and wait for the accusation. They stood facing off for what seemed an eternity.

"Your maid has informed me of your religious meetings. It appears you have been pouring lies into the women in my family. This poison that you are spreading may well bring the mutawa right to our very door. I do not need this trouble in my home. To invite the pious religious leaders anywhere near us will bring misfortune and even death. So I ask you, Isabella, what are you hiding from me?"

"What do you accuse me of hiding? Chen has searched everywhere. I can see that my rooms have been ransacked. Are you threatening me? Are you going to turn me over to the mutawa? If you do, you know they will kill me." Isabella nearly choked on the words as she spoke them. Her composure momentarily slipped before her outrage replaced it.

"I have not decided what to do with you." He nearly spat in her face. "You are not to leave this home for any reason. Do you hear me? Bahira or Uzma will not be returning." Latif turned and faced Jabbar. "You need to have a conversation with Hafa as well. Jabbar, Chen, come with me to the house." He strode toward the door in long, fierce strides, then stopped and turned back to face her. "Do not disobey me."

Isabella just stared at him, unflinching. He was waiting for her to acknowledge his demand. After several tense moments, she nodded. He swiftly turned and left with Jabbar and Chen following.

When the door was closed, Isabella waited in silence. Her heart was pounding as her fear escalated out of control. Hafa made her way toward her and whispered, "Isabella." She shook her, encouraging Isabella to focus. "Listen, they have found no evidence. Tonight, after everyone is asleep, burn everything." Isabella started to interrupt, but Hafa gently silenced her lips with her fingers. "Everything, even the Bible. If the mutawa come in here and find it, they will kill you or demand that Latif do it." Hafa stopped while gently searching her eyes. "I can see that you are on the verge of panic. I do not believe Latif would bring the mutawa onto his property by choice. He has too much to lose. Pray and do not lose heart. If I can, I will try to come to you in the next few days. Be strong; the battle is not lost." Hafa offered a weak smile as encouragement. "Let's pray quickly together, and then I must go."

Isabella forced her fear into submission and whispered, "Lord, you are our protector. Watch over your sheep. Give us strength to endure what is to come. Amen."

It had been a week of waiting as the hours inched by. She continued to hope for a visit from Hafa, but she had not returned. Sometimes on the verge of hysteria, she longed for the raging Latif to return, but he had stayed away as well. She was completely alone. In the darkest part of night, she could feel the war raging all around her. Suffocating from fear in the clutches of darkness, her heart filled with dread. It was those dark moments she feared most. She had nothing to validate the irrational belief that her life hung in the balance, but she could not shake the notion.

Right now, more than ever, she needed her Bible. But just as Hafa had instructed, she had secretly burned everything. She had taken it all outside in the deepest part of the night and found a bare place in the dirt. When everything had burned to cinders, she carefully buried the ashes in the mulch under a tree.

Meticulously, she had scratched the ground to cover up all traces of the fire. And now when she needed hope most, there was none. She thought of all the Christians through the centuries that had stood in her shoes, fearing for their lives with no assurance of rescue. A tempestuous struggle warred within her soul. Would her faith withstand the test? Could she look death in the eyes and not cower in fear, renouncing all that she believed? Today, even in this inky blackness, she felt a tiny ray of courage burning within her heart. In her prayers, she begged for liberation, but there was no denying the truth. Death was inching closer with each day of silence.

In those darkest moments, she would see the faintest light growing and giving her hope. She could even lift her voice in quiet song to her God that held her life in his hand. She remembered that Latif was only a man. He could kill her body or have it killed, but she was an immortal soul. Her life was in the control of the Creator. Hope in the midst of despair is a priceless gift. It reigned in her sanity when the minutes and hours tried to claim it. If she lived or if she died, she would not perish. If only that hope could always keep the darkness cornered, but as the days passed, the battle raged on.

Two weeks passed before Hafa stole in through her front door. It was night, but not much past dinner. When Isabella saw her friend, she grabbed her and held her like a drowning soul. When Hafa pulled away, she could see that she carried news. Isabella waited, wavering between hope and dread.

"My father has sent Uzma away. I believe she is still alive, but he has divorced her and sent her back to her parents. The last time I saw her, just after she was dragged from your home, she did not seem well. We must pray fervently for her." Hafa paused; there was a grave look in her eyes. "Latif has not decided what to do with you. He will not see me or talk to me, but he remains in the counsel of Jabbar. They are friends, and he trusts him. You know that Jabbar has been carefully trying to protect you without giving away his pure motivation. To reveal his heart now could only make things worse."

Isabella had to ask even though she dreaded the answers. "What is Latif considering doing with me? And how is Bahira?"

"Bahira is managing unscathed. Latif has laid all the blame at your feet. He has forgiven her and has even allowed her to continue to have parties just for appearances. I attended the last one and stole a few moments alone with her. At this point, I think she is okay. Of course, she is praying for you, Isabella, just as I am."

Hafa seemed hesitant to continue. Isabella smiled a weak, fragile smile, hoping to give her the encouragement to continue.

"Jabbar does not think that Latif has even considered bringing the mutawa in to investigate. The maid that replaced Mina was from Turkey. She has been paid a handsome sum and returned to her home. Latif is confident of Chen's loyalty. So at this point, you seem safe in that regard. However, according to the law of the Koran, you have committed a crime punishable by death. Latif can kill you by his own hand and receive no punishment for it. If he claims his right to kill you, there is no court to protect you and no action to stop it." A slight tear slipped down Hafa's cheek. "But I have seen Latif talk about you in the past, Isabella. I know for certain he loves you, and Jabbar agrees. But you have sliced a near mortal wound to his pride. He is still very angry. He seems to believe that a penalty must be paid for this crime that you have committed to him and to Allah."

Isabella interrupted her. "But I never hid that I was not Muslim or my belief in Christ."

"This is true, but he is angry and hurt. That is a dangerous combination in the heart of a man. Jabbar and I have prayed together about what you should do. We agree on this plan. But I must warn you it is dangerous."

Fear radiated from her friend. In response, Isabella closed her eyes and offered a quick prayer for guidance and strength. Then Hafa continued.

"Tonight, just before midnight, go to the main house. I have provided a map guiding you to Latif's bedroom." Isabella looked at the crudely sketched map that Hafa held in her hand. Until that moment, she had not even noticed it. "Go and talk to him. Talk to his heart and appeal to the love that is within him. This is a very risky plan. To follow through with this means you must disobey him, but it is the only way. After two weeks, he is still determined to find an adequate punishment for your crime. Going to him could mean certain death." Hafa swallowed and then continued.

"Bahira knows. She will be praying, and Jabbar and I will not sleep tonight, keeping a vigil of prayer for your safety. It is risky, but remember you do not go to him alone. I believe with all my heart that God will soften his heart toward you tonight. I would never suggest this if I believed otherwise."

Isabella considered the words of her friend. They shared an uncommon bond of sisterhood that bound them together. She trusted her. It was a scary, sudden plan that left little time for contemplation. Isabella thought of Queen Esther. She had placed her life in the hands of the king, but she had risked her life to plead for the lives of her people. Would God grant her the same protection while she appealed for her life? She thought of Uzma, Hafa, Bahira, and Mina. They looked to her for guidance and hope. Their faith was young and untried. Could they withstand the knowledge of her death? It was a huge load to sort through. In the end, she knew there was really no other alternative. If she lived or if she died, she would make this one last attempt for her life.

"I trust you. I know you would never do anything to harm me. I will start praying the moment you leave, and I will not stop until it is time. I will pray for wisdom to know what to say and courage to say it. Hafa, if I die, you must not blame yourself. I am in a dire situation, and my life is in the Lord's hands. If he saves me, I will praise him. If I perish, I will praise him. Your faith is strong enough for anything that comes; hold on to Jesus, Hafa. No matter what may come, do not let go of him. Promise?"

"I promise. Just as Peter said, 'Who else has the

words of life?' I believe, Isabella. But I will still have hope that he will rescue you. It may be a long shot, but I have to believe."

Hafa hugged her, and a little of her strength poured into Isabella. It was decided. Now it was time to pray.

Isabella had slipped into the murky house undetected. She had wondered if the door would be locked, but it wasn't. She quietly made her way up the stairs toward the room that Hafa had indicated as Latif's. Her heart was racing. Several times along the way, she had paused and nearly run to the safety of her home, but each time she had returned to the task before her. When questions filled her mind, she pushed them away. For a little while, she would not think; she would just put one foot in front of the other until this task was accomplished. Her courage faltered. The few meters to his room seemed like miles.

She inched her way to his closed door. There was a light on. For a brief moment, she completely lost her nerve and turned to leave. Unexpectedly, the door opened before she could walk away.

"Isabella? What are you doing here?"

Isabella froze. She could not turn and look at him, but she could not run away. She tried to determine if his question had revealed any anger, but her mind refused to function. It was stupid to just stand there. All she could hear was a rushing in her ears. She closed her eyes and urged her feet to run, but they were planted as if they had roots. What should she do? Lord, what should she do? Little by little, her courage returned, conjuring the nerve to face this. When she turned to look at Latif, instinctually she went into his arms and wept. She could not control the flood of emotion that swept through her. She had never cried like this with him. She was embarrassed and afraid, but she could not pull herself together. When she felt his arms reach around to console her, a fresh wave of emotion poured forth. Gut-wrenching sobs racked through her body as her emotions flooded out unabated. This could not have been God's plan. She was making a complete mess of the entire situation. If she ever regained control of this torrent of tears, then he would certainly cast her away. And still the tears came. After numerous attempts to stop the sobs, she felt him draw her into his room and cradle her head to his chest. Her emotion was spent; the waiting and the fear had left her exhausted. It was a long time before she finally gained a remnant of control; she was tired but slightly composed. Then she began to hiccup. She felt like a silly, blubbering little girl.

Was she mistaken? No, she was certain that Latif had just chuckled under his breath. She wanted to look into his face to read his expression, but she did not have the courage. When he finally broke the silence, he tilted her chin up toward his face. She wanted to meet his eyes, but she could not lift her gaze.

"Isabella, you make me crazy."

She lifted her eyes. She had to know. The soft, loving, brown eyes that met hers were unmistakable. Where she had expected to find anger, she could see love. She tried to speak, but the sobs were still lodged in her throat. Her face was wet from fresh tears. She was sure her eyes were red, and her nose was running. What a mess she must be.

"You just cannot behave. Your audacity thrills me more than it angers me, but I cannot handle you." He shook his head in frustration. "You are a mighty tigress with the face of an angel, and I don't know what to do with you."

Isabella finally found her voice. With meekness, she tried to explain. "I am sorry, Latif. I never intended to hurt you. I have been very afraid and alone for so many days. I needed to know what you were planning to do to me."

A deep sadness filled his eyes, and his shoulders slumped. "Do you even realize what you have done? These foolish ideas of yours have changed everything. Your indiscreet activities could have cost me everything. Look around you at all I have acquired. Do you think all this is worth sacrificing to your irrational beliefs? I don't know what to do, Isabella. It would break my heart to hurt you with the punishments that have flowed through my mind, but I cannot come to a proper solution. It is too dangerous for you to remain in my house. Even tonight, I nearly pronounced the curse that would end my marriage to you. It would be finished if only Jabbar had not refused to be my witness." Latif shook his head. He seemed to be forming the thoughts as he spoke. "He has been the voice of reason in these many dark and trying days. He loves Hafa, and for that reason alone, he has encouraged me to refrain from hurting you. But truth be told, I could not give the command that would end your life. I could not do it. Even when I believed that it was the only solution, I could not do it." His shoulders hunched in defeat.

When Isabella spoke, it was barely more than a whisper. She was afraid and that fear was pulsing through her body, but courage gave her voice to speak one last plea. "If only you might send me back home." Her eyes filled with tears, and she chocked back a tiny sob. "In payment for my life, I will never tell what happened. I know the cost for keeping me, and the cost for sending me away. But you must understand I cannot go to the authorities. The story we have shared is unimaginable. They would never accept it. It is beyond belief. Regardless, I could not hurt any of you like that. Your family has become my family in many ways. I have no desire to bring the law down around you. But you must certainly agree it is time for me to return to my family. Bahira loves you. Soon you will hold your child in your arms. It might be too much to ask, but please … please release me."

He pulled her into his arms. He was angry. She saw the torment in his face. He was silent, and she waited.

He turned her face again and then spoke. "How can I trust you? If you ever spoke of any of the events of our life, I would deny them. Hasam, Chen, and Jabbar would all testify on my behalf. How would you ever prove that you did not come to me on your own?"

"I know. You speak the truth. There are no witnesses to testify on my behalf. I gain nothing by exposing the truth. I am choosing to let it go. In return, will you consider sending me back?"

Her eyes pleaded for mercy while she was silent. Conflicting emotions wrestled within him. There was nothing left to say. It was all in God's hands. He leaned down and brushed a wisp of a kiss across her lips.

"I will consider this and let you know my decision in the morning. Go back to your room, Isabella. I have much to contemplate."

EPILOGUE

Isabella was accustomed to the heat of the desert, but the humidity in Indiana was choking her. It was August and boiling hot. Nearly two years had passed from the date she had been abducted, and now she stood outside the doors to the airport. She thought about Sam and the girls. Now that she was so close to them, how should she get in contact with them? If they believed she was dead, had Sam moved on? Considering it was more frightening than the events of the last month.

She opened the door to the sleek black BMW sedan parked at the curb. She sat her purse on the passenger seat and looked out at the bustling bodies rushing to make their next flight or arriving at their new destination. In her purse, she had a false passport with a fictitious name, a credit card, and cash. All these items Jabbar had given her as he escorted her toward the stranger with the title and keys to this car. She had wanted to hug Jabbar as thanks for all that he had done for her. They were strangers and friends that carried a common bond of salvation and their love for Hafa. He had done more to help her in the last few weeks than Isabella would ever know. In the end, they just shook hands and parted ways. For all that he had done for her, he was a friend, the best kind of friend. But he was also a man from a very different culture than her own. In Saudi Arabia, a hug from a woman was not appropriate. So their parting had seemed stiff and uncomfortable.

The people around her were so colorful. There were no black abayas, no veils, and no thobes. She was even shocked by the lack of clothing on several teenage girls that passed by the bumper of her car. She had grown accustomed to the rigid modesty of the Middle East more than she ever expected. She shook her head and started the car.

She needed to think of a plan. She considered trying to call Sam's cell phone. It was Wednesday, and she guessed he would be at work. Two years was such a long time. This should have been the easiest thing. She had dreamed it over and over the past two years, but now she was afraid. Deep in her heart, she was certain that Sam still loved her, if only there was a way to know for sure before she called him.

She flipped on the radio and searched for a station. She was not really listening, but the noise offered distraction from the churning feelings. She pulled off the road into a local fast food restaurant, bought a Coke, and parked.

She picked up the car phone and dialed her sister's number. Immediately, before it rang, she hung up. What would her family think? She thought of Latif and the relationship that they had shared. In her heart, that was a closed chapter, but she had so much explaining to do. She thought of Hafa and smiled. Even now her friends were praying for her. Saying good-bye to Hafa had been so hard. They would forever be connected from the experiences they had shared. If only she were here to give support.

She backed her car out of the parking space and just started driving. She did not know where to go, so she just drove around killing time. She wanted to see her family, but the thought of facing them scared her. She tossed around several ideas but just refused to make a decision. She knew it was time to face this. She told herself she was ready and bolstered her courage. Again, she pulled off the road into a gas station and parked. She started to get out of her car and go into the store. She hesitated and changed her mind.

She whispered a prayer and picked up the phone. She dialed her sister's phone number, listening to the buzz on the ringing line.

"Hello."

"Hello, Michelle. This is Isabella."

"Isabella? Is this some kind of joke? Who is this?"

"Michelle, it is Isabella. I have just arrived in Indianapolis. I am on my way home."

There was a dead silence on the phone. Isabella sensed that her sister was still there, but she made no response. Isabella thought she heard a choked sob, but she just could not be certain. In the moments of silence, tears seeped from her eyes. Then she heard Michelle clear her throat and begin speaking.

"I never thought I would hear your voice again. It has been so long…I really believed that you were dead." Silence returned to the line.

"It has been an unspeakable journey, a story I wish I could forget." More tears fell as she choked out the words trying to explain.

"Have you talked to Sam?"

Isabella paused. "No. I am afraid. Like you, he must believe that I am dead."

"Not Sam." She heard her sister sniff, making Isabella ache at the emotional pain all her family had dealt with during her absence. "Even when we have encouraged him to start fresh, he has been adamant that you are alive. He is still waiting for you to come home. We have all thought that he was foolish, but he could not let you go."

Isabella's eyes filled with fresh tears as hope filled her heart. "I will call him right now. And, Michelle, pray for us. I have a sad story to tell him. It may even be something that he cannot accept."

"Call him. He is a special man, and he will be so glad that you are home."

"Thank you, and good-bye. I promise I will call you later."

"Bye."

Isabella's tears of joy were almost more than she could contain. She pulled back on the road toward home and called Sam's cell number. It rang and rang. At last, his voice greeting offered her to leave a message. She hung up and called again. More ringing and the same greeting. She hung up and waited. She was frustrated. She had imagined that he would answer. She made a quick call to their home, and still Sam did not answer.

After several long moments of consideration, she dialed his cell phone again. It rang again.

"Hello, this is Sam."

"Sam…"

There was a deafening silence.

"Who is this?"

"It's Isabella. I am on my way home right now. Can you meet me there?"

More silence.

"Yes. How soon will you be there?"

Isabella could feel her heart pounding. "In just a few minutes."

There was silence on the line. He had not hung up; she was certain. She was afraid to speak. In the back of her mind, a voice taunted her. She pushed it away.

"Sam, are you there?"

"Yes."

In that one word, she heard his tears, and she felt them rip at her heart. So much had been stolen from them in these past months, but they still had their love. And just maybe it would be enough to see them through. Isabella broke the silence.

"I will be waiting for you."

"I am already on my way."

"Bye, Sam. I will see you in a few minutes."

"Okay."

Isabella continued to hold the phone, listening to the silence. She struggled with conflicting emotions as doubt whispered hopeless words of fear. She hung up the phone and pulled into her neighborhood.

When Isabella pulled onto their street, an unsettled longing filled her soul. Home. She was home. She pulled into the driveway, looking up at the two-story Cape Cod style home. It was such a simple house. To some people, it might even seem plain, but it was home. The dark red brick was just the same, and the cream-colored trim seemed to have a fresh coat of paint. She opened the car door and walked up to the little porch. She reached for the door handle. She knew it would be locked, but she tried it anyway. She was happy and so afraid, but she had hope, hope for the future; it was a powerful thing. She heard a car pull in the driveway, and she turned to see him. "Sam." It was a whisper under her breath. He was the love of her life. They stood there as the moments passed, and neither of them seemed to know what to do. When he took a step toward her, she ran across the yard into his arms.

"Isabella, where have you been? Why did you leave me?"

"Oh, Sam. I was taken so far away, and I could not return to you. Really, it is a miracle that I am even here now. I believed that I would never see you again."

"Everyone said that you were dead."

He stroked her face just to see if she was really there. When he leaned down and kissed her, tears of joy flowed from her heart. It had been difficult to bear the months of separation, but finally she was home.

listen|imagine|view|experience

AUDIO BOOK DOWNLOAD INCLUDED WITH THIS BOOK!

In your hands you hold a complete digital entertainment package. In addition to the paper version, you receive a free download of the audio version of this book. Simply use the code listed below when visiting our website. Once downloaded to your computer, you can listen to the book through your computer's speakers, burn it to an audio CD or save the file to your portable music device (such as Apple's popular iPod) and listen on the go!

How to get your free audio book digital download:

1. Visit www.tatepublishing.com and click on the e|LIVE logo on the home page.
2. Enter the following coupon code:
   1a27-9a12-0f04-c4d8-e57e-fab7-36d7-139a
3. Download the audio book from your e|LIVE digital locker and begin enjoying your new digital entertainment package today!